CARI'S SECRET

NEVA COYLE

CARI'S SECRET

A JAN DENNIS BOOK

THOMAS NELSON PUBLISHERS
Nashville

Copyright © 1994 by Neva Coyle

Published in Nashville, Tennessee, Thomas Nelson, Inc., Publishers, and distributed in Canada by Word Communications, Ltd., Richmond, British Columbia.

Library of Congress Cataloging-in-Publication Data

Coyle, Neva, 1943—
  Cari's secret / by Neva Coyle.
    p. cm.
  "A Jan Dennis Book."
  ISBN 0-7852-8171-1
  1. Unmarried mothers—United States—Fiction.   2. Young women—United States—Fiction.   3. Adoption—United States—Fiction.
  I. Title.
PS3553.0957C37   1994   94–448
813'.54—dc20   CIP

Printed in the United States of America
2   3   4   5   6 — 99   98   97   96   95   94

CHAPTER ONE

*N*ineteen-year-old Caroline Nelson took the pen and forced her hand to sign her name on the line at the bottom of the document indicated with an *X.* Not old enough to vote in the election held the day before, Cari signed a paper that would change her life forever.

She handed the pen back to Mrs. Erikson, who sat across the table from her in Hannah Nelson's dining room. The woman tried to make it easier, patting Cari's hand and saying, "It's all for the best, my dear. Now you can put this behind you and go home again. You are going home soon, aren't you?"

"This afternoon, on the four o'clock flight," Hannah answered for her. "Thank you for coming." Hannah stood to escort Mrs. Erikson to the door. "It made it a little easier."

"Good-bye, Caroline." Mrs. Erikson touched Cari's shoulder on her way to the front door.

Hannah walked back to Cari's side as soon as the front door was shut. "Cari?"

"Yes."

"You all right, dear?"

"I guess so."

At 2:15 the cab arrived, and Hannah supervised the cab driver as he put Cari's two suitcases in the trunk while Cari stood by watching. Then she tucked Cari into the back seat and slid in beside her for the trip to the airport.

"What do you think of the election? Wasn't that something?" the cab driver asked. "Youngest president we ever elected. You vote for him?"

Cari didn't respond. Hannah took Cari's hand in her own and ignored the driver.

As she waited to board her plane, Cari spoke for the first time since Mrs. Erikson left.

"Aunt Hannah?"

"Yes, dear?"

"I will miss you."

"I'll miss you too, Cari." Hannah looked at her young niece. "Your grandma needs you now, Caroline. It's time to go home and rebuild your life. Being with your grandparents is a good place to start."

"I feel empty," Cari said.

"My dear Cari." Hannah encircled the young girl's waist with her arm. "I think that is quite understandable."

"Am I supposed to cry?"

"You will, dear. When the time is right, you will. And I pray that when you do, those tears will not be tears of regret but tears that will cleanse away all the pain. I pray that Jesus Himself will wash your eyes with precious, healing tears." The loudspeaker from the ceiling overhead told them it was time for Cari to leave. "There's your flight, dear," Hannah said.

Hannah took Cari in her arms and held her tight until they heard the last call for her flight. Then she took Cari's arm, guided her toward the gate, and watched her walk down the walkway to board her flight home.

Cari had not cried, not even one tear in six months. But as her niece disappeared into the aircraft, Hannah let her own tears for Caroline flow openly.

"Final approach!" The flight attendant's words seemed more a threat than an announcement. Cari straightened her pleated blue and gray plaid wool skirt and pulled the seat belt tighter across her stomach. She pushed up the sleeves to her bulky knit sweater then rummaged in her purse for her mirror. She briefly checked her dark brown hair and rubbed her lips together, deciding against lipstick. Her hands shook as she clutched her purse and waited for the plane to land.

The aircraft's wheels screeched on the runway.

Home, Cari thought as she pushed a tear back, *I'm home.*

Descending the stairway from the plane, Cari squinted at the bright afternoon sun. Suddenly she was aware of how warmly she was dressed and how heavy the coat draped over her arm was. It had been only thirty degrees in St. Paul this morning when she left, and Aunt Hannah had insisted that she dress warmly. She was unprepared for the seventy-plus degrees of the southern California fall afternoon.

Walking in an orderly line behind the passengers ahead of her, Cari didn't dare look toward the gate. Grandpa would be there, she was sure. Hopefully he would be alone—she had so much to tell him in the forty-five minute drive from the airport to the small town of Redlands. She knew she could not keep her secret from him forever. She dreaded telling him, but looked forward to having it over. She knew she could trust her grandpa with the truth.

"Cari!" She heard a familiar voice call out. "Cari, over here!"

She caught a glimpse of bright red-gold hair bouncing along the fence. Jen! Surely Jen had guarded her secret, at least as much as she knew. She had promised she would, and Cari trusted her best friend's promise.

"Caroline." Her grandfather's voice was warm as his arms wrapped around her. "Caroline Grace." Tears ran unchecked down his weathered face. "My little Cari, you're home."

"Grandpa." Caroline felt her whole body tighten with inexpressible emotion. "Grampy," she whispered, "I've missed you so."

"Oh, missed me, did you? Is that why you never wrote to me?"

"Grandpa William Rhoades! I wrote to you!"

"Yes, I guess you did at that," Grandpa said.

Cari had been careful to write to her grandparents twice each week. She had been just as careful to tell them nothing, at least nothing of what was really happening to her and why she was so far away from them for so long.

"Come on, come on!" Jen pulled Cari out of her grandfather's arms and into her own.

"Jen, oh Jen!" The two friends clung to each other, and then Jen began to cry and laugh all at the same time.

"You okay?" Jen asked soberly.

"Don't get maternal, Jen." Cari squeezed her friend again. "I'm fine."

"Jen offered to come with me," Grandpa said, reaching for Cari's small bag. "And I was glad to take her up on it. This airport's getting bigger every time I come."

"And busier," added Jen. "Cari, how was the flight? Did you see anything from up there? Don't you just love all the uniforms? Wouldn't it be neat to be an airline stewardess?"

"Flight attendant," Cari corrected.

"Isn't it exciting to be around all the travelers? And the pilots?"

"Come on, girls. Let's get the baggage and head for home."

Jen hadn't changed much except to get taller, but Cari noticed that her grandfather was walking a little stooped and his hair had turned almost completely white. She looked at him a little closer and decided he was paler than she remembered. Had she been gone so long? A year almost to the day—a year Cari was determined to put behind her, to forget.

"Grandma insists on buying a turkey," Grandfather offered once they were headed down the freeway.

"A turkey?" *Who's coming?* Cari panicked at the thought that her mother and stepfather might show up for Thanksgiving. "I thought we'd be alone, just the three of us."

"Oh, there's to be just a few of us this year." Will saw Cari's apprehension. "About twelve, I'd guess."

Cari saw the mischievous gleam in her grandfather's eye.

"Only twelve?" Cari put her nose in the air. "Why not twenty? Why not the whole church?"

A renegade tear fell on Cari's cheek. She had missed their Thanksgiving celebration last year.

"You remember, then, little Cari?"

"I remember, Grampy."

It was the last conversation Cari had heard her grandparents have. Her grandmother was planning to have a few friends over for Thanksgiving last year, as she had each year before that. "About twelve," she always estimated.

"Why not twenty? Why not the whole church?" Grandpa challenged. He always teased Grandma about her little parties of twelve that usually grew to about twenty. But last

Thanksgiving dinner had been the only one Cari had missed her whole life.

"How is she, Grandpa?"

Will Rhoades had dreaded that question for weeks. Now he would have to tell Cari the truth. There would be no secrets in his family. He believed in living by the truth, facing each situation head on. Cari would have to know sooner or later.

"She's not too good, honey." Will wished it were not true. "She's . . . well, she's in bed." His fingers tightened around the steering wheel. He checked the rearview mirror and glanced in the side mirror before continuing. "She's paralyzed, Cari."

Caroline couldn't believe she had heard Grandpa correctly. "She's what?" Her stomach tightened in a knot.

"Paralyzed, honey. Completely on her right side." How could he prepare Cari and protect her at the same time? "Some days she seems to be getting a little better, but we have to accept the possibility that she could be this way for the rest of her life."

"Grandpa, no!" Cari fought the sobs swelling in her chest. "You said it was only a slight stroke!"

"Oh, Cari." Jen scooted up on the back seat and put her hand on Cari's shoulder. "She's very alert. She can say a few words now, and she certainly still runs the household, even in that condition."

"That she does," said Grandpa, "that she certainly does."

"She sometimes forgets common words or the names of people that she has known for years," Jen said. "That seems to upset her more than being paralyzed."

"She has good days, and she has bad days," Grandpa added. "She will be so glad to see you. She has missed you so much."

Cari felt a stab of guilt rip through her ribs. *I should have come sooner. I delayed when Grandma needed me. I should have signed the papers sooner.*

Sensing her regret, Grandpa said, "Honey, you couldn't have known how much she needed you. She wouldn't let any of us tell you. She simply wouldn't take you away from your Aunt Hannah as long as she needed you so much. Your Grandma . . . well, as testy as she can be at times . . . is totally unselfish. She knew when you came home, you'd be home for good. She wanted Hannah to have you as long as necessary."

Jen's hand tightened on Cari's shoulder, and the two friends shared a long knowing look.

Cari gazed out the window across the slopes covered with orange groves and the mountains circling where the green groves stopped. She saw the tall eucalyptus and pepper trees lining the streets. During the year away, she shut all thoughts of Redlands from her mind, yet she remembered every detail. The small, quaint city looked exactly as she had left it.

Determined not to let her guilt show, she changed the subject. With Grandma so sick, Grandpa didn't need to know just yet. They would find time to talk—hopefully before Thanksgiving.

"So, she's making you buy a turkey. And who does she think is going to cook it?"

"You, of course." Grandpa winked at her. "With her bossing you every minute. And, of course, Meg."

"Meg? Who's Meg?"

"She's our homemaker lady. How's my girl doing, Cari?" Grandpa asked.

"I'm all right, now that I'm almost home," Cari replied.

"Guess who was drafted, Cari. You really can't guess, so let me tell you." Jen began to rattle off the names of some of the boys Cari only knew through Jen and two she knew from church.

"Will there really be a war, Grandpa?" Cari's father had been killed in World War II, and Cari had known him only through his parents, William and Virginia Rhoades. Her mother wouldn't speak of him at all.

"I don't know, honey. Guess our young president has his work cut out for him. World tension is nothing new. It doesn't always mean war. I didn't vote for him, but I'll sure be praying for him."

Cari's mind wandered away from the talk of world tension and the threat of war. She looked out the window to take in familiar neighborhood landmarks. *I am glad to be home,* she thought. *I didn't think I would feel glad about anything ever again.*

Cari noticed the familiar crackling sound of the gravel under the wheels of the car as they turned into the driveway. "Here we are, honey. How does it look?"

"Like home," Cari said. "And I'm glad to be here. It's been a long time—a very long time."

CHAPTER TWO

*Y*ou go on up, Cari. Jen and I will wait down here. She has been waiting for a long time. She deserves a quiet moment with you alone."

"Grandpa? I, well I don't know . . ."

"It's okay, honey. She's waiting." Will nodded toward the staircase.

Cari looked up the familiar stairway. The picture of a young girl clinging to a granite cross in the middle of a raging sea that Grandma called "Rock of Ages" still hung in the same place. The dark-stained banister felt cool and friendly to her touch. The gray and wine-colored floral wool carpeting was soft and quiet under her feet. Taking a deep breath through her nose, Cari let the wonderful smell of Grandma's house fill her nostrils. The mixed aromas of coffee, baked goods, and Grandma's cologne gave her the courage and comfort they always had, and she quickened her steps toward Grandma's room.

"Hello, you must be—"

"Cari?" Grandma's sweet voice interrupted the woman stationed at her bedside.

Barely glancing at the stranger, Cari found the warm circle of Grandma's left arm and buried her face deep in her neck.

"My . . . Cari . . ." Grandma's tears ran down her cheeks. "You . . . we . . . home."

"Yes, Grammy. I'm home. We're together." Cari suppressed her tears and sat up to get a better look at her grandmother. Pushing a lock of the old woman's hair that was wet with her tears, she said, "I had no idea that you—that this was so serious. Grandma Ginny, why didn't you let Grandpa call me sooner?"

"Ah . . . ah . . . Han . . . ?"

"She's fine. I mean, she's fine now." Cari hated the lie. "I could've come sooner. Oh, Grammy." But before the tears could start, she straightened her back and squinted.

"What's this about a turkey and twenty or so people coming for Thanksgiving? You think I can't cook that bird without you looking over my shoulder every minute, don't you?"

Cari watched the smile she loved spread across the left side of Grandma's face, pushing her plump white cheek into a soft mound while the right side of her mouth lay stony and lifeless. Purposely, Cari bent to kiss not the left smiling side but the lifeless right cheek.

"I'm here, my Grammy. Like it or not, ready or not—I'm here to stay."

"Yup." Virginia Grace Rhoades's little Caroline was home.

"Cari, dear, I'm Margaret—most people call me Meg." The large friendly woman held out a warm hand. Cari instinctively trusted Meg and liked her immediately. "I've been taking care of your sweet Granny here."

"Eh?" Ginny grunted.

"She doesn't like to be called Granny," Cari whispered loudly enough for her grandmother to hear. "It makes her downright mad."

"Well, I'm glad to know that. It might come in handy some time." Meg laughed, straightened the covers on her patient's bed, and patted the pillow into a more comfortable position.

"Tire . . . ?" Ginny asked.

"Yes, Gram, I'm very tired. I didn't sleep well last night, and I've had a long day. I need a bath and my bed."

"Go then, child," Meg suggested. "Your Grammy's had quite enough excitement for today anyway."

Cari leaned over once more to kiss Grandma Ginny and favored the left side and felt the slight pucker of a kiss in return.

"Luz . . . u . . . ," Grandma said.

"Love you, too, Gram. See you tomorrow."

Downstairs Jen had fixed herself a cup of tea, and Grandpa was heating some milk for himself.

"How's she doin'?" Jen asked.

"Still has her sense of humor," Cari observed.

Sitting wearily in a chair, Cari leaned over and put her head on her arms. For the first time in months, she was not able to fight the tears. Her heart completely broken, she yielded to her grief and wept.

"Cari, Cari." Grandpa's eyes were wet with his own sorrowful tears. "I'm sorry I held this back from you. I was afraid that you would be so torn between finishing what you had promised Aunt Hannah and wanting to come home to Grandma. At first it was so critical, it was doubtful that you could have gotten here in time. Then she rallied, and the doctor said she was out of danger, at least for the while."

Cari lifted her head and looked at her grandfather. His eyes pleaded with her for forgiveness, but she was the one who needed forgiveness. She should have been here. If only she had faced her grandparents and told them the truth, she wouldn't have ever needed to go away. But she didn't then, and she couldn't now. Not now. She was tired, Grandpa was tired. *Later,* she promised herself, *I'll tell him later.*

"I'm tired, Grandpa, I want to go to bed." Cari wiped her face with her hands.

"Well, I've got to go." Jennifer pushed her chair away from the table and stood up. "I'll be by tomorrow before I go to work, just to check on things."

"Work? Jen, you have a job?" Cari was shocked.

"Of course." Jen stood tall and held her head in a stuck-up pose. "I'm a career woman now. I work at Woolworth's." She walked stiffly across the kitchen and opened the door. "Treat me with respect from now on, Caroline."

"Oh, I will, Jennifer," Cari laughed. "I most certainly will!"

CHAPTER THREE

*L*ooking around her room, Cari became aware that each detail remained just as she remembered it. She touched the deep mahogany-colored wood of the highboy dresser and poster bed, caressed the satin salmon-colored throw pillows as she moved them from the bed to the peach-colored chair, and felt the rough cleanliness of the white sheets as she turned down the covers. Ordinarily she would have folded back the white chenille bedspread and laid it neatly across the board at the foot of the bed, but tonight she chose to leave it on.

Her suitcases lay on the tapestry-upholstered bench at the foot of her bed. Reaching inside the smaller case, she found her nightgown and robe and decided to skip her bath until morning. She undressed quickly and slipped into bed.

Lying in the dark, Cari buried her face in the sweet smell of bed linens dried in the warm sunshine. She grabbed a pillow and hugged it close to her stomach. The pain of the past fifteen months, the relief of being back with her grandparents, and the shock of seeing her once strong and independent Grammy helpless and pale was overwhelming. Too tired to think or even cry out loud, Cari let her tears wash her face unchecked.

Cari didn't hear her grandfather come upstairs. He quietly slipped in to check on Cari before going in to send Meg to her room in the summer house and to sleep beside Grandma. Noticing the tears on Cari's face, he bent to kiss her cheek but decided against it lest he disturb her sleep. *What could be behind all those tears?* he wondered. *Where has my precious Cari been and what has she been through?* He had promised Will, Jr. before he went off to war that he would watch over Cari and her mother. He had promised he would care for them—and he wasn't able to keep either promise.

Cari suddenly bolted awake, unable to recognize her surroundings. She smelled coffee and heard the chatter of friendly voices below. Then she remembered. *Home! I'm home in my own room.* Throwing off her covers and leaping from the bed, her feet hit the floor. Then she remembered Grandma.

Grabbing her robe, she went quietly to Grandma's door and, without knocking, peeked in. Grandma was alone, propped up to see out the window.

"Morning, Grandma Ginny." Cari kept her voice light and cheerful.

"Cari . . . come." Grandma held out her healthy arm, and Cari came without hesitation for a hug.

"How are you this morning?" Cari moved a little away to get a good look at her cherished grandmother.

"Better . . . you're . . . here." Grandma held on to Cari's hand.

"Grandma, I wish I had come sooner. I just didn't realize."

"Shh . . . I . . . my . . . din't . . ."

"Yeah, I know. Grandpa told me. Even when you're sick you can be bossy," Cari teased.

"Yup!" Virginia admitted as she pinched Cari's arm. "Skin . . . ny." Virginia's face became concerned.

"Nonsense," Cari retorted. "You know what they say, you can't be too skinny or too—"

"Pooh!" Grandma Ginny interrupted. "Go eat."

Downstairs William Rhoades was listening to the radio, reading the paper, and drinking his morning coffee. Circling to his side of the table, Cari slipped her arms around his neck from behind. No words were needed and none were exchanged.

"Sleep well, honey?" Grandpa asked as Cari untangled her arms from around his neck.

"Dead to the world," Cari said. Reaching for a cup, Cari couldn't help but notice that everything was in the same old place. "I'm so glad that this is all just the way I remember it. It's nice that some things stay the same."

"Oh? Have some things changed for you Cari?"

Sensing this might be the right moment to tell him her secret, Cari carefully poured herself a cup of coffee and swallowed hard. "Yes, Grandpa, *very* much."

Grandpa put down his paper. "Pour me another cup will you, dear?"

Cari poured the coffee and turned to face her grandfather. "Sit down, Cari. We need to talk," he said.

Cari breathed a deep sigh, searched the deep blue of Grandpa's eyes, and then dropped her own eyes to the rich darkness of the coffee in her cup. She was looking for the words to begin.

"Good morning!" It was Meg, shouting cheerfully as she came through the back door.

"Good morning, Meg," Grandfather called, still looking Cari straight in the eye. He said quietly, "We'll talk later. We've plenty of time."

"I'll have breakfast on in no time," Meg said when she reached the kitchen. "First I'll check on your grandmother. She rest well?"

"I can do that," Cari insisted. "I didn't come home to be spoiled. I'm here to help."

"Not today, Cari," Meg said. "I have my orders to make sure you do nothing today."

"Oh? And whose orders are those?"

"I told you, Cari, Grandma still controls things here," William laughed.

The back door slammed as Jennifer joined the small group in the kitchen. "Any more of that poison?"

Cari pointed to the cupboard and then the stove. "The cups are there and the coffee is there."

"What lousy service!" Jen complained.

"I'm not to do anything today. Grandma's orders."

"Well then, let's not upset Grandma," Jen laughed. "I'm so glad you're back, Cari. Think you could comb your hair?" She grabbed a handful of Cari's rich brown bobbed hair and playfully mussed it even more. "Or do you think that would go against Grandma's orders?"

"I don't know. Maybe I'd better ask." Cari loved her bubbly and outspoken friend. The two of them had been friends since childhood and had spent every summer together when Cari came to stay with her grandparents. Jen kept her informed of all the changes and gossip in the youth group at church, and Jen's parents saw to it that Cari was included in as many church activities as possible.

"She wants to see Jen," Meg announced coming back into the kitchen.

"Jen? Have you replaced me here while I was gone?" Cari moaned.

"Grandma Ginny loves us both—equally." Jen teased. "She even calls me Jenny and says I was named for her. So there!"

Cari grabbed a towel and threw it after Jen, hitting the swinging kitchen door instead.

"Grandma Ginny? How you doin' this morning?" Jen asked as she came around to Virginia's good side.

"Good . . . but . . . I wor . . . ry."

"You worry? Now Grandma, you know that's a sin."

"Jen . . . Cari . . I wor . . . ry."

"I know. Me too, sometimes," Jennifer confessed. "But she's home now. We're all together again. She'll be fine. Give her a day or two to rest up, and she'll be her old self again."

"Jen . . . take . . . her . . . lunch."

"Good idea, Granny!"

"No . . . gran . . . ny!"

"Just checking the old reflexes, Grandma Ginny," Jen explained. "Seeing if your faculties are still clicking in there."

"Yup. Still . . . click . . . ing."

"You just leave it to me. I'll take her to lunch. Grandpa can bring her down at noon, and I'll treat her to a hamburger at the soda fountain."

"Good." Grandma seemed tired from the challenge of Jen's presence. "You . . . make . . . me . . ."

"Tired, mad, happy, glad?" Jen gave the old woman a kiss on the cheek as she rose to leave.

"Go," Grandma said.

"Okay, okay, you don't have to throw me out. I can take a hint."

Downstairs, Jen swept through the kitchen and grabbed her sweater off the back of a chair. "Hey, Grandpa Bill, how about bringing Cari downtown at noon so I can buy her lunch?" Without waiting for an answer, she called over her shoulder as she walked out the back door, "Noon sharp. I only get half an hour, so don't be late."

Grandpa and Cari just looked at each other and laughed. "When Grandma isn't able to boss us directly, she teams up with Jennifer. We're in trouble, Cari, big trouble."

CHAPTER FOUR

*C*ari!" Grandfather's voice could be heard all over the house.

"Up here, Grandpa," Cari called from her room. It had been wonderful to have a few days to rest and to run around downtown with Jen. Feeling a little more free each day from the difficult past fifteen months, Cari found her appetite and her energy returning. Being with her grandparents also provided a sense of security she hadn't felt for a very long time.

"I need you down here."

"Coming, Grandpa." Cari ran down to the kitchen.

"What's going on?" Meg followed Cari closely into the kitchen. "You know this is Ginny's nap time. Why all the ruckus?"

"I have something to show my Cari, Meg. Just you never mind, and not a word about it to her grandmother. You hear me?" Grandpa winked at Meg.

"Grandpa, what in the world?" Cari couldn't imagine what could have gotten him so wound up.

"Look out here." Grandpa led the way to the driveway at the side of the house.

"What's this?" Cari stared at a '54 Ford coupe. "Grandpa, you can't be serious." How could she put this in a way that would not offend her beloved grandpa? "This isn't quite . . . well, you know, it's not what people your age . . ."

"It's not for me, you little ninny. It's for you!"

Cari's heart stopped completely still for a moment, then thundered to life again inside her chest.

"Me?" Could Grandpa be crazy? She didn't even have a driver's license.

"Yes, Cari-bug, you. It's time you had a little independence, and besides that Jen drives like a maniac. I'd not worry so much if you were driving."

"Grandpa, I can't . . . There's no way I could . . . No, Grandpa, you shouldn't . . ."

"Yes, you can. Yes, I can. I gave you a rocking horse when you were five, a bicycle when you were eight, and now I can give you a car. It's not a new one, you understand. But it's been well taken care of, and there are no rips in the seat covers. Get in, try it on!"

Cari slid behind the wheel. How strange it felt to be in the driver's seat. She began to bounce slightly. "Grandpa, I can't believe it! For me? It can't be." Cari would never have dreamed of such a gift from her grandfather. "I can't thank you enough. Wait till Jen sees this!"

Grandpa showed her the radio and demonstrated how the heater worked; then he turned on the windshield wipers and checked the blinkers.

"Blinkers?" Cari asked.

"You know, to show which way you intend to turn. Come as standard equipment now, you know. I remember when they were first invented. Don't know how we ever got along without them."

Suddenly, Cari became very quiet. "I don't know what to say, Grampy." Tears filled her eyes, and the pain of the recent past threatened to overshadow her joy. William

Rhoades saw the shadow pass her eyes and decided to rescue her.

"It's not all for fun, my dear. Grandma needs you to take her to the doctor when she's better. You'll be doing the marketing for us and an errand or two now and then. You'll earn the car, Cari. I'll see to that."

"Grandma—does she know about this?"

"You don't think I'd really have the nerve to do something like this without her permission, do you?"

They had planned it together then. Cari should have guessed.

Cari jumped from the driver's seat and ran around the car once, hardly daring to believe her eyes. Then she bolted for the door, flung herself through the kitchen, and bounded up the steps.

"Grandma, Grandma, you have to see. Grandpa bought me a car!" Cari ran into her grandmother's room forgetting how ill she had been.

Then Cari stopped dead in her tracks. Grandmother was gone. She was not in her bed. "Grandma?" she called. "Grandma!" She fought feelings of panic and fear.

"Yup!" Cari heard Grandma's voice behind her. Spinning around, she was surprised to see Grandma Ginny sitting in the window seat, propped up by pillows and carefully guarded by Meg.

"What are you doing up?"

"Meg," Grandma said simply.

"Oh, no you don't, Ginny. You are the one who decided to see that business about the car for yourself. I only helped."

"Hap . . . py . . . Cari?"

"Oh, Grandma, I love you so much. Yes, I am happy." *At least most of me is happy,* she thought.

"Now you go on down," Meg scolded. "Your Grandpa wants to take you for a spin, I bet."

Cari ran down the stairs and out the front door again.

Grandpa took the wheel of the Ford, and as Cari climbed in beside him, she said, "I don't deserve this, Grandpa."

"Deserve has nothing to do with it, little love. Someday you will learn that."

The next few days were spent making plans for Thanksgiving dinner. Cari went over recipes with Grandma, who couldn't remember what spices were and why you needed them.

Cari looked out the window once in a while just to make sure the baby blue Ford was still parked in its spot beside the house. She had decided to let driving practice wait until after Thanksgiving. She needed to let the excitement of the car die down before she dared to drive it.

Finally, they decided on a menu and wrote a shopping list.

"I can help you out there, Cari," offered Meg. Gratefully, Cari went with Meg to the store, and together they found the items Grandma wanted to serve with her big turkey.

"I don't really know how to cook a turkey, Meg," Cari admitted. "Will you show me?"

"Of course, child." Meg was grateful for the invitation.

"Will you be able to be with us for dinner then?" Cari asked. "Or do you want to be with your family?"

"I'd rather be with my family, Cari. But my daughter is in Cleveland with her husband, and my son is stationed as a military advisor way off in a little country called Vietnam. Clear across the world, I'm afraid. My husband is deceased. So I am more than happy to be with you."

"Who else is coming?" Cari knew her grandmother ordinarily wouldn't have settled for less than a dozen, but this year was different. Thanksgiving dinner would be very different not only for Cari but for Grandma too.

"A family you might know, kind of new at church," Meg answered. "Jenks, no Jenkins, I think."

"No, I don't know them. But leave it to Grandma to make friends with a new family at church. Any children?"

"Yes, I think so. A nephew, or a distant cousin, I think. Shall we make pies or stop by the bakery and order them?"

"The Whipples are coming, of course," Cari babbled. "It's a tradition. Oh, I can't wait. I missed last Thanksgiving." Then Cari decided to change the subject before Meg could ask any questions. "Yes, let's make the pies."

Grandma Ginny became stronger each day, and everyone said it was because Cari was home. But Jen insisted that it was because she was hanging around to rile things up and that Cari had nothing to do with it whatsoever.

The day before Thanksgiving, Virginia talked Meg and Will into bringing her down into the alcove in the kitchen so that she could "supervise" the pie baking. Grandpa moved the table out into the middle of the floor and brought in a folding bed from the garage. Meg vacuumed the mattress, piled on several heavy quilts to cushion it some, and made it up with fresh sheets and fluffy pillows all around to make sure Grandma Ginny would be comfortable.

Slowly, Grandpa and Meg, one on each side, carried Grandma to her "post" in the kitchen.

Then putting on a fresh pot of coffee, Meg took full charge and gave orders as if it were her own kitchen. She occasionally asked for Grandma's approval, and Grandma would smile her half smile and nod her head.

"Get an apron on, Cari," Meg ordered. "Get me the flour. Where's the shortening? How much sugar's in that jar? Did we get enough eggs? Where did we put that pumpkin?"

Under Meg's careful eye, Cari "cooked up" the pumpkin, lined up the spices, cracked two eggs for each pie—a dozen since there were to be six pumpkin pies.

Cari rolled out pie crust dough, getting flour up both arms to the elbows, sprinkling a little in her deep brown hair, and smudging a big spot on the end of her nose. Ginny half-smiled, completely entertained by the sight of her only granddaughter at home at last and working in her kitchen. Suddenly, a man's voice interrupted the preparations.

"Excuse me, ladies," he said.

All three women looked to the back door with a start.

"I'm sorry if I startled you, but I did knock. You are all so busy in here, I guess you didn't hear me."

"No, we didn't, I'm afraid." Meg's eyes narrowed, suspicious and ready for inspection.

"I'm Jeff Bennett," he offered almost apologetically.

"Yes?" said Meg.

"Sarah Jenkins sent me," he explained.

"Oh?" Meg was not convinced this young man belonged in the house, let alone the kitchen.

"She sent this," he said, holding out a paper bag. Meg took it and pulled out a bowl neatly covered with waxed paper. "It's stuffing for the turkey," Jeff continued. "She asked me to bring it over so you could have it—you know, for the big day tomorrow."

"Of course." Meg's tone changed immediately. "Her special recipe. How nice of you to bring it."

So neat and clean in his gray slacks and burgundy sweater, Jeff looked completely out of place in the messy kitchen. His shoes were made of a soft leather and were a new slip-on style with two little leather tassels attached to the top of each one. His blond hair was neatly combed, and his eyes were as blue as the sky on a clear day.

Cari felt suddenly self-conscious. She had been so surprised by the intrusion that she forgot her hands were covered with flour. As she reached to smooth back a stray strand of hair she left a streak of the white dust from her temple back over her ear.

Jeff laughed a little in her direction. "That looks much better."

She realized what she had done and reached for a towel, knocking a half-full coffee cup to the floor. "Oh, my," Meg said. "Maybe you ought to just wash up in the sink while I clean up this mess."

Grateful to have an excuse to turn her back on Jeff while she composed herself, Cari turned on the water a little too hard and splashed the front of her apron. *Get hold of yourself, Cari. You are acting like a ninny,* she scolded under her breath.

Thankfully, Grandpa came in just then. "Hey, Jeff, good to see you."

Grandpa knew him?

"How's the old Ford running, Mr. Rhoades?"

The car? He knew about the car?

"It looks like I got the better of you in this deal, Jeff. She's a real honey. The car's for Cari. Cari, have you been introduced to Jeff Bennett?" Grandpa asked. Without waiting for an answer, he added, "I bought your car from him."

"Cari?" Jeff asked. "Is that short for something?"

Yeah, Cari thought, *dope.*

"I'm sorry, Jeff," Meg said. "This is Caroline Nelson, Will and Virginia's granddaughter."

"Glad to meet you Caroline." Jeff held out his hand to Cari.

"Thank you, Jeff. Please call me Cari." She checked her hand before taking his. "Everyone does."

"Well, how do you like the car?"

"I love it. I can't quite believe it. But I can't drive it yet."

"Oh? Why not?"

"I don't have my license," she explained.

"Hmm. Do you know how to drive?"

"Yes. At least I think I do." Cari groped for an explanation. "I had driver's ed in school, but I've been away for a while, so I didn't ever get my license. I have some brushing up to do, I'm afraid."

Jeff had an idea. "I guess I could—," he started, then changed his mind. "I mean, I should be going. I just came to drop off the stuffing. I have a few errands to do before I get back to the house."

Grandpa walked Jeff out the back door, and together they looked over the car again. Cari could see that they liked each other, and like men do, they stood with their hands in their pockets and kicked at the car's tires once or twice before Jeff shook Grandpa's hand and left.

"Nice boy, huh, Cari?" Meg teased.

Cari shrugged off the question and busied herself with rolling out the pie dough with so much energy that Meg had to remind her to have a lighter touch lest she spoil the flaky crust.

Grandma Ginny sighed. "Cari? I . . . go . . . to . . . up."

"Of course, Grandma. You've had quite a morning. I bet you're tired."

Grandpa and Meg carefully carried Virginia to her room. Cari smoothed the covers on the daybed and looked out at the car. Jeff's car. No, not Jeff's anymore. *Mine now.*

Turning from the window, from the memory of Jeff's unsettling presence in the kitchen, Cari went upstairs to tuck Grandma in for her nap.

CHAPTER FIVE

*J*eff turned his borrowed car toward town. *Let's see, where's my list?* Sarah Jenkins would not be happy if any item were neglected without a good reason. Jeff had a wonderful relationship with his foster mother—though before he came to live with her at age twelve, he had not trusted nor been close to any of his other foster parents.

Turning into the supermarket, he reviewed the other stops he had to make and planned his route. He'd need to keep the list handy because thoughts about Cari kept trying to push their way into his mind. He had to go to Wilson's Jewelers downtown to pick up James' watch, to the hardware store to get an extra set of keys made for Cari's car as a favor to Mr. Rhoades, and to the florist to see if the poinsettias were in yet. Sarah always set out a poinsettia on Thanksgiving to officially begin her month-long ritual of Christmas decorating, baking, and shopping.

Jeff loved the downtown street with its lovely little shops. He parked a block or two away and headed for the large clock installed in front of Wilson's. The jewelry store was his last stop.

"Good morning, how can we help you?" called Mrs. Wilson as Jeff walked in the store.

"I'm picking up a repaired watch," Jeff answered.

On his way out, Jeff stopped to look a moment in the glass cases, attractively arranged with little trinkets as well as expensive jewelry. A delicate little key ring with a plain circle of gold hanging from it caught his eye. *What a great memento of a first car that would make,* he mused. And without thinking, he asked how soon it could be engraved.

"Have any more shopping to do?" Mrs. Wilson asked. "We could have it in about forty-five minutes."

"Can you make it thirty?"

"For you?" Mr. Wilson called from the repair area. "We'll make it twenty."

Jeff walked out into the warm November afternoon. As he strolled down the street, he began to argue with himself. *What are you thinking? What will she think? Maybe you could tell her it is because the car has been special for you rather than because you think she is so . . .* He couldn't admit how much she had impressed him.

She's too young, he warned himself. *It's not a good time for you and probably not a good time for her to be interested in anyone. What do you mean be interested in? You only met her an hour ago.* Had it only been an hour? Jeff checked his watch. She had never entered his mind before, and he couldn't get her out of it now. This was not like him at all. *Where's your cool, calm, distant self?* Jeff struggled to rid his mind of Cari, but he checked his watch again. Eighteen minutes! He had two minutes to walk back to Wilson's. His heart pounded as if he were asking a girl on a date for the very first time.

Checking the inscription, Jeff's smile made the rush order worth it for the Wilsons. "Perfect," he said.

Hurrying back to the car, Jeff slipped the two car keys on the ring. He examined the gift and slipped it into his pocket.

How in the world do you plan to give this to her? he wondered. Mr. Rhoades might misunderstand and read more into his impulsive gift than was really there. *What is really there?* he asked himself. "What have I done?" he said aloud.

Cari's afternoon was busy with polishing Grandma's silver and ironing the good tablecloth and napkins. Jen was coming over after work, and they had agreed to set the table the night before. It had become a Thanksgiving tradition for the two friends—last year was the only year they had missed since they were eight years old.

"Yoo-hoo! Anybody home?" Cari heard the freezer door open and close before Jen came into the kitchen. "Boy, if nobody's home, then who made the house smell so good, elves?"

"In here, Jen," Cari called from the dining room.

Jen came in and gave her friend a warm hug. "I am so glad you are home, Cari. Last year was awful for all of us without you."

"For me, too. You know I spent Thanksgiving on the train, somewhere between Denver and Chicago."

"Oh, Cari." Jen's voice caught. "I can't imagine what you have been through. I wish I had gone with you."

"Yeah, right," Cari said. "You didn't even know why I was going then." Deciding to change the subject, she added, "And, besides, you get carsick. How would you have managed eighteen hundred miles of rocking gently on a train?"

"How did you?" Jen asked.

"Well, it's like old times, seeing you girls getting the table ready and sharing secrets." Grandpa Rhoades had entered unnoticed.

"Hey! You have sawdust all over you! Scoot, you old coot!" Jen scolded.

Grandpa threw up his hands in mock fear. "Gee, if Grandma wasn't upstairs in bed, I'd swear she was right in this room. It's spooky how much she's rubbed off on you."

"Let's go up and see her, Jen. I think she's awake. Let's ask her where everyone should sit and make her feel a part of everything as much as we can."

Entering Grandma's room, the girls were shocked to see Grandma standing, hanging on to a walker with Meg in close attendance.

Without saying a word the two friends stood open-mouthed and grabbed hands.

"Well . . ." Grandma began in her slow slurred speech, "don . . . jus . . . stan . . . there."

"There now. Take it easy, let's go back to bed now, all right?" Meg said.

"Jus . . . me . . . in . . . bed." Grandma's eyes twinkled.

"You know what I meant," Meg clucked. "Never miss a chance to correct me, do you Granny?" Grandma Rhoades kicked at Meg with her good foot as Meg lowered her to the pillows.

The two women, having only met a few months ago, were becoming good friends. Both had lived with their share of pain, loved their families, and had strong faith in the Lord. Even during the days when Meg was the only one able to carry on their conversation, they had shared a special understanding. It was Meg who had read Scripture to Virginia for long periods of time and who read all of Cari's letters repeatedly.

"Don't you breathe a word of this to anyone, you hear?" scolded Meg. "We've been planning a surprise and you two almost ruined it."

"Yup!" Grandma agreed. "Pro . . . mise. Now . . . pro . . . mise." Virginia pointed a finger at the girls.

"Grandma, I can't believe you have been keeping this a secret." Cari came closer. "How long has this been going on?"

"It's not as if you have caught us smoking out behind the barn, Caroline," Meg defended.

"You . . . goin . . . to . . . spank . . . us . . . Cari?" Grandma looked penitent and tried to thrust out her lower lip.

"This is really great!" complained Jen. "Here we thought you were really sick, and all the while you were up here holding dances and ditching school."

The two conspirators laughed, and four women converged on Virginia's bed for a hug.

"Well," Jen said, "forget what we came up here to tell them, Cari. If they can have their secrets, so can we."

Grandpa's voice thundered from below. "Are we going to get any supper here tonight, or do we have to wait until three o'clock tomorrow afternoon to eat?"

"Oh, my goodness!" Meg said. "I got so busy fussing about tomorrow, I completely forgot about tonight." Scurrying out the door, she went down to find something quick to cook for dinner.

The girls left Grandma to rest after her workout with the walker. They promised to keep the surprise a secret, even though Grandpa had recently stated there were no secrets in this family.

Happy and content, Cari and Jen decided on seating arrangements for the Thanksgiving dinner that promised to be the best one yet. For Cari, the past year seemed more distant than ever, as if it had never happened. Except when she was in her room alone—and except for the dreams.

CHAPTER SIX

I brought my stuff," Jen said.

"Your stuff?" Cari looked a little puzzled then remembered their old private signal.

"You mean you want to stay over? Oh, Jen, that would be wonderful! I haven't had a slumber party since—well, since—you know."

"I know. I thought we'd better get back in routine. So I brought my stuff."

Jen sleeping over meant drinking hot chocolate, making a pan of brownies, and moaning about all the acne they would each have from eating so much chocolate—not to mention the pounds added to their thighs by morning. Will Rhoades smiled in quiet approval and remembered how he always had to shush them every thirty minutes until they went to sleep. But that was a long time ago; they were children then. Now they were women, young women—and one was older than her years.

Will ached for Cari, but he couldn't tell her so. He would wait until she came to him. Someday they would talk, grandfather and his granddaughter. He hoped it wouldn't be too much longer.

The girls talked and snacked their way late into the night. "Shh," Cari warned, "Grampy's coming—hide!"

Cari slid between the bed and the chair on the opposite side from the door. Jen tucked herself in the corner. Will knocked on the door. "Girls, it's time for lights out. You have a busy day tomorrow."

He talked as if they were eight years old again, and the girls couldn't help but giggle. "If I have to come in there, there will be trouble," he teased.

"Yeah, right!" quipped Jen. "And just how much trouble might that be? I want to know."

"Don't push your luck, dearie," Grandpa warned. "I might have to help you finish off all those brownies."

"Oh, no! Not the brownies," Cari moaned.

Both headed for the brownie plate just as Grandpa opened the door a crack and stuck in a groping hand. "Brownies, where are the brownies?"

Cari opened the door wide and caught Grandpa in her arms. "Not only the brownies, Grampy, but anything we have here. We love you and would give you anything you want."

"How about some of that hot chocolate, then?"

"How about some hot milk instead? You know you can't have chocolate. Can you come in and sit for a while?"

"Not for long. You girls are too much for me. I'm afraid your Grandpa is getting old. I'm not up to the old tricks I used to play."

Settling down in a chair near the door, all William had to say was "Hey, you remember when . . . ?" and both girls were off, telling stories that relived the adventures and misadventures of their childhood summers.

Soon they began to slow down, and Grandpa excused himself with a yawn.

Cari and Jen climbed into the big bed and with only a few more giggles or two they finally slipped off to sleep.

"No. No!" Cari kicked and thrashed her head from side to side, but her arms were perfectly still. "No! Please, no!" she sobbed.

"Cari, wake up!" Jen was beside her friend trying to calm her. "Cari, it's me, Jen. You're home now. Wake up. See, you're in your own room. You're safe, you're safe."

"Oh, Jen." Cari was sobbing and wringing with sweat. "Oh, Jen."

Jen held her friend close and smoothed Cari's hair from her damp face.

"It was only a dream, Cari. It's over now. See, I'm here, you're here. Only a dream, and it's over."

"It's never over. I have the same dream again and again." Cari looked frightened.

"What's it all about?" Jen wanted to know.

"I can't really remember it all. Just that I'm completely bound except for my legs. And then there is this bright light, and it feels like someone is trying to cover my face and suffocate me—always the same dream."

"How often is this happening?"

"Too often," Cari sighed.

"How long has this been going on?"

"Six months."

"Have you told anyone?" Jen asked.

"I can't. Well, until now. Now I've told you. I just wake up feeling so helpless—and hopeless."

"It'll be better now, Cari. Now that you have told me, the dreams will stop, I'm sure of it." But Jen wasn't sure at all. "Go back to sleep now. I'll stay awake for a while, and if I see that bad old dream start coming again, I'll fight it off with . . . well, with my bare hands, if necessary."

"Thanks, Jen. I don't usually go to sleep again. Maybe with you here I can." And with Jen standing watch, Cari drifted off to sleep. Jen was there to keep the dream away; and while Cari slept, Jen didn't.

By 6:30 Jen heard noises in the kitchen below. Meg was probably stuffing the turkey and putting it in the oven even before she made a pot of coffee. When the smell of coffee reached the bedroom, Jen knew it was safe to go down. She didn't want to get roped into touching, let alone stuffing, a raw turkey.

Carefully she slipped out of bed, quietly opened the door, and crept down the hall toward the stairway.

"Psst." She noticed the Rhoades bedroom door open a crack. "Jen," Grandpa whispered, "can you come in for a minute?"

Jen approached Grandma's good side and bent to hug her. "Ca . . . ri?" Grandma looked concerned.

"She's sleeping," Jen answered.

"She's having dreams often, Jen." Grandpa tightened the belt on his robe. "If she'd only talk to us about it." Jen noticed that the sadness made Grandpa's blue eyes look gray.

"She will, Grandpa Will. In her own time." *I hope*, Jen added to herself.

Cari was usually up at the crack of dawn, but this morning with Jen standing guard, she roused but decided to sleep a little longer. Now she put out her hand to find Jen, but Jen wasn't there. She was alone—alone either to cry or to get up and get some of that coffee she could smell. Coffee! It must be morning. Thanksgiving morning. Dinner guests were coming, Meg needed help, and Grandma was going to surprise Grandpa today by standing at dinner. She tossed the covers back and without her usual tidiness, Cari quickly dressed in her old jeans and plaid shirt. She would come back later to change into something more festive, but now she had chores to do.

The morning after one of the dreams was always welcome to Cari, but today, Thanksgiving Day, was different. Today was not just welcome, it held the promise of celebration!

CHAPTER SEVEN

*J*t's about time we caught a glimpse of you, Cari, dear," Mrs. Whipple called cheerfully from the dining room where she was putting finishing touches on a lovely fall centerpiece. "It's been nearly a week since you've come home, and we've seen neither hide nor hair of you. Come here, let me look at you!"

Cari obediently approached Jen's cheerful mother, and when Mrs. Whipple held out her arms Cari willingly went into them for a warm embrace. "It's good to see you," Cari said. "I'm sorry I haven't been over, but I've been trying to get caught up on—"

"Don't you worry about it none, Cari." Jonathan Whipple's voice carried clear from the living room. "She's just fussin' over nothin', like usual." Cari waved hi to him and walked into the kitchen with his wife.

"Hey, lazy bones." Jen looked down her nose at her friend. "You sleep and leave all the cooking to me. Fine friend you are."

"You cook?" Mrs. Whipple took up Cari's defense. "Nothing doing. We want to eat this meal." All the women laughed aloud.

Meg was busy basting the turkey and checking the pies, each covered with a tea towel and stored on top of Grandma's new automatic washer on the back porch. Jen was assigned the task of peeling potatoes for mashing, but she agreed to do it only if she could sit down. Meg said that was no way to get much peeling done before dinner time. Cari started to take the peeler from her friend and finish the task in a proper standing position at the sink, but Meg insisted she eat something substantial since dinner was hours away yet and she would be tempted to snack and spoil her appetite before dinner time.

"Wait a minute, Meg," Jen argued, "you mean she's supposed to eat a lot so she won't spoil her appetite?"

Meg playfully snapped Jen from behind with a towel. "Fresh one you have here, Barbara Whipple. What're you doin' to get her married off and out of the house for good?"

"Ouch," complained Jen, "they're ganging up on me."

Cari poured a cup of coffee and sat down to enjoy the company of happy, close friends and family. She had missed so much this past year. But that was over, behind her. She was determined it was—even if it wasn't.

The dinner was shaping up nicely, with the turkey sending its special holiday aroma all over the house. The carrots Meg had curled the day before came out of the ice water and circled a mound of black olives, touched off with green celery sticks upright in a small crystal glass in the middle of Great-Grandma's fancy plate.

"There's scalloped corn coming, Sarah's specialty," Meg informed Cari. "And Barbara made a new gelatin salad recipe that we've yet to test." Meg winked at Barbara.

"Sure," offered Jen, "nothing makes it to my table untested. Bring it here for a real, expert opinion."

Barbara and Meg ignored Jennifer's demand as the Jenkins' car drove up in front of the house.

Cari jumped up and bolted upstairs. *I can't let him—I mean company—come to Thanksgiving dinner and find me in my jeans!* She made her way to the closet after stomping over the covers she had carelessly thrown from the bed earlier. Finding her gray woolen slacks and mint green sweater, she began to brush her hair with vigorous strokes.

"Calm down!" She said aloud. *You made a fool of yourself in front of him once, don't give him the satisfaction of doing it again!*

Glad she hadn't taken to teasing her hair like Jen was doing lately, Cari reached for a little lipstick before finding her Ivy League oxfords and white bobby socks. Grandpa had been so generous in sending her a little allowance each month during the past year. Aunt Hannah had insisted on giving her an allowance as well. Cari had carefully saved through the winter months and well into the summer before she and Aunt Hannah had gone shopping at Ward's and Lerner's, where she bought a whole wardrobe at once. She had never done that before in her life, and she was glad she had taken the extra time to carefully mix and match not only her clothes but a few accessories as well.

With a little dab of cologne behind each ear, she stood back from the mirror to assess her efforts. For a moment she stood, looking over her shoulder into the mirror; then turning around, she patted her tummy. "Okay, that will do," she said to her reflection. "Now be calm!"

Minnesota was almost two thousand miles away, and it was in the past. She was here, and this was now.

"Go home, my dear" was Aunt Hannah's parting advice. "And go on with your life."

"Maybe I will, Aunt Hannah," Cari whispered to the mirror, and she left the room to join the others below.

CHAPTER EIGHT

*W*hen Cari came down the stairs she could hear the football game starting on television in the living room and the man-talk about who was favored and players' statistics. Watching was more fun with competition, so the good friends never rooted for the same team. Every year they entertained each other with good-natured ribbing, and someone always said, "If I were a betting man, and I'm not you understand, but if I were . . ."

Cari enjoyed the sounds of a holiday at home. She walked through the dining room, where the women were settled around the kitchen table chatting. With everything else prepared, they waited for the turkey to get done, enjoying each other and the smells of the good food and the sound of the men enthusiastically yelling in support or protest of a referee's call.

Cari wandered from room to room, taking it all in, when the phone rang. Meg reached to answer it, and a frown crossed her face. "It's for your grandpa, Cari."

She knew who it was. Only one person related to Cari was not invited this year. It was Cari's mother.

"Hello?" William said into the mouthpiece. "Yes, we're all here. She's doing much better. She's coming down to eat at the table, I think." A pause. "Yes, she's here, too." He glanced at Cari. A raised eyebrow asked her if she wanted to talk to her mother. Cari shook her head and walked back into the kitchen.

"Sorry, Ellie. She's not ready. No, I didn't say she wouldn't ever talk to you. She's just not ready—not yet. Maybe someday." Cari leaned against the door, out of Grandpa's sight but where she could still hear his side of the conversation. "Give it time, Eleanor. Don't push it or . . . yes, okay, I'll tell her." After another pause he said, "Happy Thanksgiving to you, too. I will, I'll tell her. Okay, bye."

Cari leaned her head against the door frame and took a deep breath.

"It's all right, Cari," Grandpa Will said, putting his hand on her shoulder from behind. "You don't have to talk to her until you're ready—even if that's never. Hear me? Today is *our* special day. Boy, sure smells good in here."

"Get back to that game, William Rhoades." Meg shooed him out of the kitchen. "When the game is over, we'll eat. We don't want you distracted at dinner."

Jen watched her friend with wide eyes. Cari quietly slipped out the back door. Jen moved to stand up, but her mother stopped her. "Let her be, Jen. I know you hurt for her, but she'll be all right. Give her a minute to be alone, then go to her."

But Cari wasn't alone. She was crowded by memories. The memories of her mother's voice crying and yelling and accusing her stepfather. Memories of knowing that her future was uncertain and that she would not be able to stay because of the fighting that had erupted on her account. Memories of knowing she would not be allowed to live with her grandparents because of "what this would do to them." Her mother had added, "I'm so grateful your father is not here to know about this." Cari had felt as though she had somehow disappointed a father who had never even seen her.

Her last memories of her mother were not pleasant ones. The hurried packing while George Nelson called his Aunt Hannah in St. Paul, Minnesota, arranging for Cari to come and stay with her for a while. The tense, silent ride to the station to catch the 11:00 train. The darkness of the train and the discomfort of the coach class seat as she tried to shut out all the fear and anguish she felt at what lay ahead, and what was in the past.

Why did she have to call and upset this day, the best day Cari had had in fifteen months? *Why can't she just leave me alone?* Cari thought.

Cari wandered around the backyard and walked behind the guest house where Grandpa's fruit trees barely moved in the gentle November breeze. She had always walked out here to be alone, to play in the dirt, or to watch the birds try to pick at Grandpa's apricots and plums through the protective cheesecloth in the early summer. It brought back a sense of pleasantness, of sweet memories instead of the bitter ones.

"That grandfather of yours is quite a gardener."

Cari whirled around to face Jeff. "Yes, that he is," she agreed, fingering the leaf of an apricot tree.

"You like it out here, don't you?"

"I do," she said.

For a moment, they walked among the trees, slowly, quietly together—alone for the first time. Cari didn't feel awkward, she just felt glad for his company.

"I saw you leave the house in the mirror on the wall," Jeff explained.

"You're missing the game."

"I'm not missing anything," he said.

"Maybe we ought to get back inside." Cari looked toward the corner of the house.

"Are you ready?" Jeff asked.

"Sure."

"See you inside then," he said as he walked around the other way and in the front door, leaving her to return through the kitchen door.

"You doing okay?" Jen asked when she came back in.

"I'm doing okay," Cari answered.

The friendly banter between friends getting hungrier by the minute resumed. As the game's score became so lopsided that the winner was determined well ahead of the end, the men wandered one by one from the living room.

Meg's sense of timing was never better than when she announced that the turkey looked perfect and that if the whole group didn't sit down at once the bird would be as tough as a buzzard within minutes.

Grandpa and James went upstairs for Grandma. The other men brought chairs in from the kitchen while Jen and Barbara filled the water glasses. With the holiday conversation surrounding her, Cari began to regain the joy of the day. Jeff watched with interest as he noticed the strain of the phone call fade from her face.

Now, if I could just make her smile, he said to himself, *I would really have a Thanksgiving to remember.* He reached in his pocket and touched the little gold key chain. *Maybe it wasn't such a dumb idea after all.*

The phone rang a few more times before the day was over, and Jeff watched Cari wince slightly each time, then relax as friendly chatter revealed it was only Thanksgiving well-wishers calling to send their love to Grandma and Grandpa.

What is causing her so much pain? Jeff asked himself. After dinner, before Meg could start to clean up, Grandpa gave his usual speech about being thankful for friends and family together. Then he encouraged each person to say what he or she was thankful for, starting with Virginia.

"I . . . go . . . last," she said. Grandpa passed to James, who said he was thankful for his family and of course, his precious wife, Sarah. Sarah was thankful that they had found such friends since moving to Redlands and that Jeff could be with them this year. Jen was especially thankful for her job at Woolworth's, except when she had to work in housewares, which she hated.

"I'm thankful that my car has a new home," offered Jeff, which brought a hint of a smile to Cari's face. *Almost,* Jeff noted, *almost a smile.*

"I'm thankful that I am home," Cari said. She didn't add anything more because she was afraid she would cry.

"Now Grandma, it's your turn," Will said after everyone else had spoken.

"Yup . . . my . . . turn . . . Meg." Meg went to Virginia's side, and the two women struggled a little as Grandma Ginny made it to her feet.

"I'm . . . thank . . . ful . . . to . . . stand . . . a . . . again." Virginia held her head a little straighter than she had for weeks, and her sentence was longer than any she had uttered since the stroke.

Grandpa quickly went to her side, and Meg stepped away. Kissing Grandma on the cheek and turning to the cheering family, he said, "You know, when she fully recovers the use of that hand, I'll be in for it, for sure."

Jeff watched Cari's face for the smile he wanted to see. *It's there, right under the surface, I know it is.* And he determined to see it before he went back to L.A. on Monday.

Finally, the men went back to their places in the living room where they read the paper and complained over the Christmas ads. The television was turned on again for the news and final football scores before the Mitch Miller Thanksgiving Special Sing-A-Long.

Meg and Barbara insisted on cleaning up, dividing the leftovers between all three households. Jen curled up on the daybed after Grandma was taken back up to her room, and Cari walked out to the porch to carry the pies into the dining room table for dessert. Glancing over her shoulder to the baby blue Ford, she saw Jeff looking it over and polishing the chrome on the side view mirror with his sweater sleeve.

Quietly she slipped out the back door, and this time *she* surprised *him.* "Sorry you sold the car, Jeff?"

"No, Cari, not at all. Well, almost not at all."

"Why did you sell it?" Then she was sorry for being so forward. "I mean, it's none of my business, I guess."

"I needed the money, Cari." Jeff became serious. "I've worked every semester since I was a junior in high school. I finished law school last June and have tried to work part-time while I study for the bar exams in February. I wanted to have a little more time to study—passing the bar exam is all the pressure I can stand for the moment."

Cari felt as if she had overstepped, but Jeff continued.

"This way, I can afford a small room near the law library in L.A., and I'm able to come home once in a while. If I pass the bar, early next year I will have to get a job in a law firm somewhere. I don't know where that will be, or if I'll be able to come home as much. I thought I'd better take advantage of your grandfather's offer while I could."

"Where's home, Jeff?" Cari ventured.

"Here, with the Jenkins." He didn't offer an explanation, and Cari let it go.

"It's getting cool. Maybe I'd better go in."

But Jeff couldn't let her go back just yet. "Wait. I mean, how about listening to the car radio for a little while?"

Cari shrugged. "Okay, I'll get the keys."

"I have a key," Jeff said without looking directly at her. He reached in his pocket, brought out the key, and opened the driver's door. "Here, you sit here, in the owner's seat."

Going around to the other side, he slid in beside her. "I never sat on this side before. It's kind of strange over here."

"I know what you mean," Cari said. "I'll have to get used to this side pretty soon."

"Here's your keys, ma'am." Jeff ceremoniously handed her the key ring.

She looked at the keys dangling from his hand and took them, noticing the little gold key chain. She studied it a little closer and noticed '54 engraved on the little gold circle that hung on the ring. "This is lovely, Jeff, but—" She turned the circle over.

Cari was spelled out in lovely scroll lettering and below, in very small block letters, was engraved *JB.*

Jeff looked straight into Cari's blue eyes. Noticing for the first time that they were dark blue, not brown as he had first thought, he almost missed what he had wanted to see all day. Cari smiled.

CHAPTER NINE

*M*eg scurried around the kitchen the morning after Thanksgiving, getting all the last bits of leftovers rearranged in the refrigerator.

"We could have fed double the guests we had," she complained. "That's the way it always is. We won't have to cook for a week."

"We won't have to eat for a week," Cari offered. "I ate more yesterday than I have for a whole month." She began to wash the cooking pots that had been soaking overnight.

"Not . . . hurt . . . you . . . a bit," Grandma observed from her daybed in the alcove. Cari noticed that her lifeless hand was lying in her lap today, not beside her as it usually was. It was encouraging to see even that little movement.

"I want . . . to see . . . a—oh, what's . . . it called?"

"What's that Grammy?"

"A book . . . a paper book."

"You mean a magazine?" Cari asked.

"Yup. Tha's right. A . . . room . . . to build . . . a room."

"Boy, let her downstairs, and she wants to remodel the house." Grandpa had been standing on the back porch, and now he joined the women in the kitchen.

"Yup," Virginia said, "want . . . to . . . help . . . me?"

"Nope," he said. "Ginny, if you want to build a room, you will have to hire a younger man. I'm getting too old and too tired for such projects anymore."

"What is she talking about?" Cari asked.

"She wants to build on a room out back so she won't have to be upstairs and away from everyone so much," Meg explained.

"Big window." Virginia gestured with her stronger hand.

"That's a great idea, Grandma. Next time I go to town I'll find you a remodeling magazine with lots of good ideas. Jen will help me find just the right one."

"Great," William muttered. "With four women against me, I guess it's settled no matter what I say."

The women who loved him so much would never have gone against him had he been serious in his objection, but as a matter of fact, it was he who had suggested the idea to Virginia in the first place. Besides, the stairs were getting a bit much for him, going up and down to see his wife and now carrying her up and down a couple of times each day.

Meg mentioned that she had met a nice man at church who worked on just such projects and went to her purse to get his number.

"How is it you carry his number in your purse, Meg?" Grandpa teased. "You his agent or something?"

Meg produced the number. "I'm just efficient, William Rhoades, nothing more." And with a warning glare, she put the group on notice to drop that part of the discussion.

"I'll call him, then. On your recommendation, of course." Will couldn't resist making a parting remark on his way out of the kitchen to answer the phone.

"Cari, it's for you. It's Jeff," Grandpa announced casually.

"Me?" Cari quickly dried her hands and went to the dining room.

"Want to go to lunch?" Jeff's question was quick and direct.

"Eat? After yesterday? I'm not hungry." Cari was hesitant.

"Let's go downtown and spy on Jen at work," he suggested. "Then if we get hungry, we'll be close to the soda fountain. Maybe she could get away and join us on her break." Jeff was hoping that the offer of Jen's company would entice Cari to go with him.

Cari thought it over a little and then accepted. "Want me to drive? I do have a nice car I've never used."

Jeff laughed. "I don't mind taking your car, but I do mind having you drive. You don't have a license, and since I am almost an officer of the court—"

"Okay, you can drive *my* car. But when I get my license it will be different—you understand, of course."

Cari went back to help in the kitchen, and when she explained that Jeff would be over in a few minutes, they shooed her away to get "presentable." In her room she decided to wear her brown slim legged pants and pink sweater. The brown was the same color as her hair and the pink set off her youthful skin perfectly. She pulled one side of her hair back with a pink comb and smoothed a little lipstick across her full mouth. *Maybe I should buy some mascara,* she mused. As an added touch, she pulled a brown and pink striped scarf from a little box and tied it around her neck. She grabbed her small leather purse, checked to make sure her keys were there, and for a moment fingered the key ring Jeff had given her.

She heard a car drive up and heard Sarah Jenkins call a friendly greeting to Meg before driving away.

"Jeff's here, Cari," Meg called up the stairs.

Downtown, Jeff and Cari parked the car in one of the angled parking places near the end of State Street. Jeff put some change in the parking meter before they walked the few blocks back to Woolworth's. They stopped once in a while and looked in the windows, noticing all the Christmas decorations and happy shoppers. Pausing at Wilson's Jewelers, Jeff waved at the proprietors inside. They smiled and waved back.

They had a wonderful time together, and close to noon Jeff suggested it was time to surprise Jen.

"She's working in housewares today," a clerk told them. "Oh, great," Cari said, "she'll be in a fine mood."

Jeff and Cari found her in the back sorting dozens of cookie cutters a customer had knocked from a display to the floor. She muttered as she worked and was getting more frustrated by the minute as she tried to untangle the mess without cutting her fingers.

"Wow! I'm glad to see you two." She looked at Cari, then at Jeff. "I thought I'd see you here today."

"Oh, yeah?" Jeff asked.

"Yeah."

"When can you go to lunch?" Cari asked.

"I'm due for a break in fifteen minutes. Want to meet me somewhere?"

The trio arranged to meet at the soda fountain and decided that if it were busy they'd cross the street and go down the block to the lunch counter at Key's Drugs.

While they were waiting, Cari wandered through the cosmetic section with Jeff following at a safe distance. Cari looked at the mascara, noted its price, and browsed a little more. She felt self-conscious with Jeff watching her look at makeup.

After lunch Jeff had a surprising idea. "Want to go to the DMV?"

"The what?"

"The Department of Motor Vehicles."

"Why?"

"To renew your learner's permit."

Cari's heart began to pound. She would need to renew the permit if she were to learn to drive Jeff's—no, her—car.

"Well, I don't know. I guess I have to go sometime."

"Today is as good as sometime, maybe better."

When they left the DMV an hour later, Cari tucked the cherished paper in her purse. She was proud of her high score on the written test in spite of not reviewing the material.

"Want to drive home?" Jeff's question caught her completely off guard.

"I can't." Cari panicked.

"Why not?"

"I just can't."

Jeff sensed it was not the time to push her. "How about tomorrow?"

"Tomorrow?"

"Great! Tomorrow it is then."

"Jeff, wait. Maybe I should . . ."

"Why wait? Wait until when?" Jeff was insistent. "Tomorrow. I'll come by at ten in the morning and get you and the car, and you'll have your first driving lesson."

"Well, it won't really be my first. I did have driver's ed, you remember."

"Okay, then. We'll find out how much you remember."

Jen was thrilled to find out that Jeff was going to take Cari driving; Grandpa was relieved, not sure if he could actually handle the tension of a new driver behind the wheel. Cari was nervous and could hardly sleep that night. She wasn't sure if it was because she was going to finally drive her car or because she was going to be with Jeff again. Trying not to sort it out she focused on Monday, when she would be past tomorrow's experience. But she tried not to remember that on Monday Jeff would be gone, back to his studies.

Jeff proved to be a patient and calm instructor, and Cari learned about clutches and flywheels and why she should never pop the clutch. Jeff knew the little idiosyncrasies of his treasured Ford and instructed Cari to pump the gas four times, then keep her foot off the throttle while turning the key in the ignition. He warned her that on cold mornings she might have to try it once or twice before it actually started.

Cari commented that California didn't know a cold morning compared to the mornings in Minnesota. She wished at once that she could retract the comment.

"What is Minnesota like?" Jeff asked.

"Well, it's beautiful," Cari said. "Very green in the summer and very white when it snows. But it's gray in between and depressing at times."

"Why were you there, Cari? I don't quite get it."

Cari didn't want to discuss her stay in Minnesota with anyone—especially not Jeff. Her eyes pleaded with him not to ask any more questions about her stay there, and he momentarily avoided her gaze, acting as though he didn't notice.

Cari took a deep breath and began what sounded to Jeff like a rehearsed speech.

"I went to take care of my stepfather's aunt. She needed someone to help her after a bad accident at work. She broke the large bone in her thigh when she fell from a ladder and—"

Jeff interrupted her practiced answer. "What was an old woman doing on a ladder? Was she a construction worker or a fireman?"

Jeff was glad to hear her laugh. "No. First of all, she isn't so old. Not too much older than my mother's age, I guess. And she's a librarian." *Can we talk about something else?* Cari begged silently.

"But she is your stepfather's aunt?" Jeff sounded confused.

"I don't know their whole family history. But Aunt Hannah is wonderful, Jeff. She really helped me during . . ." Cari paused.

"I thought you went there to help her."

"It went both ways. Say, you really are a lawyer, aren't you? May I get down from the witness stand now, Mr. Bennett?"

Jeff knew he had pushed Cari as far as he dared this time. He wanted to know so much more about this lovely young woman. Why hadn't her mother come to see her? Why was her last name Nelson and not Rhoades? But for now Jeff changed the subject and began to talk about car maintenance and oil changes.

Cari concentrated more on his facial expressions than on his words and was only slightly impressed by his knowledge of the car. She noticed how the veins stood out in an attractive pattern on the backs of his hands and how his shoulders fit nicely into his ski sweater. She saw his class ring and noticed how he could slip his fingers through his hair to keep it perfectly in place.

Will Rhoades observed the young people from a place on the back porch. He was putting in glass windows to replace the screens for the winter—such as it was in Southern California. The new automatic washer was installed there, and the windows helped keep the porch a bit warmer on wash day.

He was happy that Jeff seemed to like Cari, but he was just as glad that tomorrow afternoon Jeff would be catching the bus back to L.A. and would probably stay there until Christmas. By then, he and his granddaughter would have time together. Then they could talk—or at least he would try to make an opportunity to do so.

On Sunday, Cari offered to stay home with Grandma and give Meg a chance to go to church for the morning service for a change. For weeks, Will had been attending the morning service while Meg stayed at home with Virginia, and Meg had been going to the Sunday evening service, leaving William in charge of his wife's care. Meg resisted, insisting that Cari would probably want to see friends other than Jen and that they would be expecting to see her in church.

"Meg . . . go . . . ," Virginia insisted. "Maybe she isn't . . . ready yet."

Meg agreed and left Cari and Grandma Ginny at home, alone for the first time since Cari's return last week. *Virginia wants her to stay home,* Meg decided, and she got ready in time to go with Will.

"What shall we do with our morning, Grammy?" Cari asked.

"Look at my . . ." Virginia held up her magazine on room additions.

They planned and discussed ideas and looked at copies of *Better Homes and Gardens* for decorating ideas. At about 11:30, Cari put leftover turkey and dressing in the oven to heat for dinner. She set the table while Grandma napped on the daybed and contentedly waited for Grandpa and Meg to get home from church.

Checking on Grandma, making sure she was sleeping and could not accidentally roll off the daybed, Cari wandered out to the backyard and around to the back of the guest house to Grandpa's work shop. He was a master wood-carver, and as a small child Cari loved to watch him work his magic at making whistles and pull toys. Since his retirement from his dental practice, he had been able to spend more time doing what he loved best—working in his shop.

Noticing that the door was padlocked, Cari remembered where Grandpa kept the key on the back porch. She quietly went into the house, careful not to wake her grandmother. She took the key from its nail and let herself into the workshop. She took in the familiar sights and smells of the wood shavings and ran her fingers across what was probably going to be a gift for Grandma, a small chest lined with cedar.

Moving from the main area to the shelves at the back, Cari noticed a larger piece of wood draped with a canvas. Almost ready to peek under, Grandpa's voice surprised her. "Cari! Don't!" She spun around to face her grandfather's angry tone. Immediately, he softened. "I'm sorry, Caroline. I didn't mean to scare you. Hey, it's almost Christmas—don't you know you are not to be peeking around Santa's workshop this time of year?" He took hold of her arm and pulled her close. "I really didn't mean to scold you, honey. I love you so much. I'm sorry."

"I'm the one who's sorry, Grampy. I had no business snooping around in here. I hadn't been here in so long, I just wanted to . . ." Cari's eyes were filled with tears. "When I saw it was locked, I should have stayed out."

"It's not locked against you, honey. Times have changed. We have had a few stories of prowlers in the paper lately. I just wanted to protect my tools and projects, not keep you out. Honest. You can come here anytime. Just don't be peeking, promise?"

"Keeping secrets from me Grandpa?" Cari asked. Then she wished she hadn't.

"Don't we all have secrets from time to time?"

"Yes, I guess we do. Sometimes I wish we didn't though." Cari heard Meg's insistent voice call them to dinner. "We better go eat." But suddenly she wasn't hungry anymore.

"Go ahead, I'll be right behind you." William stayed until Cari was out of sight around the corner of the guest house. He checked under the canvas. "Stupid thing! I should have gotten rid of it before she came home. Now what can I say—how could I have explained this?" William kicked at the canvas covered project and left the workshop. Locking the door behind him, he put the key on the leather key holder in his pocket—just to be on the safe side.

CHAPTER TEN

*A*fter dinner, Grandma asked to be taken back up to her room, where she would be when Sarah Jenkins came over to read the Sunday school papers she had picked up in church. They'd had a standing appointment ever since Virginia's stroke, and it gave Meg a little time to herself. Cari checked the clock in the kitchen. *It's 2:30. Sarah is coming around three. I'll make sure there's a fresh pot of coffee and get some of that pumpkin bread out of the freezer.*

Grandpa's afternoon was spent, as usual, with the Sunday paper and a football game on TV. He almost never saw the final score because he would doze behind the paper most of the afternoon. He was already half asleep when Cari checked in on him on her way to the kitchen.

Cari loved the quiet scene and had pictured it many times while she was away. But today, she was restless. She still could not understand Grandpa's sudden outburst in the workshop. She didn't believe for a minute that what was hidden under the canvas was a Christmas surprise, but she would never openly question him. When the time was right, he would tell her.

Jen sent a message for Cari home with Meg. She promised to wash the family car today and would come over later, before the youth group met at five.

"Hello! Anyone home?" Cari could hear Mrs. Jenkins' cheery voice from the front porch. Grandpa roused to let her in, and Sarah went upstairs.

Preoccupied with her own difficult mood, Cari was glad that everyone was too busy to notice that she decided to stay in the kitchen until time to serve Mrs. Jenkins and Grandma their coffee.

"Hi," Jeff said standing in the doorway to the kitchen.

"Oh—" Cari's hand flew to her throat.

"I didn't mean to scare you," Jeff apologized.

"That's makes twice today."

"Twice?"

"Yeah, Grandpa earlier and now you," she told him.

"Sorry," Jeff apologized again.

"Never mind." Cari's answers were short, too short, and Jeff felt very uncomfortable.

"This a bad time, Cari?"

"Yes, well, actually—no." *It's not the time that's bad, it's me,* she thought. "I guess I'm not in the best of moods. Maybe It's a Thanksgiving let down. Sometimes I can't believe I'm here. As if the last year didn't really happen. Like I never left."

"Why did you leave, Cari?" Jeff asked, pinching a bit of pumpkin bread from the plate she held in her hand. Jeff didn't look in her eyes because he didn't want to see the request to mind his own business he knew would be there.

"It's a long story, Jeff. What time do you leave for the bus?"

"I could go now if you'd like."

"No, that's not what I meant."

"Is that what you want?"

This is not going well, she thought. *Everything I say is coming out wrong.*

"No, I'm glad you came. I really am."

"You don't sound like it."

"Jeff Bennett, are you picking a fight with me?" she teased, trying to change the direction of their conversation. "If you are, tell me. In the mood I'm in, I could give you a good one."

"I do not want to fight with you, Cari. We don't know each other well enough to fight."

Cari laughed, but Jeff had heard that laugh before. It came from only being amused, not from being happy. What could have hurt her so deeply? And why should it matter to him? He wondered if he should pursue the question or just stay out of it. Certainly he had enough trouble with his own painful past; he didn't need to take on Cari's.

"Jeff, you didn't answer my question. What time does the bus you take leave?"

"Five-thirty. I get back to L.A. close to eight, and I will be in my room before 9:00 or 9:30. I may even have a little energy left to do some reading before I hit the books on Monday morning."

"Is it really hectic?" Cari didn't have any idea what studying for the bar might be like.

"It can be. Right now, with studying for the bar and competing for a law position, I'm pretty pressured. My last year in law school was like cramming for exams for the entire term."

"So what's after the bar exam?" Cari asked.

"Work. Well, after a few months of sending out applications and interviewing, I hope it's work."

Jeff had taken a chair at the kitchen table, slouched down in it just a little, and crossed one ankle across his knee. He didn't look like a person who needed to catch a bus out of town in an hour or so—he looked pretty settled and comfortable. Cari found a place on the opposite side, facing him.

"Is that coffee fresh?" he asked.

"Sure, you want some? Oh, my goodness. I made it for Sarah and forgot all about her."

"Don't worry about it. She drinks tea anyway."

Why am I so uncomfortable? Cari wondered. *I feel totally stupid whenever there isn't something to occupy my hands or something to do when I am alone with him. Keep it together, Caroline,* she warned herself. *He'll be gone soon, and you'll be wishing him back.*

"I won't be back until Christmas." Jeff answered Cari's unasked question. "Since I don't have a job, I'll be able to spend a few weeks at home."

He looked for her reaction. But Cari was afraid to hope that he would want to see her again. She simply looked at him, unaware of how sad her eyes were or how anxiously Jeff was searching them for encouragement.

"Oh," she said simply, "that's nice."

"Cari, I . . ."

Cari looked at the slices of pumpkin bread still on the plate and poked at them with her finger. The silence between her and Jeff grew longer and her heart pounded louder.

"Cari?" Jeff wanted to look into her eyes one more time.

Just as she looked up at him, a car door slammed in the driveway.

"That must be Jen." Cari felt both relieved and sorry. "She said she'd be stopping by." Cari's voice was barely above a whisper.

"I wish she . . ." Jeff dropped the sentence with a deep sigh just as Jen came in through the back porch.

"Hi, you two. Having a snack?" She didn't notice, or at least pretended not to notice, the silence hanging in the room like a heavy fog. As she walked to the cupboard for a cup, neither Jeff nor Cari spoke. "This coffee fresh, or is it left from this morning? Doesn't look too bad to me. Is that pumpkin bread from Thanksgiving?" Turning she looked at Jeff, then at Cari, realizing she had interrupted. Without a moment's pause, she changed her course. "How's Grandpa? Think I'll go see." And with a whirl she backed through the kitchen door and disappeared into the dining room.

"Sarah will be down soon. She is taking me to the bus station." Jeff's voice was quiet, and it was as if Jen had not even been there. "Cari?"

"Thank you for the key ring," Cari said softly.

"You're very welcome." And he meant it.

Jeff heard Sarah coming down the stairs, and he rose to leave.

"When I come back for Christmas, I'd like that cup of coffee."

Cari closed her eyes for a moment. "I completely forgot about it, Jeff. I'm sorry."

"That's okay. Like I said, I'll get it later." Jeff winked, and she felt hot as the blush spread up her neck to her face.

CHAPTER ELEVEN

*B*y Cari's second week home, the Rhoades household settled into something of a routine. Cari spent most mornings with Grandma Ginny going over ideas for the room addition, which had grown in their plans into two rooms joined by an archway.

A meeting with the contractor had given birth to another idea. Since the addition would come to within twenty feet of the guest house, a covered patio joining the two buildings was added to the plans.

Grandma had insisted on installing one of those new sliding glass doors so she could see into her garden. She loved to watch the birds come to splash about in the bowl held aloft by a cement cupid, and she wanted to "keep an eye on my roses."

With the plans all finalized, the work was scheduled to begin immediately after the holidays. But the yard work to be done in preparation for the project needed to begin at once. Grandma wanted her iris bulbs dug up and replanted as well as several rose bushes moved. James Jenkins offered to help Grandpa do the digging, but he actually did the work with Will watching and offering advice.

"One of these days, we need to have a talk, Cari," Grandpa said over supper one Tuesday evening.

Cari's heart leaped and she swallowed hard. "Yes, Grandpa, a nice talk." But Grandpa let the matter drop, and Cari didn't press for an appointment.

On Thursday that week, Grandpa asked Cari to go with him to the bank.

"The bank?" Cari was more than a little curious.

"I want to open a personal checking account, and I want you to go with me."

"Don't you already have an account there?" Cari knew Grandpa was a regular customer at the local bank.

"Not a checking account. I haven't really believed them necessary before now." For years, Grandpa spent the Friday morning before the first of every month driving around paying his bills in person. "Now I think it might be a good idea. You might as well come along. You don't want to wait until you're my age to learn such things, do you?"

It was settled. Cari would go with Grandpa to the bank and learn about checking accounts.

After filling out the papers and making the opening deposit, the bank clerk passed a signature card to William. He signed it and passed it to Cari for her signature as well.

"Me?" Cari was surprised.

"Yes, you. We need two signatures on this account, and Grandma's not about to get mixed up in these matters, now is she?" Grandpa seemed irritated that Cari should question him—and in front of the bank clerk, no less.

Leaving the bank and heading out to car he announced, "Now each month we will sit down together and pay the bills. We can mail them, or you can drive downtown to pay them." No discussion, just a decision. Cari didn't argue; she knew that when her grandfather's tone was this serious you didn't question him.

"How about driving up to Oak Glen and getting some apples?" Grandpa suggested. He and Cari had made apples a Labor Day ritual for as long as she could remember, but this was December, just two weeks before Christmas.

"Grandpa, the apples are all gone by now." Cari saw the frown cross his face. Sensing his disappointment at being denied the outing, she quickly added, "But how about some oranges. Is the fruit market open in Yucaipa?"

Driving up Sand Canyon Road, Grandpa grew silent, and Cari saw his hands tighten on the wheel. "Is it time for our talk?" she asked quietly. She had dreaded this time, and now her heart pounded as she waited for his answer.

"Yes, Cari-bug, it's time." William Rhoades found a place to park on the side of the road and turned the car around so that they could see far across the expanse of orange groves in the valley below and the San Bernardino Mountains rising in the distance. It was an exceptionally clear, typical December day.

"Cari," he began, "there can be no secrets between people who love each other the way you and me and your grandma do." Cari could feel the guilt stab in that familiar place under her ribs again.

"There's been a secret, do you know that, Cari?"

"Yes, Grandpa, but I . . ."

"It's okay," Will tried to comfort her. "It couldn't be helped. I'm just glad you understand that this is the time it has to come out in the open."

"The open?" Cari couldn't bear the thought of anyone else, especially her beloved grandparents, knowing the awful truth about her and the year she spent with Aunt Hannah.

"Yes, unhidden. It is time that the subject is no longer forbidden. It's time we all acknowledged the truth—it's time to make our adjustments to the inevitable and go on with our lives as normally as possible.

"Cari, don't cry." Will noticed the tears beginning to fall from Cari's eyes into her lap. Suddenly the spectacular view from the front window of the car didn't matter anymore. Nothing mattered anymore except that she was about to be able to speak of the terrible anguish built up in her for the last year and four months. It was almost over, and her new beginning was within reach.

Grandpa began slowly. "It's been about six months since I found out. I didn't tell Grandma about it at first. I didn't know how she would take it. We had no idea she was so close to having a stroke..." His voice broke, and he reached in his pocket for his handkerchief and blew his nose.

"Was it when Grandma found out that she got sick?" Cari's eyes were wide with terror and her voice was thick with sobs. *I have caused my grandmother to have a stroke, I almost killed her!* Cari's mind was running wild with the implications. *Mother said it would kill her to know the truth. She was right. I almost killed my Grammy.*

"The doctor assures me it had nothing to do with me telling her. Her blood pressure had been dangerously high for months." William straightened himself in the seat and rolled the window down for a little air. "But I couldn't keep it from her any longer, Cari. Please don't hold this against me." Grandpa put his head forward on the steering wheel as the sobs shook his body.

"Grampy! Grampy! It's not your fault. I wanted to ..."

"I know, Cari. Your mother said you wanted to come sooner but that she wouldn't let you leave Aunt Hannah." Reaching over he took Cari's hand in both of his and stroked her small arm. "It's not your fault. You didn't know."

"Know? Know what?" Cari realized that she and Grandpa might not be talking about the same thing.

"Cari, dear, please be brave. Okay? Can you be brave?"

"I can try, Grandpa."

"That's my girl. Now, you have to know. I can't let it go another day without telling you." Then looking deep into Cari's dark blue eyes, he said, "It's my heart, Cari. It's not doing too well; in fact, it's doing pretty bad."

"Your heart?" Cari asked quietly.

"Yes, dear." William looked relieved as he said it.

"What does that mean? Can you take medicine? Can you have an operation? What?" Cari's guilt had given way to confusion and fear.

"It means that even if Grandma gets better, I will probably get worse."

Cari couldn't believe what she was hearing. She had felt so guilty for keeping a secret from them, and all the while they had been keeping their own secret. Suddenly, everything began to make sense.

"The new addition. That's for you, too, isn't it Grandpa? The stairs are too much for you." Cari began to piece the puzzle together. "That's why you nap so much and why Meg, practically a stranger, has been given the run of the house." She looked out at the distant mountains but was seeing truth and sense. "That's why you want me on the bank accounts. And why you want me driving as soon as possible."

Then she saw something else. "Is that also why you got acquainted with Jeff and have all those little conversations with him in private?"

"Yes," he said. "It's all clear now, isn't it?"

More than clear, she thought. *I'm Jeff's assignment! One of his very first clients.*

"Grandpa," Cari began, suddenly calm. William didn't think he had ever seen her more mature or more beautiful. "Am I . . . I mean, what will happen to . . . well, to Grandma and me if something happens to you while she is still sick?" William could also see her blue eyes filled with pain.

"I asked you if you could be brave enough to hear this, Caroline. Now I must ask if you are grown up to hear the rest." Cari felt anything but grown up.

"I must hear it, mustn't I?" Caroline knew she didn't have a choice. It was time for the truth, all of it.

"It's out in the open now, honey. We don't have to sit in the car and talk about it. Let's go home. Grandma is waiting, and she wants to be there for the last part of this conversation."

William turned on the car's engine, pulled out onto the road, and left the oranges for another day.

CHAPTER TWELVE

*C*ari sighed. She couldn't quite believe all she was hearing, let alone understand it. Trusts, wills, titles, grant deeds, burial accounts; it was overwhelming.

Grandpa had pulled out a brown leather portfolio from the bottom drawer in the large oak secretary in the living room. In an organized fashion, he tried to explain to his only grandchild the arrangements he had made.

"Cari—" He paused amid the stack of papers in front of them on the dining room table, "Do you understand what I am telling you?"

"I only understand one thing. You are preparing me for your death." Caroline's big eyes were brimming with tears.

"No Caroline," William Rhoades said firmly. "I am getting you ready for the future. So you won't be caught unprepared."

"If you die!" Cari's voice cracked, and she looked away from her grandparents out the window to the front yard.

"Cari, my dear Cari." It was Virginia's voice that brought her attention back to the matters spread out in front of her. "I . . . I am sorry." Ginny paused to weigh each word carefully.

"I am the one . . . the one who should be ready to handle . . . everything. But . . . I . . . can't. I could have another stroke and not die. But can't take care . . . of necessary things. Decisions can't . . . wait."

Cari felt her throat tighten with suppressed sobs.

"We have to depend on you, Cari," William said. "We wish it weren't so."

"Oh, Grandpa, please don't apologize. Grandma, don't apologize." Cari took a deep breath and carefully touched the papers lying about on the table.

"This is the hardest part to talk about, Cari." William pulled the final papers from the portfolio and made eye contact with his wife.

Grandma reached for Cari's hand and held it while her husband continued.

"In the event—and mind you we don't know when that will be—we have already made funeral arrangements."

"No, Grandpa, please don't—" Cari could no longer stifle her sobs. With tears streaming down her face, she rose and rushed around the table to her grandfather. Throwing her arms around his neck, they cried together. Virginia looked through her own tears at the two most beloved people in her whole world.

"Come, Cari-bug, come on, now." William said. "It's hard to face the realities, I know. But remember, we don't know when. Please believe me. I'm not ready to kick off just yet." After giving her a moment, he asked, "Can we finish now?"

Cari pulled up a chair to the corner of the table so that she could sit between her grandparents. Wiping her tears away with a sleeve, she said, "Okay, Grandpa, I might as well hear it all."

Grandpa told her about the funeral home and explained the prepaid plan he had selected for himself and Virginia. He also showed her the papers concerning the burial plot he purchased years ago with six unused grave sites. "There were eight, but Baby Franklin is in one, and your daddy is in the other. We've had them ever since Franklin died."

Grandpa and Grandma never referred to their stillborn son as anything less than a person. He was their son; they would see him in heaven, and there would be an eternity to make up for the life they had never had together. William, Jr. had died in World War II. His hero's death was still a tragedy to the family devastated by the loss. Cari's father died before she was born.

The two sons had been buried with two empty spaces in between. "I will be here," Will said, pointing to the site beside his soldier-son. "And Grandma will be here, right beside her firstborn baby."

And the other four? Cari wondered as she looked at the diagram more carefully.

"What is done with the rest of the spaces will be up to you." Grandpa looked at Virginia again. "You probably won't have to decide that for many years to come." Cari was relieved that something could be put off until later.

"Perhaps, your mother . . . ," Virginia suggested cautiously.

"Well, you never know." Grandpa interrupted and went on before Cari could react to the suggestion.

"There is one more thing, honey." William blew his nose and ceremoniously refolded his handkerchief and put it back in his pocket. "Jeff has copies of all these papers, and tomorrow we will be going back to the bank to put these in a safety deposit box."

"Jeff?" Caroline was shocked. "Why Jeff?"

"Because Mr. Lambert, my old friend and lawyer, is worse off than I am. As bad as my heart is, I will probably outlive him. I wanted someone we could trust who would be around to help you with all this. And, Caroline, I do trust Jeff."

"He hasn't even passed the bar exam yet," Cari observed.

"He will. And if he doesn't, he'll go with you to a lawyer to make sure you get a good one. I've named him as executor of the will and administrator of your trusts."

Strangely unmoved by this last piece of news, Cari felt her senses overloaded and her emotions taxed beyond any further surprises. She would have to wait until all of this penetrated her mind to react to Jeff's decided involvement in her life.

"Grandpa, does this have to go into the safety deposit box tomorrow? Could I have a few days to look at it all again, just in case I have questions?"

"What did I tell you, Ginny? The girl has a good head on her shoulders." Cari felt the old familiar stab of guilt between her ribs. "Of course," he told Cari. "Take as long as you wish."

Caroline carefully reorganized the documents, placed them inside the portfolio, and replaced them in the bottom drawer of the secretary.

William reached for the phone and called James to come help carry Grandma upstairs. It had been a long day, and for the first time he decided to take his good friend up on his offer to call for help, anytime, day or night.

CHAPTER THIRTEEN

*A*fter Grandma was settled upstairs, she and Cari shared a short prayer. "Cari, I love you so much." Virginia's speech was surprisingly clear, especially in light of the difficult discussion they had held around the dining room table.

Cari kissed her grandmother and gave her a long hug. "I love you too, Virginia Rhoades. Now that our affairs are in order, do you think we could just focus on that?"

James was downstairs talking with Grandpa, and Cari reached her room just as she heard the back door squeak as it shut behind him as he left. Meg came in to check on Virginia, then took an extra minute to say goodnight to Cari and tuck her in.

Cari lay awake, listening for Grandpa to make the climb upstairs to bed. Hearing nothing, she slipped from her bed, put on her robe and slippers, and quietly made her way downstairs. The lights were on in the kitchen, but the living room and dining room were dark. She walked out to the back porch and saw that his workshop light was on. Trying not to let it squeak, she carefully opened the back door. Silently, she crossed the yard in the moonlight and crept to the workshop door. Hearing the familiar scratching sounds of Grandpa sanding and then blowing on his work to clear it of sawdust, Cari didn't disturb him but went back in as quietly as she came out. Back in her room she sat in the window seat where she could see the light from the workshop's window reflected on the lawn below.

Finally, when the light went out and she heard Grandpa lock the doors behind him, she returned to bed. She heard him come up the stairs ever so slowly and quietly shut the door to the bedroom behind him.

She was suddenly aware of how tired she was. Overwhelmed, she turned over to face the door. Then once more she got up and opened her door a few inches—just in case either of them called out to her in the night.

During the next few days, Cari made all the Christmas preparations Ginny requested. Jen helped some, but with the Christmas season in full swing, Cari's friend was working long hours and was exhausted when she got home. Cari decided to wait until after the holidays to tell Jen about her new responsibilities. She needed to sort them out, anyway, and get used to the idea before she would be ready to tell anyone.

Meg busied herself in the kitchen, baking Christmas breads and cookies for everyone on Grandma Ginny's list as well as a few friends of her own from church. Meg prepared an especially large basket of Christmas treats, and as she was tying it with a bow, William began to inquire as to who this special basket was for.

"None of your nosey business." Meg pretended to be offended. "It's Christmas, you're not supposed to be askin' any questions, Billy Boy."

"It's that contractor fellow, isn't it?" William's eyes gleamed with the fun of teasing her.

"Never you mind, I said." Meg stiffened.

"He's been over here quite a bit, looking over the dirt being moved, where the roses were planted, measuring a half dozen times the same thing over and over."

"Grandpa, leave her alone." Cari decided to join in the game. "When she wants us to know she has a boyfriend, she'll tell us."

Meg threw up her hands in mock despair. "What'll I do with these people, Lord? Busybodies, the lot of them."

Grandma watched the ruckus from her post on the daybed in the kitchen alcove while she looked over the remodeling and decorating magazines.

"Better be careful . . . you two." Grandma warned without looking up. "She'll get married and leave us . . . then what will we do?"

"You joinin' the enemy now, Ginny?" Meg pleaded for an ally. "Three against one is not a fair fight."

"Isn't it three against two?" William said back over his shoulder as he hurried out the back door.

"Hmmph," commented Meg as she busied herself re-arranging things in the refrigerator.

Cari talked Grandpa into going with her on Saturday night to meet Jen and pick out a Christmas tree. They made an evening of it and stopped for hot chocolate before coming home with their selection. They decided to trim it on Sunday night after the evening church service. While Sarah sat with Virginia on Sunday afternoon, Grandpa and Meg put a stand under it in order to have it ready for decorating later that night.

Cari skipped the evening service as usual, not wanting to leave her grandparents alone. Earlier in the week she had retrieved the decorations from their storage place in the garage and sorted them. She had tested all the light strings and replaced the burned out bulbs.

"These decorations were sure dusty, Grandma. Who put them away like that?" It was an idle question, not needing an answer.

"You did." Ginny's answer made Cari's head snap up as she looked at her grandmother.

"I did? But I wasn't here . . ."

Grandpa was reading the paper from his favorite rocker in the corner. "We didn't have a tree last year," he said matter-of-factly from behind the business section.

"What?" She couldn't believe it.

"We didn't feel like it. It was a very quiet Christmas," he explained.

"But this year . . . this year . . . we are together," Virginia said. This year's holiday would be one of celebration, not like last year. Last year everyone was separated, torn apart by a mistake—Cari's mistake, a mistake still lying secret between them. They didn't know the truth—a truth that would hurt them even more.

I've hurt them enough, Cari decided. *I'm not going to hurt them with the truth, not now, at least not before Christmas.*

Cari's thoughts were interrupted by the sound of a car driving up and voices outside. "Jen and Meg are here," she said. "Now Christmas can officially begin."

"Hey! Let's get that tree going!" Jen always entered the house talking, with no thought for any conversation that might be going on.

"In here, Jen," Grandpa called, "just waiting for you to give your professional advice."

Cari was kneeling on the floor, absorbed in seeing how many ornaments needed their little wire hangers replaced and did not look up until she heard Grandpa's greeting.

"Well, hello there. This is certainly a pleasant surprise."

Jeff! Grandpa pounded him with questions. When did he get home? How long is he going to stay? How're the studies coming? When's the bar exam scheduled? Cari was glad that Grandpa was so curious. It gave her time to gather herself as she tried to calm the fluttering in her stomach.

"I hope you don't mind," Jen said to Grandma. "He looked so lost there at church all alone."

"Mind?" Virginia said. "Certainly not."

"Hey, you're looking pretty chipper, Mrs. Rhoades," Jeff observed.

"Mrs. Rhoades?" Grandpa teased. "Sounds pretty formal to me."

"Please, call me . . ."

"Everyone calls her Grandma, Jeff," Jen explained.

"Grandma?" Jeff held out his hand to Virginia and her wide, mostly one-sided smile gave him the permission he needed.

"Cari"—Jeff moved in her direction and squatted beside her—"how are you?"

"Confused," she said simply. "I can't remember what goes on the tree first. Jen?" She looked up at her friend. "You better take over from here."

CHAPTER FOURTEEN

*W*hen the tree was about half decorated, Cari noticed that Meg hadn't come in with Jen and Jeff.

"She had another ride home," Jen announced with a wink. "I told her to invite him over, but she wasn't sure he would come."

"I guess you're in charge of refreshments then," Grandpa said to Cari. "Have any of that cider left? Do you mind heating it?"

Cari was glad for a chance to escape and have time to regroup. She felt like such a fool thinking Jeff might have been interested in her for any other reason than that she was to be his first client. Taking a deep breath, she leaned over the sink for a moment before reaching for the china cups that Grandma put on the top shelf, saving them for Christmas time.

"Need some help there? You're kind of short." It was Jeff.

"Yeah, thanks." Cari tried to be casual. She heated the cider in an enamel sauce pan with two sticks of cinnamon and a few whole cloves. "I didn't expect you home so soon."

"I said I'd be coming home for Christmas."

"I know, but Christmas is still a few days away."

"Want me to leave, Cari?"

"No. I didn't mean . . ." Why did she always have to say something that Jeff could misunderstand? Her frown was from the anger she felt toward herself.

Jeff was puzzled by her reaction. He could have sworn that he had seen a little interest if not some feeling for him the last time they talked. He took a step back toward the table, found a chair, and sat down. "Got any cookies to go with the cider?"

Cari busied herself arranging some of Meg's delicious cookies on one of Grandma's special Christmas plates, and she found some solid red napkins to complete the festive ensemble. She poured the cider into a glass carafe and found the holder and a candle warmer to keep it hot.

Back in the living room, Cari and Jeff carried on small talk about the weather, the room addition, and how the driving lessons were coming when the phone rang. "May I speak to Jen, please?" It was Mrs. Whipple. She had run out of sugar and needed Jen to bring some home as soon as possible. She was baking for the church's bazaar the next day and sounded like it was a full family emergency. Jen offered her apologies and slipped out the back door, promising to return later to give Jeff a ride home.

"Take your time, I'm in no hurry." He smiled at Cari while talking to Jen.

"I'm tired, Cari," Grandma said from the couch. "Looks like you two will have to finish the tree yourselves. Will someone help me up to my room?"

Cari and Jeff carried Virginia slowly up the stairs, one step at a time. The climb was exhausting for Ginny, and she asked to be left alone to rest a while before Meg got home to put her to bed. Jeff said goodnight and left Cari and Virginia alone.

Cari kissed her grandmother. "Don't you like Jeff?" Grandma asked in her slow deliberate speech.

"Of course, I do, Grammy. It's just . . . I mean, it's just a little confusing for me. Is he supposed to be my friend or my lawyer?"

"More or less."

Grandma's answer didn't clear up any of Cari's confusion. "What?"

"Maybe more than a friend, maybe less a lawyer." Virginia's smile gave Cari more information about her grandmother than it did the attractive young man downstairs. "Grandmother Rhoades, you are trying to make a match here, aren't you?"

"I don't decide such things, Cari. You know that."

"I know nothing of the sort." Cari loved Virginia but knew she wasn't above meddling when she thought she saw a chance for a good romance. Somehow Ginny's answer didn't make it any easier to go back downstairs, but it did make Cari more anxious to do so. She checked her reflection in the mirror on the way out of the room and decided to freshen up—just a bit.

Downstairs Jeff and William were discussing investments and whether or not savings bonds were as safe as the government said they were. "I don't know," Will was saying as Cari entered the room, "the government takes plenty away from you at tax time, then wants to borrow more. Makes a body wonder."

Jeff noticed Cari as she went back to decorating the tree. "Need some help?" he asked. Without waiting for an answer he took the box of ornaments from her hand and stretched to hang them on the back of the tree where she couldn't reach. Grandpa sat contentedly watching the young people, grateful that Cari's sunshine was once more filling the house and making Christmas seem right again. Now if that little cloud that threatens her from time to time would just go away for good. Well, maybe Jeff could help with that too.

"Jen called while you were upstairs with Grandma. She's decided to call it a night and wondered if it would be okay for Jeff to take your car home and bring it back tomorrow."

This is a plot, an outright plot to put Jeff and me together at every opportunity! Jen's as bad as Grandma, Cari thought, but she said, "Of course, it's okay. I don't have my license yet and the poor thing just sits most of the time anyway."

"Thanks, Cari," Jeff said, but he was thinking it was Jen he needed to thank, and he would the very next time he saw her.

Just then, Meg came in through the kitchen. "Sure smells good in here. Is that cider still hot?"

"You're in kind of late, aren't you Meg?" Grandpa's eyes held a teasing flicker but his voice was even and serious.

"Never you mind, Billy Boy. I'm over twenty-one and quite able to handle myself. Don't you worry none at all. I won't do anything to bring shame on your house." Meg and William laughed, but Cari screamed silently in pain, turning quickly so no one would notice. And no one did except Jeff, who chose to change the subject and comment about two green lights too near each other on the tree.

Finally, Meg joined in for the final touches with the tinsel, and when the tree was finished she went up to check on Grandma.

"I'm going up too. Goodnight, Jeff."

"Goodnight, sir."

"Goodnight, Grandpa," Cari said as she kissed his cheek. She went to gather the few dishes and cups from their refreshments, and Jeff took the tray from her as they headed for the kitchen.

"Cari," Jeff asked, plunging his hands into the dishwater before she could stop him, "what was that all about in there?"

"I don't know what you're talking about," she answered shortly.

"I saw you turn away. I saw it, Cari. I saw the pain in your eyes. Are you going to talk to me, or do I have to torture you for the truth?" He held a handful of soapy bubbles above her head with one hand and held her tight around the shoulders with his other arm.

"Jeff, please." He let go of her, and she moved toward the pantry to put away the rest of the cookies. She came back toward him and said in a very direct manner, "You may know everything about my legal affairs and every detail about my financial future, but you don't know everything there is to know about me. I'm not what you think I am. I'm not what my grandparents think . . . or hope I am or want me to be."

Jeff dried his hands on a nearby towel and leaned against the sink facing her.

"I'm waiting to hear whatever you want to tell me."

She took a deep sigh that held a hint of a sob in it. "That's just it, Jeff. I don't want to tell you." *That's a lie,* she thought, *I do want to tell you, but I'm afraid to.*

"That's clear enough. I don't like it, but until you are willing to tell me whatever it is that's bothering you, no one will force it out of you."

"Thank you, Jeff." Her eyes, those deep, dark blue eyes, met those of Jeffrey Bennett, and in that moment, he knew it was hopeless, knew he was smitten—but good.

"I really . . ." He hesitated. "I'm concerned about you."

She was well within his reach. He wanted to take her in his arms and press his lips against her forehead, her lovely face, and kiss the pain away from her eyes. In that same moment, Cari wanted it too—and then, hearing Meg coming down the stairs, they stood frozen, looking at each other until she came into the kitchen through the dining room.

Jeff took a deep breath and said, "I guess I'd better say goodnight, then. I'll have your car back before noon. That okay?"

"Yes, anytime is fine. I really won't be using it myself." She attempted a little laugh.

"Want a driving lesson?"

"Yes, I do," she answered simply.

"Good, then I'll see you tomorrow." Meg's back was turned as she faced the unfinished task in the sink. "Night, Meg," Jeff said.

"You too, Jeff." Meg didn't turn around to see him lightly touch the end of Cari's nose with his index finger.

CHAPTER FIFTEEN

*C*ari strung lights along all the eaves of the house with Jeff's help and under Grandpa's supervision. Each small evergreen along the driveway was also strung with the multicolored lights. The days leading up to Christmas Eve were happy, and Cari finally started feeling a little more distant from her long year in Minnesota.

"I've had a letter from your mother," William told Cari at supper one evening. "She wants to see you over the holidays."

Cari's eyes dropped to her dinner, and she began to move the food around on her plate. Suddenly her appetite was gone. *Wants to see me. Whether or not I want to see her, she wants to see me.*

"Is that so much to ask, honey?" Will questioned his granddaughter. "You don't have to see her until you are ready. But she is your mother, after all. And she wants to see you."

"Can I think about it?"

"Yes, you certainly can. She will have to wait until you are ready. This relationship is on your terms now, Cari."

William wished his son's wife would drop her persistence about Cari. Years ago, when she let that drunken bum into her life, she should have let them have Cari permanently as they had asked. Summers and holiday vacations were the only times they had their only grandchild, and those visits came after an expensive court battle. During these times, they tried to make her life somewhat normal and happy.

When Cari was five years old, William and Virginia were devastated to hear Eleanor announce that she had signed papers permitting George to adopt Caroline, changing her legal last name from Rhoades to Nelson.

On the weekends, George wanted to "go out on the town" and insisted that Eleanor accompany him, or threatened to find a woman who would—leaving Cari with a babysitter down the hall from their apartment. At eight years old, George declared her old enough to stay home alone, with the doors locked, and most weekends she watched TV until she fell asleep on the couch.

Cari stayed mostly to herself in her room while her mother worked at a local diner. Many weeks went by that she didn't even see her mother because she was at work when Cari arrived home from school and asleep when she left in the mornings.

By the time she was twelve, Cari had taught herself not to listen to George's lewd jokes, and she didn't understand many of the remarks he made about her body as it began to mature. Eleanor often warned him about his attitude toward Cari. She lived in fear of what he might do to Cari while she was working, so she bought a deadbolt for Cari's bedroom door and had an extension phone put in her room. "For emergencies," she said.

As Cari grew into a beautiful young woman, William Rhoades knew her presence in the Nelson household only caused more tension. As Cari's mother grew older, she also grew hard and unattractive with bitterness toward her second husband.

Cari looked forward to the summers she would spend with her grandparents and passed the time in between studying and reading, becoming a very good student. By the time she reached high school, Cari was disgusted by her stepfather's filthy jokes and his continual drinking.

Eleanor's stubborn refusal to let Cari spend the school year with her grandparents and go to school in the Redlands with Jen became a strong point of contention between mother and daughter. Any time she brought the subject up, either it erupted in a family fight, or George put his foot down as her "legal guardian" to end all discussion.

Every year, the first few days of visiting her grandparents were spent shopping for new summer clothes, and the last few days were spent shopping for school clothes to take home to face another dismal year in the city, living with her overworked, haggard mother and her drunken stepfather. It took Cari several days to shake the depression when she came to Redlands each year, and she always became very quiet during the last week of her visit.

William sensed that same old depression and patted Cari's hand. "You don't have to decide tonight, honey. There's plenty of time." Then changing the subject he turned to Meg.

"What's this I hear about you not spending Christmas day with us?" Meg turned, putting a large bowl of home-canned peaches in the middle of the table.

"That's right, Billy Boy. I have a date." Her eyes were dancing with the thought of such a thing. Bringing the corner of her apron up she dabbed daintily at her nose and the corners of her mouth.

"A date?" Cari pretended shock.

No one was really surprised because Jack McKenzie had been calling or coming by at least once a day, and Meg rode with him to church these days instead of taking Will's car.

"A date." Meg's expression was triumphant.

"To do what? Where're you going?"

"We're going to help the Salvation Army serve dinner, and then we are going over to Mac's daughter's house for a bit of a celebration later in the afternoon. Who knows, if you give us a gracious invitation, we might end up here sometime in the evening, just to say a Merry Christmas to you folks."

"And you, Cari," Grandpa asked, "do you have a date for Christmas as well?"

"Certainly, I do, Grandfather my dear. Right here with you and Grammy." Cari was looking forward to their usual game of Chinese checkers, a tradition which began when she was ten. "And this year, I'm going to win again," she warned.

Because of Grandma's illness, Cari anticipated a Christmas different from the traditional one. Usually, the holiday meant at least two days of company coming and going, with the punch bowl constantly being refilled with Grandma's secret recipe orange punch. It meant the dining room table would be filled from noon Christmas Eve until long into the evening Christmas day with homemade cookies, breads, and finger sandwiches for the many friends who would drop by for a minute or stay for a few hours. Occasionally, there was a small gift or two exchanged, but for Grandma, her friends' company was all the Christmas gift she ever wanted.

This year, Meg had loaded every extra shelf of the pantry with homemade goodies using Grandma's recipe book and adding a few of her own favorite recipes. Virginia had

---

finally shared her punch recipe, and a large batch was waiting in the refrigerator. It was hard to tell when Christmas officially began, for within just a few minutes, a celebration could be in full swing and the house full of guests who'd had no formal announcement or invitation.

Cari and Jeff had taken down the large punch bowl and had washed it and all its matching cups. Meg had ironed the white damask tablecloth, which Virginia saved for only this occasion. Cheery red and green napkins had been arranged in a fancy fan pattern beside the cookie platter and the center of the table exploded with the bright colors of an evergreen flower arrangement Jeff had picked out at the florist and presented with a flourish as his first official gift to his new "Grandma."

"I feel so strange leaving you with no dinner arrangements," Meg confided to Cari.

"Don't be silly, Meg." Cari recalled the years when the table became overloaded with the food brought in by others to add to the Christmas fare spread by her grandmother. "If that doesn't happen this year, there's some of the soup you made and froze last week, and I bet if I look deep enough in the freezer, I could still find some Thanksgiving turkey."

Jeff dropped by the afternoon before Christmas Eve and asked Cari to go with him to the Christmas Eve service at church. She had managed to avoid all but one Sunday morning's church attendance, avoiding him in the process. Grandma was sitting on the daybed in the kitchen and was a witness to his invitation.

"Cari, you go."

"But Grammy," she protested.

"I insist." Grandma tapped the floor with a cane she used to try to reach things rather than bother anyone.

Meg also joined Jeff's cause. "I'm not going anywhere until Christmas morning. Go and stay out as late as you want."

"I guess it's settled then. I can't take you all on at once and expect to win."

"Uh, just one thing," Jeff added. "Could we take your car?"

Cari laughed. "That's why the man pays so much attention to me. He can't part with his car." But she knew it wasn't true.

Jeff feigned insult, and Meg teased him for using Cari as an excuse to see the car. "Shame on you for using such a young innocent for your own selfishness." She chased him into the dining room with a broom.

Cari pushed away the sudden feeling of shame and hoped no one noticed. She was fortunate that this time Jeff was too busy defending himself from Meg's attack to witness her reaction.

It was good to be home, Cari decided as she shook off the threatening depression. *I belong here.*

CHAPTER SIXTEEN

*C*ari had carefully selected a new red wool straight skirt and a soft ivory sweater with pearl buttons; then she added a tiny white linen collar as an afterthought. Her hair was getting longer and she took the time to set it in a soft curly style in the new "brush rollers" Jen brought the last time she stayed the night. She pulled it back on one side, catching it with a small pearlized hair barrette and letting the other side fall in soft loose curls toward her shoulder. Adding nylon stockings and gray t-strap flats dressed up her outfit nicely, and she was glad Jen had insisted that she purchase the small matching clutch purse.

Her fluffy ivory-white bolero jacket completed the holiday ensemble of red and ivory that was intended to make Jeff catch his breath as she came down the stairs. But before he could say something about how she looked, Grandpa beat him to it.

"You look very nice, Caroline." William knew it was an understatement.

"Thank you, Grandfather," Cari answered formally.

"Do you have a date with this young man, my dear?"

"Why yes, Grandfather, I do. May I introduce you to Jeffrey Bennett, a new lawyer in town, I believe."

"Well, not yet, but maybe soon." Jeff was relieved he didn't have to join in the conversation until now. He needed the time to adjust to the sight of Caroline so sophisticated and so disarmingly beautiful. He was sure no one he had dated during college and law school could hold a candle to her beauty.

"Cari?" Grandma's voice came from the living room where she was seated for the evening.

"Look at you, Grandma. You look so wonderful." Cari was taken aback by her Grandmother's lovely new hostess gown of royal blue brocade and velvet collar and cuffs. She bent to kiss her cheek and noticed she was wearing a little perfume and that she had added a touch of rouge and just a hint of lipstick. Her graying hair seemed to sparkle in the light from the Christmas tree and from the candle burning on the coffee table.

"So do you, Caroline. You look beautiful. Red is one of my favorite colors on you. I knew it would look wonderful on you the minute you showed it to me." Then reaching into her pocket, Virginia brought out a little treasure, something Cari had remembered her grandmother wearing every Christmas—a small brooch made in the shape of holly leaves set with emeralds and three berries of garnet. "Put this on her coat, Jeff. My fingers can't hold something so small anymore."

The heirloom looked perfect on Cari's lapel. "Thank you, Grammy," she said simply. Cari looked beautiful and happy as she walked out the door with Jeff following behind.

"Don't hurry, children," Grandpa Rhoades called out the door. "We might be having a party here and you kids would just get in the way."

On the way to the car, Jeff and Cari passed the next door neighbors coming in with a plate full of Swedish meatballs. "They were serious, weren't they?" Jeff asked.

"About what?"

"Having a party."

"They never have a party. They just have friends who can't stay away on Christmas. It's a tradition."

Cari enjoyed the short Christmas Eve service and was warmly greeted by several friends of her grandparents who asked about Virginia's health. Several said they were planning to stop over on their way home. Jeff wondered if Cari was needed at home, and she reminded him that Meg was there and that they had been ordered out of the house— "No kids, remember?"

Cari was grateful not to have to face any questions about her mother. She was happy to just be with Jeff, who suggested they take a walk through Prospect Park. "We have a Christmas moon," he had commented. "Let's not waste it."

There were other Christmas strollers in the park, and Jeff and Cari found a bench overlooking the decorated houses on Highland Avenue. As they sat in silence, they heard Christmas carols being played on chimes rolling out across the small celebrating city.

"Glad to be here?" Jeff asked Cari.

"Yes, it's good to be home."

"I didn't mean home, I meant here, on this bench—with me."

Cari looked at him in the moonlight. "Yes, Jeff. Very glad."

Jeff took her hand and tucked it under his arm. "I'm glad too."

"I have a present for you, Jeff." Cari said.

"You do?"

"You want it now? Or are you old fashioned about Christmas presents waiting until Christmas morning?"

"I'm not so old fashioned." He was curious.

Reaching into her small purse, Cari produced a long slender velvet box tied with a single strand of elastic gold cord. "I hope you like it."

Inside Jeff found a gold Cross pen engraved with his initials. Cari had shopped at Serr's stationery store and had debated between a gold pen and a black pen. Deciding finally that even though Jeff would soon be a lawyer, black was too stuffy for him, she placed her order in plenty of time for Christmas.

"Cari, I love it. Even in the moonlight, I can see my initials." He carefully turned the pen over in his hand, felt its balance, and tried to write on a scrap of paper he found in his wallet. He squinted to see what he had written on it and handed it to Cari. She said she couldn't see it until she was in better light and tried to stuff it in her purse with Jeff playfully trying to retrieve it.

He quickly put his arms around her and pulled her closer as his lips brushed her hair. "Thank you," he whispered. Cari felt his breath on her temple before she pulled away.

"Now, my present for you." Jeff could hardly let one more minute go by without giving her his gift. "Open it."

She tugged at the red velvet bow tied neatly around the small gold box lined in red satin. A little gold vial rested there, and Cari knew she had never seen anything more beautiful. She caught her breath then whispered, "What is it?"

"It, my dear Caroline, is a full dram of genuine perfume. Use only a half-drop on the inside of each wrist. It is potent—believe me, I know."

Opening the vial very carefully, Jeff lightly touched the inside of each of Cari's wrists with a little of the expensive liquid. She held her wrists one at a time up to her nose and inhaled the wonderful fragrance.

"Like it?" Jeff asked.

"Oh, Jeff, it's wonderful. Here, smell." She put her dainty hand up to his face and impulsively Jeff kissed the inside of her wrist. She jerked her hand back suddenly, catching Jeff by surprise.

"I'm sorry, Cari. I didn't mean to . . ." Jeff was shaken by his own impulsive act.

"Jeff . . ." Cari's eyes were filled with tears.

"Cari, don't cry. I didn't mean to make you cry . . ." Jeff reached for her shoulders. "I don't ever want to do anything that will make you pull away from me."

"It's just that . . . I . . ." Cari groped for words.

"Don't you want me to like you, Cari?" Jeff hated to ask the question, fearful of the answer.

"Jeff, you don't understand. I can't . . ."

"What is so terrible about me? Is it because I am so much older than you?" Jeff became more insistent.

Cari pulled away from his hands, and he let them drop from her shoulders. She carefully tucked the perfume vial back in its box and put the small box inside her handbag.

"No, it's not you at all. It's not that I don't want you to . . . well, care about me. I don't deserve to be with someone as special as you."

Jeff angered at the statement. "As special as me? And what do you think is so special about me? You're special, Cari, not me."

Jeff stood up and looked at her. When she finally met his gaze, he made a small ceremony of putting his pen in his shirt pocket. Changing the subject, he said, "Now I feel like a real lawyer. I have my own gold pen to flash in front of clients and say, 'Sign here, please.'"

Holding out his hand to her he said, "Come on, Cari. Let's go see if your grandparents' party is worth crashing. I'd say it's been an almost perfect evening so far, wouldn't you?"

"Almost," Cari whispered. In silence they walked toward the car. As Jeff reached in front of her to open the door, Cari caught his hand. "Jeff?" He faced her. "Want to smell again?" She put her wrist up to his lips and gently pressed it there until he kissed it again. This time she did not pull away.

CHAPTER SEVENTEEN

W ith the holidays nearly behind them, the Rhoades
family began to talk about taking down the lights and
packing away the Christmas decorations. Cari decided they
should be packed more carefully this year.

With the bar exam less than six weeks away, Jeff had no
choice but to return to his small studio apartment near the
law library the day after New Year's. He would need to put
in more hours of study and memorization each day than
ever before. Jeff knew that many young lawyers took the bar
two, even three times before passing; but he was determined to pass the first time. Having to take it over would
mean another six months of intense preparation, and his
meager finances were carefully budgeted until February
tenth—no longer.

Jen was breathing a sigh of relief now that the Christmas
rush was over and complaining that she had been so busy
she had not even been able to attend church on Christmas
Eve because she had her own packages to wrap—after
helping out in the gift wrap department at work, she said
she thought about sticking pretaped bows to paper bags
and leaving it at that.

Meg clucked about how much food was left over and
wondered how they would ever dispose of it all. Virginia
looked once again over her magazines for last minute ideas

before the work on her room addition actually began. Meanwhile, William Rhoades sat looking at all the "fussing females" surrounding him and complained about being outnumbered. Though he knew his health was failing, he felt very content. Only one thing would make him any more peaceful—if he and Cari could talk about her year away.

"What're you doing New Year's Eve?" Jeff's voice sounded rich and wonderful to Cari even over the phone.

"Thought I'd watch Guy Lombardo on TV with Meg," Cari answered.

"I think she has a date with Mac," Jeff said.

"Then with Jen."

"Jen is going to church."

"Then I guess I'll be alone."

"Want to be with me?" Jeff asked.

Cari didn't even have to think about her answer. "Yes, I would."

"Good, I was hoping you'd say that. I'll pick you up about 8:30, we'll go out to some fancy restaurant and then to church for the midnight service. How does that sound?"

Cari wished they could skip the church service and said so. "Listen, Caroline," Jeff's tone was firm, "this is a very important year for me. I plan to pass the bar, get a job, and well, who knows what else. I need to begin the year at church. It's important to me. And I want to be with you, too. Can't I have both?"

"Of course, you can. I'll be glad to go to church with you."

Good, Jeff thought, *it'll be good for you, too.* But he didn't say so out loud.

"Do you think it is ever possible to put the past behind us once and for all?" Cari asked Jeff as he turned on the car engine after the service.

"Yes, Cari, I do." Jeff was thoughful for a moment. "Want to go back to our Christmas bench?"

Caroline remembered the park bench overlooking the small city. "That sounds very nice."

Once they were sitting on the bench, Jeff put his arm around Cari and pulled her close to him. They sat in silence and looked at the city lights mingled with the light-strung houses below. "I guess this is the last night for the Christmas lights." Jeff sounded a little sad.

"It's been a nice holiday," Cari said.

"It's been my very favorite," Jeff responded.

"It has?"

"I have a little something for you. Kind of a New Year's present." Jeff retrieved a small square box from his jacket pocket.

"Jeff, you didn't have to . . ."

"I know I didn't. But in a way I did. I think it answers your question."

"My question?"

"You know, the one about putting the past in the past." Jeff handed the little unwrapped box to Cari. "Here, open it."

Carefully lifting the lid, Cari found a little disc of gold tucked inside a miniature velvet bag. Jeff produced a small flashlight so she could read the inscription:

New things 2 Cor. 5:17. On the other side was *'61.*

"You can put it on your key ring."

"Jeff, this is so beautiful. What does it mean?"

"It is a favorite Bible verse of mine. It says that when a person is in Christ, he is a new creature. That all things from the past can pass away and brand new things, a new future can come." Jeff took Cari's face in his hands. "You have not let Christ give you a future, Cari. You are somehow living in the past."

Cari's eyes filled with tears. "I don't think I can . . ."

"No, Cari, you can't. But Jesus can. If you let Him." Jeff kissed her forehead gently. "Cari, I pray that God will somehow help you see how much He loves and cares for you. I pray for you to have a better—a happy—new year." He encircled her in his arms and whispered into her hair, "You may have had a terrible year, Cari. I don't know what has happened to you, what you've been through, or why you went away to your Aunt Hannah's. But don't make it worse by shutting God out."

Jeff noticed Cari's face streaming with tears and lifted her face to his own. "God loves you, Caroline. You would be very easy to love." Cari closed her eyes and felt Jeff's warm kiss. Lifting his lips from hers, he said, "Happy New Year."

On New Year's afternoon, while Jeff and William watched the Rose Bowl game on TV, Jen and Cari caught up on girl talk in Cari's room. Meg and Virginia sat together in the kitchen cooking up still another idea about the remodeling project. It was all so perfect that Cari had almost forgotten about last New Year's day.

"Cari?" Jeff's voice carried easily up the stairway to her room.

"Coming!" Cari answered and leaned over the banister toward him.

"Telephone." Jeff's voice was matter-of-fact, but his eyes showed concern.

"Is it my mother? I don't want to talk to her yet. Can Grandpa talk to her?"

"It's not your mother. It's Aunt Hannah."

"Aunt Hannah?"

Cari started down the stairs and reached the phone while Will and Virginia exchanged fearful glances.

"Hello? Aunt Hannah?" Cari's voice reassured each person in the family that she was genuinely glad to hear from the mysterious aunt living in the Midwest. "How are you? You are? Are you keeping warm?" Looking at her grandfather she said in a whisper, "It was twenty below there this morning."

"What's happening with your leg?" Cari listened for a moment. "Oh, Aunt Hannah, that's such good news. Will you be able to go back to work soon?"

Cari listened a long time with *yes*es and *uh-huh*s punctuating the conversation. "Aunt Hannah has a lot to say, I guess," surmised Meg to Virginia.

"She did? She called you?" Cari's voice developed an edge that made Jeff uncomfortable.

"Did she think you could talk me into it?" Cari shot a worried look to her grandmother.

"Yes, I discussed it with my grandfather. I decided that she could get along without me two Christmases as easily as one, Aunt Hannah. I just don't feel like talking to her at the moment." Cari fell silent and listened for a few minutes longer.

"Maybe, maybe by Easter. But I will not—do you hear me, Aunt Hannah? I will not see George."

Jeff observed that the edge to her voice became sharp with anger. "I never have to see him again. It's my choice, this time, not his."

"Aunt Hannah, I miss you." Cari's voice softened noticeably. "I wish you could visit out here and meet my grandparents. You would all get along so well. It's not so far. I made it all by myself, so could you. But let me tell you, the plane is a far better way to come than that stupid train."

Jeff couldn't believe she had traveled more than halfway across the country alone by train. He could feel his anger growing, and Jen noticed his temples begin to throb and his face redden.

"Yes, I do sometimes. I think about it. But I did the right thing, I think. Maybe I'll never know for sure." Cari guarded her responses to Hannah's questions, not wanting to give herself away to the listening family. "How long before you return to work? Oh, I see. Well, it would almost give time for a little trip to the warm sunshine, Aunt Hannah." Cari paused, then laughed. "Will you at least think about it?"

Aunt Hannah's response appeared to be neither an acceptance nor a refusal of Cari's request. "Thank you for calling. I love you too. Okay, I will. Happy New Year. Bye."

Cari turned from the phone to face Jen and Jeff staring at her from the stairway, looked in the kitchen into the faces of Meg and Virginia. Even Grandpa Will was staring at her from his chair in the far corner of the living room.

"That was Aunt Hannah," Cari announced. "She was calling from Minnesota. She misses me." Cari grew quiet and the family did not press her for answers to their many unspoken questions. Cari suddenly wished that she had told her beloved grandparents and Jeff the truth—all of it. She was almost sure that they loved her enough to hear it and love her still. Almost.

"Mother called her and asked her to call me. She thought Aunt Hannah could persuade me to see her." Cari told them all from the third or fourth step up the stairway. "She was wrong. Aunt Hannah wouldn't even try."

Jeff looked at Will and silently asked for an explanation. Cari's grandfather just shrugged his shoulders. "Someday, when she is ready, maybe she'll tell us. Maybe not. Until then, it's best we back off and not pressure her."

Jeff nodded in agreement, but he wanted to run up the stairs after Cari, shake the truth out of her, and hold her until all her pain went away. Then he wanted to protect her from ever again being hurt so deeply.

How could he leave her and go back to the city to study when he couldn't even concentrate on a football game because of her?

Becoming a lawyer had been the driving force in Jeff's life. It had been his passion, his one goal in life. But then came the day he met her, smeared with flour and awkwardly embarrassed. Law was no longer the driving force in his life, nor his passion—Cari was. He wouldn't admit it, but he couldn't deny it either. Being near her was his only goal. He had to pass the bar the first time. There was no alternative.

CHAPTER EIGHTEEN

$\mathcal{U}$pon his return to the city, Jeff plunged headlong into his studies. He had given himself a stern talking to on the bus about Cari, warning himself not to rush her and reminding himself of the ten year difference in their ages. A young girl her age could fall head over heels in love with someone this week and change her mind the next. Cari hadn't even gone to college where she might meet someone she liked better, someone nearer her own age. Jeff decided he would not think about her and where he wanted their relationship to go. He would only concentrate on passing the bar exam—so that he wouldn't have to be away from her any longer than necessary.

Cari also had a conversation with herself about Jeff. He needed to close from his mind their relationship and how much closer they had become over the holidays in order to study—she knew that. She also knew that it would be better for her if she could do the same. She would get out her grandfather's legal papers once again and try to understand them as best she could. She would write down her questions and ask Jeff when he came home.

Jen's hours were cut at Woolworth's following the Christmas rush and yearly inventory. She moaned with relief but worried about needing the money too. In a conversation with Cari, she confided that to be secure in the retail business, she needed to be a manager. But to be a manager she had to have more than just a high school education. Cari agreed to go with her to Valley College in San Bernardino to get information on a merchandising program they were offering.

Alone in her room, each time Cari was tempted to think about Jeff, she read the Valley College catalog again. She began to think about attending school. The spring semester began in the first week of February, and she still had time to register.

Her grandparents enthusiastically agreed that going back to school was a wonderful idea for Cari. She was very bright and had been a good student in high school. They also thought school might give Cari a chance to put her past even more in the distance. They didn't realize that Cari carried her past with her every minute and that probably nothing would ever change that.

Jen and Cari signed up for as many classes as possible together to share rides and be together as they had always wanted to be in high school. However, some of their classes did not overlap and they reluctantly separated for part of their day.

Cari couldn't decide between the nursing program and physical therapy, but noticing that many of the basic classes were the same, she asked for permission to make the final decision at a later date. Settling into a school routine gave Cari's day some direction and kept her busy in the evening studying.

Jeff—as prepared as he could possibly be, considering how easily distracted he would become with thoughts of Cari— headed for the examination room. Hoping for the best, he prayed to pass.

When it was all over, he gave the examiners the Jenkins' address. He returned to his room, packed up his things, and left the little studio apartment. He had called a delivery truck to pick up his books.

Headed for Redlands on the bus, he let his thoughts turn to Cari. For the first time in six weeks, he let himself think of her without feeling guilty. It would be a few weeks before he knew if he had passed the bar exam. In the meantime, he intended to rest, help with the Rhoades' room addition, and see Cari as much as he could. She hadn't written to him except for a small card of encouragement signed with only her name. He hadn't contacted her either, other than sending two little notes. One said, "Here I go, ready or not. Please pray."

Cari had tucked this note in the Bible on the night table beside her bed, and she read it again and again. Although she hadn't prayed in a very long time, she began to say short prayers for Jeff. But Cari believed her prayers were being stopped before they reached God. Especially when heaven realized who they were from.

The second note asked for a ride home from the bus station. Cari kept it in her purse, looking at it now and then, eager for the day and time he had written down to finally arrive. She had a surprise for Jeff.

When he got off the bus, she saw him first. He looked tired.

"Jeff." She was barely a yard away when he saw her.

"Hi." Jeff wanted to take her in his arms and hold her, right there in front of the whole world. But he was carrying his backpack, a suitcase, and a briefcase. He didn't have a free hand, much less free arms.

Together they gathered the rest of his luggage and took the bags to the car. It was then that Jeff realized Cari had come alone. She had come all this way in the '54 Ford all alone. He just stood there and stared at her. Though she ignored his reaction at first, she began to giggle; then finally she turned with a wide grin.

"Put your eyes back in your head, Jeff. I am a licensed driver."

"You are? How did this happen?"

"James. He came over every day for two weeks and then took me to the DMV for my driving test. I passed the first time."

"Let's hope I did, too." Jeff's voice was full of worry and weariness.

"I've prayed for you, like you asked."

Closing the trunk on all his belongings, he caught Cari by the arm, pulled her closer, and said, "Congratulations. I'm very proud of you."

"Thank you, Jeff," she said, allowing him to pull her into an awkward embrace before she pulled away. Offering the keys, she said, "Want to drive?"

"Want me to?" he said. She nodded, and they headed back home.

Waiting at the Jenkins's house, Diedra Bennett paced back and forth. "Mind if I smoke?" she asked Sarah.

"Well, I don't . . ." Sarah started to object, but Diedra interrupted.

"Thanks." Without even a little hesitation, Diedra pulled out a cigarette and lit it, blowing smoke toward the ceiling. "When did you say he would be here?"

"Should be any time now."

Sarah was uncomfortable with Diedra and had always been. She was a nervous woman, hardened by years of alcoholism and abuse. She seemed to seek out men who would beat her and eventually leave her. Then she would move on to a new man, who would treat her no differently.

It was the abuse of one of these boyfriends that prompted authorities to remove Jeff from her care when he was three years old. Living first with one foster family, then another, he finally came to the Jenkins at the age of twelve. He hated his mother by then. Every time she visited him, he had begged her to take him home to live with her, but she always had an excuse and said, "Maybe later." But later never came. Jeff's birthdays went unnoticed, and Christmas gifts that Diedra promised never came. Yet she never let go entirely. And she always seemed to come to see him at the worst possible moments. Today was no different.

Jeff and Cari loaded themselves with as much of Jeff's luggage as they could carry in one trip from the car. As they stepped onto the porch, Jeff noticed the smell of cigarette smoke. He dropped his belongings, and Cari saw the look of anger and disgust on his face. Then she was shocked to hear Jeff utter a single word of vulgarity.

"Jeff!" Cari dropped the backpack and put his briefcase on a nearby wicker table. "What's wrong?" She came quickly to his side.

"Only one person I know would have the ill manners to smoke in Sarah's house." Jeff's jaw was set, and Cari knew he was clenching his teeth.

She touched his arm and found his muscles tight as he opened and closed his fist. "I haven't seen her since my high school graduation. What the—what is she doing here?"

Suddenly the door flew open. "So there you are! Jeffrey, my baby." Her voice was high and thick with sweetness. "Aren't you going to even say hello to your mama?" She opened her long skinny arms to her son. Jeff remained where he was, ignoring the invitation to embrace his mother.

"Cari, this is my mother—such as she is. Diedra, meet Cari." He looked past Diedra to Sarah, who looked frightened and uncomfortable. He could see a handmade "Welcome home, Jeff" taped to the wall behind the sideboard in the dining room and a brightly decorated cake with his name on it. Walking past Diedra, he purposely put his arms around Sarah. "How's my *real* mom?" he whispered into Sarah's ear.

"What do you want, Diedra?" he asked with one arm still around Sarah's shoulders.

Even as a grown man he needs my protection from her, Sarah thought.

"Well, I've been thinking . . . you know, about all the times you wanted to come home with me." Diedra started her nervous pacing again, taking drags on her cigarette as she walked.

"I was a kid then. I didn't know any better," Jeff said.

"But I couldn't then. I was . . . well, involved."

"Yeah, with a different man every time I saw you."

"But that's all changed now, Jeff, I promise. I've changed. I'm alone now, all alone. I need you, Jeff, I really do," she whined.

"What about all the times I needed you? Where were you then? You gave me to strangers, you left me with people you didn't even know." Jeff was nearly crying now. "You didn't come back or even call to check on me for two years. By then I had been passed to three different families. I know what it is to be alone. But I'm not alone any more. You didn't want to be my mother then, and I won't let you be my mother now. Do you have any idea what I think of a woman who would bring a baby into this world and then give it away to be raised by strangers?"

Cari felt her rib cage about to explode with fear.

Diedra stared at Jeff. "I didn't expect you to be so cruel, Jeffrey. You don't know how hard life was for me. You can't know what I have lived with."

"Or how many!" Jeff yelled back. "I don't even know who my father is, and you probably don't either. Get out. Out of this house and out of my life. And don't come back."

Cari began to back toward the door. "Where're you going?" he yelled. Then realizing how he sounded, he said, "Please don't go, Cari."

"Jeff, I think it's best if I . . ."

"Let her go. This is family business, anyway," Diedra said curtly as she lit another cigarette.

"What do you know about family?" Jeff argued, turning his back to Cari. "You give your own son to strangers and then talk about family?"

Cari could endure no more. She turned, tears blinding her eyes, and found the door. She ran to her car and fumbled in her purse for the keys. *Oh no! Jeff has my keys,* she remembered. Getting out of the car, she began the three-mile walk home. When she reached the end of the block she could still hear the argument between Jeff and his mother—the mother who gave him away to strangers. The mother Jeff hated because of it.

He will hate me too, she told herself. Cari felt the same ripping through her heart that she had felt that day in May. That awful rainy May day when . . . she let the flowing tears turn to sobs and began to run. Home . . . she had to get home.

CHAPTER NINETEEN

*C*ari arrived home just as it was getting dark. She came quietly in the back door and was glad to find Virginia and Meg huddled over the remodeling plans in the living room and Grandpa napping in front of the TV. She moved silently to the stairway and was almost to the landing halfway up when she heard her grandmother call her name.

"Cari, is that you dear?"

"Yes, Grandma, it's me." Cari tried to sound normal.

"I didn't hear you come in. I usually hear the car door."

"Jeff has the car, Grandma."

"Cari?" Virginia thought she heard strain in Cari's voice. "Want to join us and hear our latest idea?"

"Maybe later. I have an English paper due. I'm going up to my room." Cari continued up the stairway just as the phone rang.

"It's for you, Cari," Meg called from below. "It's Jeff."

"Can I call him back later? I need to study," Cari lied.

She waited for a moment and then guessed that Jeff had accepted her excuse. She threw herself across the bed and buried her face in her pillow, but she was spent from crying all the way home. Exhausted, she fell into a fitful sleep.

A few minutes later Meg softly entered the room with a tray. "Want some dinner, Cari?" Cari jerked awake, and for a moment thought the day must have been a bad dream.

"Thanks, Meg." Cari said as she reached for her English book. "Guess I fell asleep."

Meg looked over her shoulder at the troubled young woman, and without further comment made her way back to Virginia in the living room.

"I think you're right, Ginny. She is very upset about something. Poor thing, eyes all red and swollen. Looks like she's been crying long and hard."

"Call James. I need to go up to her."

Meg came back from trying to reach James and said he was at a church committee meeting and was planning to stop by about nine on his way home. "Guess we'll just have to wait," Meg said.

"Should I go to her?" Will asked.

"Yes, my dear, I think you should."

Grandpa knocked lightly on Cari's door. "Can I come in?"

Cari opened the English book and tried to look as if she were reading. But she was too late; Grandpa opened the door and saw her.

He decided on a direct approach. "What's wrong, Cari?"

"Wrong?" Cari tried to sound cheerful. "Nothing's wrong."

"That's not true, and you know it. You come home from picking up Jeff, go to your room without a word to any of us, and when he calls you won't talk to him." Will sat down on the bed beside his granddaughter. She opened her mouth to offer her excuses, and he put his hand out to stop her. "In addition to that," he reached for a small mirror on the dresser, "look at your face. Something is wrong, honey. Can't you talk to your grandpa?"

"We just had a silly argument, Grandpa. That's all. How bad can it be? I let him use the car, didn't I? It's nothing. We'll work it out, I promise."

Will was not one for pressing someone to tell something they weren't ready or willing to tell. So he just stood and made his way to the door.

"Well, if there is anything, *anything* at all you need to talk about, you can always come to your grandma and me. You know that, don't you, Cari?"

"Yes, Grampy, I know that." Cari hugged him before he left the room.

Slowly he descended the stairs. Going to his chair in the living room, he had a frown on his face and deep concern in his eyes.

"Something's wrong, isn't it?" Virginia knew her husband's expressions well.

"Yes, my precious, it is. Very wrong."

"Do you think she told him?"

"I can't imagine that she did. There's no way for us to find out without giving it away to him if she didn't." William rubbed his chest. "I guess we'll have to be patient a little longer. This waiting is hard on me, Gin, and it's getting harder every day."

"Do you think we ought to call Eleanor?" Ginny asked.

"What good would that do?" Will wondered aloud.

"It might force the issue."

"She doesn't think we know what this is all about," William continued. "Thank God for Jen. For such a flighty girl, she sometimes has a good head on her shoulders."

"Maybe we ought to call Jen then. She might be of some help."

Jen came as soon as she got the Rhoades' phone call. After a short briefing, she walked unannounced into Cari's room.

"Hi!" Jen greeted her friend as if nothing were wrong. "How's the old English assignment coming? I've been struggling with it myself and decided to come over and pick your brains. Wow! You look like you've been run over by a train! I might as well drop out now; if it's that hard for you, it will kill me."

Jen dropped on the floor beside her friend's bed.

Cari just stared at the ceiling.

"Hey, what gives?" Jen asked.

Rolling over on her side, Cari propped her head up on her hand. "Jeff hates me."

"What?"

"He hates me. Or at least he will."

"Get off it, Cari. What in the world makes you say such an outrageous thing?"

Cari told her about Jeff's mother and the awful things Jeff had yelled at her. She described the tone of his voice and the wild angry look in his eyes.

"If he hates her for leaving him with strangers, what do you think he will think of me?"

"It's different with you, Cari."

"No, it's not."

"Yes, it is. Much different."

Cari began to cry. "He has such bitterness and anger. I never saw this side of him before. I was so scared. I'm still scared. He'll never speak to me again once he learns the truth. I've lost him, Jen. How much will one mistake cost me? How long do I have to pay?"

Jen held her friend and let her cry.

"Don't you think it's time to tell your grandparents?"

"No . . . I—"

"You what? All you think about is yourself. Don't you think they have a right to know what is tearing you apart and causing your nightmares? Don't you think they deserve the truth?"

"Jen, you don't understand. It will kill them." She parroted her mother's words.

"Oh, pooh. They might be sick, but they are strong. They can take much more than you give them credit for." Jen paced back and forth now. "I think it's you."

"Me?"

"I think you are trying to protect yourself from being hurt again. You aren't thinking about anyone else but yourself. You can't tell Jeff because of how he might react, not because of how he would feel. That's thinking about yourself, Cari, not him. You won't tell your grandparents because you are afraid they might not love you anymore— that's not thinking about them—but you." Jen paused with her finger pointed right at Cari's nose.

"You're being unfair. What do you know about this anyway?" Cari was getting angry.

"Plenty. And what's more, I know I am right. Come out of your cocoon, Cari. There's a real world out here." Jen walked out the door shutting it firmly behind her. She took a deep breath, hoping she hadn't been too hard on her friend. Her anger was a pretense. She hurt for Cari, but feeling sorry for her wasn't helping. It was time for a change—maybe even a little interference.

CHAPTER TWENTY

*J*en had a few brief words with Will and Virginia before leaving. She advised them to give Cari a day or two and to encourage her to patch things up with Jeff while Jen worked from the other end. The Rhoades decided to hold off on calling Cari's mother unless things didn't straighten out over the weekend.

"If you hear commotion during the night, don't be afraid; I will try to get Jeff over here and it could take a while."

Jen drove to Jeff's house. It was already ten o'clock, and she didn't know if anyone would still be up. She saw the flickering of the TV set on the window blinds and decided to see if he was in his room instead of knocking on the front door. She circled around the back and opened the gate. The neighbor's dog barked and lunged at the chain-link fence, causing her heart to leap into her throat.

"Shh! You mangy mutt," she scolded in a loud whisper, which caused the dog to bark and carry on even louder.

She made her way to Jeff's bedroom window, and seeing there was a light on, she rapped on the pane, lightly at first, then louder.

The blind went up, and she could see Jeff's face as he squinted out to see what the commotion was all about. "Jeff, it's me. Open up."

Jeff slid the window open. "What are you doing out there, Jen?"

"Waiting for you to help me in."

"No, wait, I'm coming out." He grabbed a jacket and walked out the back door.

Sarah heard the commotion and opened the front door in time to see Jeff and Jen walk toward the street.

"It's okay," Jeff called back toward the house. "It's just Jen." He turned back to Jen. "What's this all about?"

"That's what I want to know. I just left Cari. She's a mess. What did you do to my friend, anyway?"

"It wasn't about Cari, Jen. It was about my mother. She was here when we got home, and we had a terrible argument. I said some pretty terrible things to her—things I have wanted to say since I was a little kid but never had the nerve. I don't know—having both Cari and Sarah here gave me the courage to stand up to her once and for all. She wanted me to live with her. Can you imagine? I'm twenty-nine years old. She didn't want me when I was nine—no, she waited until I was twenty-nine. Can you believe it? She's a tramp, Jen. A real tramp." Jen listened as Jeff vented his anger again.

"I have a brother—a sister too, I think," Jeff continued.

"You think? Don't you know?"

"No, not for sure. You see, the social welfare system conveniently provided my mother money to live on when she was between men and full-time babysitters in foster homes when she didn't have time to be a parent." Jeff was clearly disgusted with his mother's lifestyle. "I never went back to live with her because I was beaten by one of her excellent choices in men. My brother was not so lucky. He not only was raised by many foster homes, but in between he lived with her. I am not sure what happened to her little girl—I can only imagine."

"I'm here because of Cari," Jen said.

"This has nothing to do with Cari." Jeff looked at his watch. "And besides it's late. After I've calmed down, I'll take the car back and we'll talk it out. I can make her understand, I'm sure I can."

"It's not Cari who needs understanding, Jeff. It's you. I am not here because of your mother—well, not directly. I am here because of what your fight with your mother did to Cari."

To Cari? Jeff couldn't believe that his fight with his mother could have done anything to Cari except unnerve her. She had left almost unnoticed, out of politeness, or so he had assumed.

"What do you know about Cari?" Jen was trying to find out if she had ever told Jeff about the time she spent in Minnesota.

"Just that she's had a rough time. I am assuming that her stepfather beat her or something, and she had to leave home."

"Why would she go to his aunt if that were the case?"

"I have no idea. I've been waiting for her to tell me."

"I think it's time she did. Get in the car. Follow me to Cari's. It's time you two had a talk."

"It's late, Jen. Maybe we should wait until tomorrow." Jeff was exhausted. It had been a very long day.

"It's late now. But it might be too late tomorrow."

Jen parked on the street rather than risk Cari hearing the cars drive up on the gravel driveway, and Jeff did the same. Together they walked around the back and found the back door unlocked. "Grandpa is expecting us," Jen said with a grin.

Jen went quietly upstairs, noticing that a few dim lights were left on by Cari's thoughtful grandparents. Pausing at their door, she listened for a moment and heard Grandpa blow his nose. She opened the door a crack.

"Psst!" She hoped she didn't alarm them.

"Come in, Jen," Grandma whispered. "Did Jeff come with you?"

"Yes, he's down in the kitchen. Now I've got to get her down there. Hey, you two, say a little prayer for me." She turned to go to Cari's room. Pausing at the door she added, "It could get a little loud—don't worry, okay?" Will waved her off and laid his head on his pillow. He was tired, and he could rest now. Jen and Jeff were about to have the truth out of Cari at last.

Jen opened the door without knocking, and Cari jumped. "I'm hungry. Let's go out and get a hamburger."

"It's almost midnight, Jen. I'm not going anywhere."

"Boy you're a real sport. Then make me a sandwich."

"Make your own."

"I'm trying to make up with you, Caroline." Jen's tone was insistent. "Can't you even give a little?"

"You need food to make up?"

"It helps."

"Oh, Jen, come here. I can't stay mad at you for very long anyway. You're my best friend. What would I do without you?" Cari jumped from the bed and grabbed her friend in a tight hug.

"Yeah, yeah." Jen pretended toughness. "Then feed me. I'm starving. Put on a robe first and comb your hair. I don't want to eat with a slob."

"You bring your stuff?" Cari asked.

"No, but I could go get it while you fix me something to eat," Jen suggested.

"No way. You always leave me with the kitchen work. You can sleep in something of mine."

Downstairs Jen stepped back from the swinging door to the kitchen. "After you, my dear." And Cari went in before her to meet Jeff head on.

"Jeff? What is this?"

Cari turned to leave the room, and Jen blocked the door. "No you don't. It's time you and Jeff had a talk. A real talk. I'm not budging an inch until you two are sitting down and discussing what happened this afternoon."

Jeff reached for Cari's hand, but she drew back from him.

"Okay," he said. "Have it your way. I'm sitting here, clear across the table from you. You are safely out of my reach. I promise I will not touch you. But I'm not leaving until I get the answers I came for."

Cari's eyes filled with tears. Looking at Jen, she thought, *How could you be so cruel?* She looked from Jen to Jeff, who sat silently, waiting. Finally, taking a deep breath she said, "Well, I might as well get it over with."

"You might as well sit, too, Jen. You know the truth but only part of it. You might as well hear it all."

Jeff, putting his elbow on the table and leaning on his hand, asked, "Is there coffee? I could sure use some." Cari got up to put a pot on to perk and used the time to try to figure out how she would begin.

Turning back to the table, Cari sat down across from Jeff. He was watching her every move. She couldn't bring herself to look at him directly. *Well,* she thought, *here goes.*

"I think you were too hard on your mother today."

"What's the use!" Jen stood and threw up her hands.

"Jen, let me do this my own way."

"Give her a chance to talk, will you, please?" Jeff begged. He looked back at Cari. "Too hard on her. You don't know anything about this. How can you say I was too hard on her? You weren't there on all the birthdays she skipped. How many Christmas promises did your mother break? Don't tell me I was too hard on my mother. You don't know her, and you don't know how it was."

"I may not know her, but I know how it was."

"Get off it, Cari." Jeff was getting angrier.

"Calm down, both of you," Jen warned. "This will get you nowhere—and fast."

The three friends fell silent. A few minutes passed before Cari spoke again. "Jeff, I just think you're looking at all this from your side and only your side."

"Oh? Okay, Miss Nelson. Let's hear your version of what my life has been like, since you have known me for all of three months."

"It's not my version I'm trying to give you, Jeff. It's a perspective from my point of view."

"Her point of view," he said in a mocking tone to Jen.

"Quiet down and listen," Jen reprimanded Jeff. "We're listening now," she said to Cari.

"You only know how it was for you. How do you think it was for her? I'm not excusing her lifestyle. Nor do I excuse her for not remembering your birthdays and Christmas all those years. I'm not defending her either."

"Sounds like it to me."

Jeff's attitude bothered Cari. "I just want you to know that it can be just as hard for a mother to be separated from her child as it is for the child to be separated from his mother."

"Yeah, right," Jeff said flatly. "And how would you know that?"

She looked into his sky blue eyes and could see how tired he was. She searched his face for any affection for her and finding none, she said simply, "Because I know." She dropped her eyes into her half-empty coffee cup.

"*What?*" Jeff couldn't grasp what he was hearing.

"I said, I know." Cari couldn't bring herself to explain any further.

Jeff stood up so suddenly he almost knocked his chair to the floor. He ran his hand through his thick blond hair and pushed it away from his face. He looked at Cari, then leaned over the table, putting both palms flat and his face closer to hers. His eyes filled with tears, and his forehead wrinkled with the pain of what he had just learned.

"You know?" he asked in a coarse whisper. "You know?" he said louder.

Cari covered her face with her hands and began to weep. "How could I have been so stupid . . ." Jeff moaned. Suddenly he remembered how Cari had flinched at his touch, how she had avoided answering questions about her year with Aunt Hannah. He remembered the pain on her face when Meg said that she would never bring shame on the Rhoades' house. And today, when he had railed at his mother for leaving her son with strangers. He could have cut out his tongue for hurting her like this.

"Jeff, please." Jen tried to touch his shoulder.

"You had to force this, didn't you, Jen?" He turned his rage toward the redhead. "You couldn't leave it alone, could you?"

"Cari," he said from the back door while he put on his jacket, "I don't know what to say." But she just laid her head on the table and continued to cry.

He took the little gold key chain from his pocket and laid it carefully on the table beside her. "I'll use Sarah's car."

Cari lifted her face. He looked deep into her eyes, and after a moment she looked away. *I've hurt her so much,* he thought, *she can't even look at me.*

"Jeff, please try to understand," Cari begged as he turned to go. *He will hate me now, just a much as he hates his mother.*

"I can't take anymore today," he said as he opened the back door. "I can't believe this has happened."

Jeff's heart felt as if it were made of lead. *How could I have possibly done this to her?* "I guess we need some time to sort this all out," Jeff said.

He's trying to find a gentle way to say good-bye, she thought. "Yes, maybe we do," she answered, trying to make it easier for him.

"Wait, I think this is . . . ," Jen said, trying to keep them from parting with such misunderstanding. "I don't think that . . . ," she tried again.

"Leave it alone, Jen," Jeff warned. "You've done enough for one day."

Cari pushed back her chair and looked at Jen. "He knows now. Satisfied?" She disappeared through the dining room door and ran up to her room.

Jen turned back just in time to see Jeff walk out the door. Following him, she offered to give him a ride home.

"Thanks, anyway. I think I'd rather walk," he said over his shoulder as he trudged into the darkness.

CHAPTER TWENTY-ONE

*S*tanding alone in the driveway, Jen couldn't decide who was being more stubborn, Jeff or Cari. One thing for sure, she didn't like the idea of going up to Cari's room and facing a night of discussion and argument about Jen forcing their discussion. Deciding to go home, Jen locked the Rhoades' back door and left.

During the next few days, Jen threw herself into her studies more than usual and only saw Cari on their fairly quiet rides to the campus together. Usually the girls had a lot to talk about and enjoyed being classmates after all these years of wanting to go to the same school. But these days, they said hello and little else.

Finally, a few days later, Jen cautiously approached the subject with an apology.

"Sorry? For what?" Cari asked.

"For interfering between you and Jeff. It's just that I thought the two of you could talk this out. I thought it could be worked out between you."

"Some things just can't be fixed. Not by you, not by anyone. I guess it was never meant to be. Jeff cannot forgive me for doing the same thing his mother did to him. How can you reason with the unreasonable? I am just sorry that I didn't tell him up front. It would have saved a lot of trouble."

"Do you miss him?" Jen was trying to focus on the traffic and her conversation at the same time.

"Yes, Jen, I really do."

"Do you think you're in love?"

"Who knows? I thought I was in love once before, remember? If this is love, it sure is a lot of bother."

"I'm not going to fall in love," Jen said.

"Yeah, I bet."

"No, I mean it. I want a career. Falling in love would just get in the way of my plans. First I want to be established in my career, then maybe I will have room for a man. But until then, I'm going to keep my nose to the grindstone and work, work, work."

"We'll see," Cari teased.

Weeks went by and the girls began to prepare for final exams. Studying together, many times late into the night when Jen "brought her stuff," gave them a closeness that even sisters rarely share.

Soon the end of the school term was near, and Jen had found a summer job. Cari decided to take some summer courses.

"We'll still find time to be together, won't we Jen?" Cari was nervous about taking a different path from Jen's even for the summer months.

"Of course, silly," had been Jen's promise.

"Have you heard from Jeff?" Jen's question caught Cari off guard.

"No," Cari said quietly. "He never wants to see me again, you know that."

"I don't know that, and neither do you. You are both so stubborn, that's all."

"That's not all. I have disappointed him, and he can't forgive me. I should have expected it."

"Are you going to church on Sunday?" Jen asked.

"Of course," Cari answered. "It's Mothers' Day. I wouldn't disappoint Grandma on Mothers' Day."

Mothers' Day would be Virginia's first Sunday back to church since her stroke last October. The family was excited, and Meg had promised a special Sunday dinner even though Will had protested that Sunday was Meg's day off.

"Will that be hard on you, Cari?" Jen asked.

"Oh, I don't know. I've been a few times since I came home. I don't think anyone will think it's strange that I am there. Especially since it's really Grandma's day."

"That's not what I meant. I meant—well you know, Mothers' Day . . ."

"I hadn't even thought of it."

"Oh great," said a disgusted Jen. "I had to think of it for you."

"Look at it this way, Jen. I gave birth to a baby, but someone else became a mother." Cari sighed deeply and closed her eyes and her heart against the pain.

Preparations for the grand day for Virginia's "coming out" were fully underway, and in the excitement, Cari found it possible to only think of her grandmother's joy. Grandma walked with a walker now, and since the room addition was finished and she and Will had settled in, she seemed content and happy to be able to get around in the house with little assistance. A physical therapist had been coming over to the house twice each week since the beginning of January, and soon Virginia would be expected to make weekly visits to the clinic instead. Life seemed ever so sweet to the little elderly couple—their Cari was with them, and she finally seemed to be overcoming the heartbreaks of her young life.

"I heard Jeff called last night," Jen said one day.

"Grandma doesn't keep any secrets, does she?"

"What did he want?"

"He's my lawyer now. He passed the bar."

"Cari, that's wonderful news. Very few pass on the first attempt. Aren't you proud of him?"

"I guess. I don't think of him much anymore."

"You liar." Jen said. Cari got angry and left the room. Jen decided to find out if Jeff was doing any better than Cari.

Dropping by the Jenkins' at dinner time, Jen was sure she would find him at home. "Hi," she said when he answered the door.

"Hi, yourself. Haven't seen you for a while. Let's see, late one night in February, wasn't it?"

"Jeff, I want to apologize for what I did that night," Jen started.

"You didn't do anything, little friend. I did it. Royally, no less."

"I heard you passed the bar."

"I did," Jeff said without emotion.

"Well, did you celebrate?" Jen asked.

"No. I guess I forgot."

"This will never do. Come, young professional lawyer man, I'm going to take you to dinner."

"Dinner, on a part-time salary?"

"Okay, Mr. Bigshot, you can pay."

After ordering, Jen and Jeff settled into catching up on each other's news before their spaghetti came. Jen told Jeff all about her classes and her career goals. Then the conversation turned to his plans.

"I thought that I wanted to be with a law firm in the city, but I've changed my mind, Jen."

"To what? You decide to become a barber or something?"

"No, I'll stay in law but on a much smaller scale."

"I'm listening."

"I've a chance to work with Mr. Lambert. Do you know him? He's Will Rhoades's lawyer. He's wanting to retire soon. I can work with him and take over his practice when that time comes."

"Well, what do you think of that."

"That's what I want to know from you. What do you think of that?"

The practice Jeff referred to was the small firm handling William's affairs. Jeff met Mr. Lambert when they were discussing Cari's financial situation and some ideas for future investments on her behalf. The older lawyer was impressed with Jeff's abilities and his interest in family law. He suggested Jeff might want to consider settling down in a smaller town instead of joining the rat race in the large city. There were many well-to-do families in the Redlands area, and family law could be a very lucrative business while offering plenty of time for other interests—golf, civic involvement, and so forth—or so Mr. Lambert said.

Jeff had discussed the opportunity with Will and had found him supportive. "That's how Dr. Dugan took over my practice, Jeff. He came to me as a young pup, right out of dental school, and we worked side by side until he got to know my patients and the business, then we made arrangements for him to buy me out. Provides a big part of my income today. But you know all that already. I've put most of it in trust for Cari."

As Jeff told her of Will's support, Jen sat back in her chair, pulled a bread stick from the basket, and stuck it in her mouth like a cigar. "Then, my boy, it's settled. You must become one of uppity-ups of Redlands. Soon you will need a big house up on the 'hill,' right on Sunset Drive itself."

Jeff just laughed and shook his head. "Well, not for a while anyway."

"With a pool." Jen winked.

Then changing the subject, Jeff asked, "How's Cari?"

"Miserable. How're you?"

"Miserable."

"What I don't understand is why the two of you can't at least get together and be miserable."

"It's too late for me with Cari."

"Poof," Jen scoffed.

"It is, Jen. I hurt her. I've wished I could change that whole scene a million times."

"How could you have changed it?"

"I could have excused her and sent her home. I could have sent Diedra away. I could have told Sarah to take Cari in the kitchen. But most of all, I could have looked at the whole situation from my mother's point of view. I never did until Cari forced me to."

"Excuse me? Did you say you heard what Cari said that night?"

"Of course. It made sense. I was just too tired to see it right then. And when I did, it was too late. The things I said to Diedra were cruel and senseless. That conversation may have helped me, but it devastated Cari."

"Let's get out of here." Jen grabbed Jeff by the hand and pulled him from the booth.

"What about my spaghetti?" Jeff moaned.

"Later—oh, yeah, pay the lady." She motioned for the waitress.

"Mind telling me where we're going?"

"You'll see, you'll see." In the car Jen sat well back into her seat. Pointing toward the windshield, she said, "Home, Jeff. Home."

CHAPTER TWENTY-TWO

I think you're wrong, Jen." Jeff began to worry about Jen's plan.

"What if I am? Is there anything more you can lose?"

"Yes. Every chance, as few and as slim as they are, of ever settling the differences between Cari and me."

"Jeff! I know this will work. Trust me."

"Right." Jeff didn't trust Jen's plan, nor did he trust her instincts. His instincts told him to wait. He had waited years to meet someone like Cari; a few more weeks or even months couldn't hurt, nor would his feelings for her be likely to change if he gave her a little more time. She had, after all, been through quite an ordeal in the last couple of years. Meeting him as soon as she came home may have been too soon. Time could be on his side. Waiting was a risk, but Jen's plan seemed even more risky.

"Jeff. You and Cari have totally misunderstood each other, thanks to me. I saw it happening and didn't do anything to stop it. Please, let's try to get this straightened out once and for all so we can all get on with our lives and be happy."

"Only if she agrees to see me," Jeff said as they pulled up in the Rhoades' driveway behind Cari's car.

Jen went in alone to approach Cari. She called Jeff a chicken for sitting out in the car, but he was doing the polite thing, she guessed.

"I'm sorry," Virginia told Jen, "she's out with a classmate. Studying together for a debate or panel discussion, I think she said."

"Oh?" Jen surmised the assignment was for one of the two classes they didn't have together, art or speech. "Did she say who?"

"Sam. Wasn't that the name she said, dear?" Will asked Virginia.

"I think it was. Yes, it was. Sam." Virginia agreed.

"Did she say when she'd be home?"

"By 10:30, she said. She's so good about not wanting us to worry. She'll be here promptly at 10:30, or even a little before." Virginia was very proud that Cari was always home when she said she would be.

"Would you mind if Jeff and I came back to talk to her then?" Jen was aware that the elderly couple would probably be in bed by then.

"Another one of your late night confrontations, Jen?" Will asked.

"Well, something like that. If someone doesn't do something to make the two of them sit down and talk—"

"And listen," interrupted Virginia.

"Then, it's okay with you? Great." Jen bounded out the back door to Jeff.

"Jen, this is ridiculous," Jeff said when she told him they should come back at 10:30.

"Do you want to get this straightened out or not?"

"I'm still hungry. You yanked me out of the restaurant before I could eat. Now we sit here on some sort of stakeout while we wait for Cari to come home. Let's at least go get a burger."

"Jeff, you are such a complainer," Jen teased. "I'm hungry myself. The Burger Bar's only a little way from here."

"Who did you say she was with?" Jeff asked.

"I didn't say."

"Do you know?" Jeff insisted.

"Yes. Well, I don't know. I mean it's a classmate. They're studying."

"Jennifer. Do you have a name of this classmate?" Jeff was getting irritated.

"Sam."

"Sam?" Jeff's eyebrows shot up. "Who's Sam?"

"I wish I knew." Jennifer squeezed her eyebrows together and wrinkled her forehead. "To tell you the truth, I'm a little worried."

Cari and Samantha Slater were sitting in Samantha's car waiting for the waitress to pick up the tray hanging on the driver's side window.

"I think we did quite a bit tonight, Cari," Samantha said. "If we could meet again on Saturday, we could finish this up. We'll have a great presentation, don't you think?"

But Cari was not listening to her classmate. Her attention was drawn toward a car coming around the corner. Who could miss Jen's red hair, held back in a ponytail and bobbing from side to side as Jen carried on a very animated conversation with her male passenger. As they entered the drive-in, Cari slid down in the seat. Samantha's eyes grew big as she wondered at her new friend's strange behavior.

"Sam, do you think we could go home now?" Cari asked from her slouched position. "I mean, *right* now?"

"Sure, Cari." Sam flashed the lights twice and started the engine. "Sorry, miss, we're in kind of a hurry. Curfew, you know." The waitress looked at Cari hunched down in the seat. She shrugged her shoulders, took the tray, and walked away chewing her gum.

"Now what was that all about?" Samantha asked as they reached the curb at Cari's house.

"It's just that a friend . . . well, it's hard to explain. Would you mind forgetting about it for now?"

"Sure, consider it forgotten. Now, how about Saturday afternoon? Two-thirty okay for you? I usually help my folks around the house, but I should be done by then."

"Two-thirty would be great. See you then," Cari called over her shoulder as she crossed the lawn to the house.

Just as Samantha drove away, Jen and Jeff rounded the corner at the end of the Cari's street. They looked at each other as the mysterious car pulled away from the curb. Neither recognized the car, and they couldn't see the driver.

"I'd better go in," Jen said opening her door. "You wait here."

"Boy, you're bossy. Remember, if she hesitates any at all, I'm for giving this a little more time." Jeff wasn't at all sure this was the best idea. He checked his watch—10:15. "If you're not back in five minutes, I'm leaving."

"Hitchhiking home?"

"Okay, ten. But only ten. Then I'm leaving."

Jen let herself in through the kitchen door. Cari was rinsing a glass out under the faucet, and she put it in the drainer beside the sink when Jen came in.

"Hi," Jen said.

"Hi." Cari didn't want to face Jen. Not tonight, not after seeing her with Jeff.

"Were you out?" Jen asked.

"Yeah, I was. You?" Cari kept the comments as short as she could. She didn't want to get into this with Jen. She needed to think before they talked.

"Who were you with?" Jen asked.

"You are asking *me* who *I* was with?" Cari felt tears sting her eyes, and Jen became a blur in front of her.

"Who's Sam?"

"What business is that of yours?" Cari's cheeks began to burn with anger.

"I came by earlier. Grandma told me you were with Sam, that's all."

"Did you come to get my permission, Jen? Did you think you had to ask me before you went out with Jeff?" Cari didn't want to continue, but the words kept tumbling out. "Well, for your information, you don't have to have my permission, nor does Jeff. I've no hold on him. And he has none on me." Cari began to cry while Jen stood in utter disbelief.

"What in heaven's name are you talking about?" Jen's mouth was dry, and she clenched her fists tightly at her sides.

"Were you waiting for the coast to be clear, all the time talking about me and Jeff getting together someday? Was that all just talk, Jen, or were you waiting to hear me say I was not interested in him anymore?"

"Cari, listen to me. Jeff and I were just—"

"I know, Jennifer. I saw you."

"So you saw us? Then you know that—"

"I know that all this time you have been pretending that you wanted me and Jeff to work things out. You've been playing both ends against the middle. I can't believe you've done this, Jen."

"Done what? What do you know about what Jeff and I were doing?"

"Didn't you hear me? I said I saw you."

Jen took a deep breath and turned away from her mixed up friend.

"You know, Cari, you are so stubborn. You give Jeff a hard time, you won't listen to his side of what happened, then you get mad when you see him with me." Jen could feel her temples throbbing and her hands began to ache from being clinched so tightly. She opened her hands and began to rub them together. "Why should it matter to you, anyway, Cari? You went out with someone else, didn't you?"

"Me? Who?"

"Caroline, I know you were out with Sam What's-His-Name."

Cari laughed, and her laugh sounded empty and even a little angry to Jen. "Right, Sam. Yeah, I went with Sam. And you know what? I'm going with Sam again on Saturday."

"You're making the biggest mistake of your life, Caroline Nelson. And it seems there is nothing I can do to stop you."

"You're wrong, Jen. Going with Sam is not a mistake. This conversation is a mistake."

"First you misunderstand Jeff. Now you misunderstand me. Do you just go around misunderstanding people on purpose? Cari, are you so convinced that everyone will betray you sooner or later?"

"I guess so. It happens, doesn't it?" Cari turned and left Jen standing in the kitchen. "Turn out the lights and lock the door when you leave."

Watching Jen leave the house, Jeff could sense her anger by the way she stomped across the driveway.

"Need I ask how she responded to your suggestion?"

"I didn't get to make my suggestion." Jen's teeth were clenched and her eyes were filled with tears.

"What happened?"

"You don't want to know, Jeff. Believe me, you don't want to know."

"Time, my friend. Like I told you. This is going to take time."

"Right," Jen agreed as she pulled the car out into traffic, heading in the direction of Jeff's house. "And so will finding out who Sam is while we are waiting," she said.

A couple of blocks down the street Jeff broke the silence hanging thick between the two friends. "Who's Sam?"

"I don't know," Jen said quietly. Then turning to Jeff, her frown broke into a broad grin. "Yet," she added.

*V*irginia usually woke up early in the morning. However, this morning she woke up exceptionally early, excited about going to church for the first time in nearly eight months. As early as the doctor would permit, she had worked with a physical therapist at home and had been careful to adhere to the prescribed exercise routine with Meg's help. She had refused to go back to church until she could walk and finally gave in to the use of a walker. William had insisted on the type that had a little fold down seat, just in case she needed to rest. Every time he saw her sitting in it, he would comment, "I'm sure glad you chose that one, Ginny."

Being downstairs gave her more independence because she didn't need anyone to help her move from place to place. Meg's assistance had grown into a deep friendship, and Ginny was unwilling to let her go. Will didn't complain. He adored his precious Virginia and would have done anything she wanted. Besides, he too enjoyed the company of Meg and without her help Cari might not have felt the freedom to go to college. Will was determined that she get an education, and having Meg to take care of her grandparents seemed to help Cari decide to go to school.

All in all, the household seemed to be one full of love and contentment for the elderly couple except for one thing—the secret that still haunted Cari, the secret she believed had been so carefully guarded from William and Virginia.

Virginia thought about the lovely young girl sleeping upstairs and wished she were able to climb the stairs and check on her as she had so many times during the years. Shrugging her shoulders, Virginia slowly walked with the aid of her walker toward the kitchen where she put on a pot of coffee.

Cari dreaded this day. Mother's Day. If it weren't Grandma Virginia's first day back at church, she would have skipped going as she had so many Sundays since she came home. But this was Grandma's big day, and Cari wasn't about to spoil it by showing her own feelings of sadness. Not today. Today she would focus on Grandma and her victorious return to the church she loved and missed so much.

After dressing, Cari made her way downstairs, but she skipped breakfast. Just before going out the door she produced a lovely gardenia corsage and pinned it on her grandmother's shoulder. "You look as good as it smells, Grammy."

At church, Cari braced herself against the tributes given, one for a mother and one for a daughter. During those times she concentrated instead on how people responded to Grandma as she came in the front doors of the little church. Many people had come over before the service and began to greet her. Virginia's right hand was still not strong so she kept it under the little blanket tucked over her lap and took the outstretched hands of well-wishers with her left.

Cari stood as the congregation sang the last hymn before the sermon and noticed Jeff sitting across the aisle and a little farther back. He nodded and smiled at her, and she managed a little smile in return.

She's very uncomfortable, Jeff thought. He wanted to be next to her, giving her his strength and love, but in the last three months she had closed him out completely. *That stupid argument!* he scolded himself. *What else could she do but protect herself from further hurt?*

The pastor chose Proverbs 31 for his text, and Cari began to feel feelings of condemnation surface again. She wasn't a virtuous woman, and she never would be. She straightened the skirt of her pastel yellow shirtwaist dress, looked at her matching flats, and pulled at the white gloves she had chosen to go with her white, straw pillbox hat. *I might as well wear bright red, paint my lips and fingernails just as bright, and wear black stockings and spike high heels,* she thought.

Finally, the pastor began to conclude his sermon with a tribute to all mothers everywhere, praising them for the diligent prayer warriors and caring parents they all were. Cari felt nauseous.

A few mothers would be singled out for recognition, the pastor announced. He presented Amy Talbot with a long-stemmed rose for being the youngest mother present; Nelda Sorensen for being the mother with the most children present; and Abigail Smith for being the oldest mother present. Cari gripped her purse so tightly that she heard something inside crunch. Grandma patted her hand and smiled. Cari looked down at her lap for fear she would burst into tears in front of the entire congregation.

The pastor also named Virginia for a special honor as the mother most missed. "But she's back with us after her long illness," he added, and an usher rushed over to where she sat and gave her a long-stemmed rose as well.

The pastor asked that all the mothers stand for a prayer of blessing. Cari couldn't take anymore. As all the other mothers stood for their prayer-blessing, Cari bolted out the door and into the ladies' room.

Jeff saw Cari leave. "See to it that Will and Virginia get home, okay?" he said to James and Sarah. Then without waiting for an answer, he followed Cari out and waited at the ladies' room door.

When she came out, he grabbed her arm and propelled her out the front entrance, around the building, and to her car. "Give me the keys," he said simply.

Cari's vision was blurred by tears. She opened her purse and held it out for Jeff to retrieve the keys himself. He put her in on the passenger side, and going around to the other side, he slid in behind the wheel. He started the car and began to drive. Reaching the freeway, he noted the gas gauge and headed toward the mountains.

After several minutes, Cari asked, "Where're you taking me?"

"Somewhere we can talk," Jeff answered, and Cari fell silent and stared out the window, seeing nothing.

Neither of them spoke until they were almost to Forest Falls. The canyon carved so many years ago by the powerful forces of nature was always a wonder to Cari. She loved the small stream and the babbling sound it made as it tossed over rocks and swished around little curves, making its way to a far distant valley.

Parking the car in a clearing, Jeff took her by the hand; she didn't pull away. His heart ached for her. Together they sat with the wonder of the mountain displayed in front of them, the canopy of the trees shading them from the sun, and the distant stream singing a lullaby as background music.

Finally Jeff broke the quiet. "Cari, today has to be hard on you."

"It's his birthday," she said softly.

Jeff's head snapped around to look at her. "What did you say?"

Cari closed her eyes, and Jeff saw the tears falling in streams down her lovely young face. "It's his birthday. My son's first birthday."

Not able to contain his feelings toward her any longer, Jeff slid across the seat toward her and enclosed her in his arms. She found a welcome place on his shoulder and went limp against his chest.

"Cari—" Jeff's voice broke with emotion. "My dearest Cari." He began to stroke her hair with his hand and rested his lips on her forehead. Cari began to weep, softly at first; then against her will, sobs began to break from the deepest, secret part of her heart.

Jeff's tears mingled with hers as he let her cry out the incredible pain of the past twenty-one months. Finally, when the tears subsided, she straightened up. "What about Grandma and Grandpa? How did they get home from church?"

"James and Sarah took them. Sarah made a salad and dessert, and she and James were planning to go there for the afternoon anyway." Jeff tried to pull her close again. "Don't worry about them, Cari. It's time we talked about us."

Cari resisted the temptation to snuggle close to Jeff. "Why do you shut me out?" he asked. His voice revealed his hurt.

"I don't mean to, Jeff." Cari reached up to take off her small white hat and loosened her gloves. "I just don't know how to let anyone in anymore."

"There's this wall between us," Jeff said, "and it seems to have a locked gate keeping me on one side and you on the other."

"I know."

"The gate," he continued, "isn't locked from my side. You are the one who is keeping it locked. Can't you unlock it and let me in?"

"I think I lost the key," Cari said.

"If you could find the key, would you open the door?"

"I don't know."

"Cari, I want to be on the other side of the wall where you are. Do you want me to come over there with you?"

"I can't unlock the gate. I can't find the—"

"That's not what I asked. I asked if you wanted to get rid of the wall between us."

Cari thought for a moment. "Yes, I think I do. But—"

"No *but*s. If that's what you want, and you can't seem to unlock the gate, then I will have to find a way to get over, under, or around the wall." Jeff touched her face with his hand and turned her head to look deep in her dark blue eyes. "Do I have your permission to scale the wall, Caroline?"

"Yes, Jeff, you have my permission."

Jeff traced the side of her face with his thumb and gently held her chin in his hand as he carefully leaned his head forward to touch her lips with his own.

Cari's heart raced with Jeff's nearness. He wanted to be with her; in spite of everything he knew about her, he kissed her. She didn't pull away until he released her.

"Cari, we need to have the misunderstandings between us cleared up."

Afraid to speak, she looked in her lap and nodded.

"First of all, the argument between me and my mother was between us. It had nothing to do with you."

"That's because you didn't know about me then."

"Yes, you're right. I didn't know then, but I do now. And I'm telling you, the situations are nothing alike."

"They seem alike to me." Cari felt the tears beginning again.

"That's where you're wrong."

"Wrong? I don't think so," she said.

"Listen to me." Jeff pulled a little away from her and turned sideways in the seat so that he could face her. He rested one arm on the steering wheel and put the other up across the back seat where he could still reach her if he wanted to.

"I'm listening."

"When I was two years old, one of my mother's boyfriends beat me so badly that I had to be treated in the hospital. After a few days, she came to the hospital and was told that if she didn't tell who beat me so badly, she would be arrested for child abuse and neglect." Jeff paused and looked beyond Cari to the mountain in the distance. "She finally told them that her boyfriend was responsible, but she wouldn't leave him. She had no way to support herself, and going on welfare was out of the question. Though her boyfriend was violent, he had a nice house and plenty of money. Social Services said that if she didn't press charges they would place me in foster care. Because it meant that she would have had to lower her standard of living, she let me go rather than press charges."

Jeff talked about his early childhood without much emotion. "I don't remember this incident. My earliest recollection of my mother is when I was about three or four and she came to visit me. I wanted her to take me home, and I remember crying when she left.

"'Be a good boy,' she said. 'I'll come see you on your birthday and bring you lots of nice presents, okay? You be a strong little man and stop that crying, right now. If you don't, I won't be able to come and see you again.'

"I stopped crying," Jeff said. "Until she was out of sight, anyway. I don't remember anyone comforting me, only a vague recollection of someone putting me to bed and telling me that I could only get up when I could behave better."

Cari turned to face Jeff and leaned back on the door. "How awful." For the first time, she felt some of Jeff's pain.

"She didn't come on my birthday that year. I sat on the couch in front of the window, and with every car that came by, I jumped up to see if it was her." Jeff grew silent, reliving the disappointment.

"The people I lived with didn't give presents. They felt that they were giving me a home and that was supposed to be enough." Jeff looked straight at Cari. "Can't you see the difference between what my mother did to me and what you did *for* your son?"

Before Cari could answer, Jeff saw the frown begin to overcome her beautiful face. "Look Cari, my mother had a choice. You had a choice, too. But that's where the similarity ends. She made the wrong choice; she chose someone else over me. You chose to think only of your son and gave him a chance to be a part of a real family, a permanent family."

"But I wasn't married to my baby's father." Cari had never spoken the words aloud before, and they felt strange—foreign.

"Neither was my mother," Jeff said. "And she wasn't married to my brother's father nor my sister's." Jeff's expression pleaded with Cari to understand. "Yours was a mistake, hers was a lifestyle. You can go on with your life, she's stuck with hers."

Cari watched Jeff's blue eyes fill with tears and felt his hand reach to stroke her hair.

"Caroline, I can't believe how I've hurt you. I never want to hurt you. I . . . well . . ." Jeff reached into the back seat and somehow produced a long stemmed rose and dropped it in Cari's lap.

"What's this?" Cari's eyes opened wide.

"This, my darling Caroline, is not for the oldest mother, the youngest mother, or the mother with the most children. It is for the most unselfish mother I have ever met."

This time it was Cari who moved across the seat into Jeff's open arms. She peppered his cheeks with little kisses, saying "Thank you" with each one.

Jeff accidentally hit the door handle with his elbow, and as the door opened, he caught himself before he fell backwards. Laughing, he said, "Hey, it's a beautiful day. Want to go for a walk?"

CHAPTER TWENTY-FOUR

*I*n the days that followed, Grandma noticed a much happier Cari about the house. Her homework was always a priority, but Jeff called every day or dropped by in the evening. Jen was content seeing her best friend's happiness, and most of the time she took the credit for getting them together again.

Grandma Ginny was taking over more and more, if not the actual work, the running of the house. Meg was delighted for Virginia to plan the menus, make the shopping lists, and put the housecleaning back on her preferred schedule. The two of them pored over cookbooks and supermarket ads, and they dreamed up projects to keep Will busier than he wanted to be.

In the second week of June, Virginia announced that her days of working in the yard were over and that they should hire a gardener to do some landscape work and maintain the yard. Of course, Meg's contractor friend, Mac, always had a suggestion about such things, and Grandma interviewed the young man he recommended.

Cari had been totally consumed with final exams and didn't get involved in hiring the gardener beyond a comment of encouragement now and then. "Please, just leave the roses and the fruit trees," was her only request.

Ginny planned what she wanted where she wanted as she sat in a rocker on the new patio—a potted plant here, a small cement bird bath over there, and lots of ivy. And all the while Meg took notes so they wouldn't forget any of their plans when the new gardener came.

As the yard project got underway, Meg and Ginny inspected the work each day and planned their suggestions for the nice young man the next time he was to come. "Hot, dirty work, wouldn't you say, Meg?" Virginia often commented. And Meg always agreed and added how blessed she had been not to have had to work as a field hand after her husband died in the war.

"Left me with two little babies to care for," she'd recall. "God has been faithful, though. I've never begged for a penny nor borrowed a dime." Meg had lived on her husband's military benefits, and while she had raised her children simply, she had not seriously wanted for anything. Taking jobs as an invalid's companion from time to time provided company for her and enabled her to sell her house and live on the income she received from investing the proceeds.

Virginia always listened intently to Meg, and learning more and more about her close friend's life made their friendship deeper. Once in a while Virginia shared her life. She talked of her sons and said that even though she and Will had not agreed to Will Jr.'s marriage, at least they had Cari. What a blessing she was to them following her father's death. "Right smart, too," Meg would add.

Cari passed her exams with high grades and was relieved that the semester was over. Almost sorry that she had decided to continue classes through the summer, she toyed with the idea of getting a summer job instead. Her grandfather brought such discussions to an end, saying that she was just pushing her future further into tomorrow by doing such a thing and that he wouldn't hear of it.

"But Grandpa, I could be making a dollar seventy-five an hour," she would argue.

"Then I'll pay you a dollar eighty to stay in school."

She would chuckle and try to negotiate for a higher wage, with neither of them giving in. Cari delighted in such games with her grandfather. She knew she would continue in school but loved the sport of challenging him.

One evening about an hour before dinner, Ginny and Meg had decided to try something new in the kitchen, and Cari excused herself and walked out to the backyard for a peek at the fruit trees. She wanted to see if the peaches were ripe yet.

"Well, well, look who we have here!" The male voice coming from out back by the workshop door took Cari by surprise. She spun around to stand face to face with Richard Potter.

"I wondered what ever happened to you, little Caroline." His voice became thick as he looked Cari up and down. "So is this where you live? You never would tell me."

"What do you want?" Cari's voice was noticeably shaky.

"Well, what do you have to offer?" He reached for her arm. "We had a mighty good time that summer, didn't we Cari?"

"Leave me alone."

"You used to say that before, but you never meant it, now did you? I bet you don't mean it now. Hey, what ever happened to you? You sort of disappeared into thin air."

"How did you find me?"

"Find you?" Richard let go of Cari's arm and laughed. Reaching for the pack of cigarettes he kept rolled up high in the sleeve of his T-shirt, he said, "I haven't looked for you since that night a couple of summers ago when you stood me up. I work here, and well, I can't believe it—here you are."

"You mean *you* are the gardener?"

"Yeah. And what are you, the maid? The cook?"

Cari turned to go back to the house, and Richard called out to her, "Well, little servant girl, I guess I'll be seeing you from time to time then." Cari heard his laugh as she rounded the corner and headed for the back porch.

At dinner she asked casually, "Who's the gardener?"

"Someone named Richard Potter," Grandpa said.

"You know him?" Cari asked.

"No, Mac recommended him. Seems he married Mac's cousin's daughter, Sharon Mason."

"Sharon Mason?" Cari was shocked.

"You know Sharon?" Virginia said.

"Yeah, she came to youth camp with us one year, and to the youth group a time or two. Lived kind of on the edge, though." Cari wanted to drop the conversation now and ask Jen about it later.

"Had to get married, I understand," Meg offered.

"Really?" Ginny said. "To that young man?"

"Mac said she's expecting again—and the first baby's barely a year old. That's why he tries to keep him working. Not too regular on a job, I guess."

Standing suddenly, Cari upset a glass of ice water, making everyone scurry for a tea towel to catch it before it ran to the floor. "I'm sorry, Grammy." Cari's face was ashen. "Would you please excuse me? I guess I'm not that hungry tonight. I think I'll do some reading up in my room." Cari ran up the stairs and, once inside her room, leaned against the door.

Sharon Mason married to Richard Potter. *Expecting her second baby!* Cari added up the months. Sharon's first baby was just over a year old. It couldn't be true. Richard had said that he was in love with Cari! That he thought of nothing and no one but her day and night. He said that when she wouldn't meet him in back of the library, he would sit there all alone just in case she changed her mind. He said that he was going into the Marines and that he would most likely be sent overseas as soon as he finished basic training. He said that he needed to know that he had someone back home who loved him, really loved him—someone who loved him enough to let him have wonderful memories to carry with him no matter where they sent him.

Jeff! How could Cari tell Jeff that she had run into Richard in her own backyard. If she told him who Richard was, he would have Grandpa fire him, that she knew for certain. Then she would be forced to tell her grandparents—as well as Jeff— the whole story, not just the parts she chose; and she would have to tell Meg and Mac too. Worse, it could force her to tell them before she was ready, before *they* were ready. No, this wasn't something she could tell Jeff, not just yet. Not until she was ready to face her grandparents.

Somehow she would have to handle Richard herself. How, she didn't really know, but for now, she would simply avoid him.

"That boy's here every time I walk out the door," Meg said a few days later. "He's always on his way to trim some bush or water some patch of grass."

"Well," Grandpa said from behind the weekly paper, "we pay him a flat rate. He could be here all day every day, and it doesn't cost us a cent more."

"The yard never looked better, Meg. You have to give him that."

"I think he's trying to run into Cari," Meg muttered.

"Don't be silly," Will said, "he's a married man with a baby and another on the way." But Will decided to mention it to Jeff, just to be safe, for Cari's sake.

CHAPTER TWENTY-FIVE

*J*eff drove to the library where Meg said Cari was studying, found a parking place, and locked Sarah's car before walking in. Looking around, he spotted Cari's Ford and crossed the street toward the library. As he reached the door, he glimpsed a lone figure in the shadows at the end of the long corridor. The man looked familiar, but Jeff discarded him as he caught sight of Cari in the main room with reference books spread all around, busily writing. She was so intent on her project that she didn't see Jeff approaching until he pulled out the chair opposite hers.

"How you doing?" Jeff asked.

"Almost finished." Cari smiled at him. Her decision to enroll in the summer semester meant that she would be in classes in the mornings and busy with her studies most afternoons as well as a few evenings each week. "Trying to stay ahead of it all is really a challenge," she said, "but I am glad I decided to go straight through the summer. Probably won't get a tan this year, but then I didn't get one last year either."

"You're very pretty without one," Jeff said as he reached across the table and put his hand on hers.

"Ahem." They looked toward the noise into the face of a disapproving librarian.

Jeff jerked his hand away with a little chuckle. "I guess," he whispered to Cari, "that I'd best leave you to study alone."

"Don't go," Cari whispered back. "I need to talk to you."

"Let's get out of here, then," Jeff said, "and go somewhere we can talk out loud."

Richard leaned back against the building as Cari and Jeff left the library and walked across the street toward Cari's car. He watched with interest as Jeff unlocked the driver's door. Cari got in and scooted over, and Jeff slid in under the wheel. He saw Jeff turn to Cari and pull her closer to his side of the car. He took a long slow drag on his cigarette as they drove away.

"Is this business," Jeff asked her once they were out of the library lot, "or personal?"

"Legal," Cari said.

"Legal? Then let's go to the office." It couldn't have been a more perfect setup. Jeff had come to the library hoping that he could persuade her to go look at his office. He was settling in and had gotten his very first client that morning—his first client besides Cari, that is.

Once they reached the office, Jeff made Cari close her eyes as he guided her toward his office door.

"Okay," he said, stopping her in front of his door, "open your eyes."

As her eyes began to focus, Cari looked straight ahead at the nameplate newly installed on the door: *Jeffrey D. Bennett, Attorney at Law.*

She looked at Jeff then back to the name plate. Running her finger over the piece of polished brass, she felt the delicate scrolled engraving.

"Jeff, it's beautiful." Then turning to him, she said, "Congratulations," reached up, and put her arms around his neck in a warm embrace.

"Thank you," he said, and suddenly he became very uncomfortable with Cari hugging him right there in the reception office.

"Won't you come in, Miss Nelson?" Cari straightened and held herself in the most businesslike posture she could and said formally, "Thank you, Mr. Bennett, I will." She walked in and sat in one of the brown leather wing-backed chairs placed opposite a large dark walnut desk. Jeff walked around to take his seat opposite her. She glanced around the room, scanning the bookcases to find his law degree hanging discreetly in the corner behind his desk. She noticed the empty place below it. "That's reserved for my license." Jeff pointed to where she was looking. "The state bar takes its sweet time sending them out. All I have to show clients is my temporary license. Now, ma'am, what can I do for you?"

"I want a divorce," Cari said.

"A divorce?" Jeff was puzzled.

"Yes. My mother arranged for my stepfather to adopt me and for me to take his last name. I don't want to be in the same house with him ever again, and I don't want his name. She doesn't have the good sense to divorce him, but I do."

"I see." Jeff began to take notes. He asked her about the dates of the adoption, whether she had access to any legal documents, and so forth. Jeff looked at his young client and wondered, *What did that man do to you, Cari? Will I ever know for sure?*

"I don't have any papers. Is that a problem?"

Jeff shook his head. "Probably not. It's just that papers would make it easier. We'll make a search of the court records. Which county was the adoption filed in?"

"Los Angeles, I guess. I don't really know for sure."

"Why do you want to do this, Caroline?" Cari loved to hear Jeff say her whole name but shrugged off the feeling in order to concentrate on the answer to Jeff's question.

"I want my own name back," Cari said simply. "I want to be Caroline Rhoades again. I want to do it for me, and I want to do it for my grandparents too."

"I see." Jeff wrote a few notes on his yellow legal pad. "You are still a minor, you know. It will be difficult to do this without your parents' signatures."

"Really, Jeff?" Cari felt her insides begin to tremble. "Will I have to talk to them about this?"

"It would be the best way. But, it's not the only way. You could file to become an emancipated minor."

"A what?"

"That's when you ask the court to make you a legal adult before you come of age."

"Can I do that?"

"We can try." Jeff took a little more information and said, "I'll get to work on it as soon as possible." He put the notes away in a drawer of his desk. "Hungry? How about ice cream? I think Winn's is still open."

Afterward, Jeff pulled the Ford back into the library parking area. He looked around to see if the man he noticed in the shadows was still there. Seeing no one, he relaxed. The car he had borrowed from Sarah stood alone in the library parking lot. He parked Cari's car next to it and turned off the engine and the lights.

Turning in the seat to face Cari, Jeff put his arm on the back of the seat and loosely around her shoulders.

"Now, Cari, on the personal side." Cari looked up at him. "Is getting rid of your stepfather's name so important? You'll be twenty-one in—let's see—how long?"

"A year and a week."

"Fifty-three weeks. Could you possibly wait?" Jeff made a mental note that Cari's birthday was next week.

"No. I don't want it a minute longer, let alone a whole year." Cari played with the scarf that had been tied around her neck earlier in the day. She refolded it and retied it loosely around her neck. "When I graduate from nursing school, I want my own name on my certificate."

"Nursing? Then you've decided to major in nursing?" Jeff knew that she had been trying to make up her mind as to which program she would complete at Valley College.

"I think so." Cari frowned a little. "It's a new one-year program. Once I have this next semester of basic courses finished, and I can become a Licensed Practical Nurse by June of next year."

"Don't you want to become an R.N?" Jeff didn't want her to settle for anything less than the highest goals she could possibly achieve. He had confidence that she certainly was bright enough to do anything she set out to do.

"I want to graduate while Grandpa . . . well, before anything happens to him."

Jeff pulled his precious Cari into a gentle embrace, and she laid her head on his shoulder. Jeff's heart began to pound with the love he felt for this young brave girl.

"Cari, I . . ." Jeff couldn't finish his sentence. Cari had turned her face toward him, and he kissed her gently—with no further demands.

Cari turned her car toward home and thought about the surprise visit from Jeff. *Just in time,* she thought, as he seemed to be these days. *Just when I needed him.*

Remembering his touch and his gentle manner as he asked her the necessary questions about her stepfather, thinking about his kiss, Cari pulled the car into the garage without noticing that Richard stood in the back corner. He had left the library, gone past the apartment to have another argument with Sharon, and left again. He drove around in his pickup truck and decided to check to see if Cari's car was home. Noticing that her side of the garage was empty, he had parked his truck a little way in a nearby orange grove and waited for her in the garage.

Cari felt the hair on her arms stand up as soon as she smelled cigarette smoke. "Cari," Richard spoke from the darkness, "I want to talk to you."

Cari lunged for the doorway. As she reached the back bumper of her car Richard caught her arm and spun her around. "Talk, that's all I want."

She tried to pull away, but Richard's hold on her arm was too tight. "You're hurting me," Cari complained.

"Be quiet," Richard hissed as he pulled her tightly to him. "Do you want old Meg out here asking questions? Do you want your precious old lady upset?"

Cari let herself go limp and yielded to Richard's tug toward the dark corner of the garage. She couldn't risk Grandpa getting upset. There was no telling what it would do to him.

"What do you want?" Cari said, calming herself.

"Talk, Cari. Talk like we used to. Remember our long talks?" Cari felt her stomach tighten and thought she might be sick. He tugged her scarf from around her neck.

"No, don't." Cari stiffened as Richard tightened his grip on her.

"What's the matter, Cari?" Richard said gruffly. "You used to like being close to me."

"No," Cari protested, "I didn't."

"You don't mean that, Sweetheart." Richard tried to kiss her, and she jerked away from him. "You have always said *no* when you really meant *yes*." Cari groped for a way to reason with him.

"Get away from me, Richard. You're married."

"Is that it? I'm married?" Richard laughed as he caught her arm again. "It's not a real marriage, Caroline." Cari hated to hear her name spoken in such a mocking tone by this disgusting man. She felt his arm encircle her waist as he pulled her toward him. *Keep him talking,* Cari silently warned herself.

"Looks like a real marriage to me," Cari answered.

"Wouldn't be a marriage at all if she hadn't gotten herself in trouble."

"She got *herself* in trouble?" Cari couldn't believe what she had heard.

"Yeah, well you know . . . we had to get married."

"No one has to get married."

"Yeah? Well, what did you expect me to do? I had to do right by her. Mac found out about it and came looking for me. I had no choice." Richard tightened his grip around Cari's waist. "Now, if you hadn't stood me up, maybe I wouldn't be in this pickle with Sharon. Maybe we could've . . ." He tried to find her mouth with his own just as she managed to pull free from him.

Richard let her go, tucked the scarf he had taken from her in his back pocket, and reached for the pack of cigarettes he kept rolled in his T-shirt sleeve. Cari stepped away from him a few feet. "I've only hated two people in my life. You, Richard Potter are one of them."

"That will change. Hate and love are very close. Both are very intense, and both are full of passion." He winked.

Cari uttered a small sound of disgust.

"I will make you change your mind, little Cari." Richard folded his arms across his chest. "You wait, I'll find a way.

You'll see." Then tossing his cigarette onto the floor of the garage, he stepped on it as he walked past Cari. "Good night, Sweetheart, see you soon." He teased the air in front of her nose with her scarf. "Try not to wake the old folks when you go in." Cari could hear him laugh as he climbed over the chain link fence and disappeared through the darkened orange grove.

"Hi," Meg said from the sink as she rinsed out Grandpa's hot milk mug. "You must have seen Jeff." Cari nodded. "I thought so when you didn't come home after the library closed."

"Yeah, I saw him." Cari hoped her face didn't give her away. "I saw his office too," she said blankly.

"I bet it's nice."

"What?" Cari seemed distracted. "Oh, yes. It's very nice. My grandparents asleep?"

"Almost." Meg wiped the counters.

"I'll see them in the morning, then." Cari walked from the kitchen, through the dining room, and up the stairs to her bedroom.

Without turning on the lights, she closed the door and walked around to the window overlooking the orange groves. She heard a pickup engine start in the distance and caught a glimpse of the taillights as Richard turned his truck onto the main street.

"I hate him, I really do." Cari closed her eyes against the thought and fell across the bed as she wept.

CHAPTER TWENTY-SIX

*W*e heard Cari come in last night, but she went straight upstairs," Will commented to Meg at breakfast. "Did you see her?"

"Yes. She said she'd see you both this morning," Meg answered.

"Was she all right?" Ginny still worried about her granddaughter.

"I think so." Meg paused with a bowl of hot cereal in her hand. "Does Jeff smoke?"

"Well, no, of course not." Will seemed surprised by the question.

"And Cari doesn't." Meg placed the bowl in front of Virginia and Will. "Then I wonder . . ."

"Meg? What's that you wonder?" Virginia asked.

"She smelled like cigarette smoke."

"Jeff and I went to Winn's last night." Cari interrupted from the doorway. "There were lots of high school kids there. Many of them smoke these days." She leaned to kiss the top of her grandfather's head.

"Not healthy," Will muttered.

"What's that?" Ginny asked.

"Cigarettes—and someday they'll be able to prove it, mark my words."

"Write it on the calendar, Meg," Cari teased. In spite of Cari's cheerfulness Virginia noticed the dark circles under Cari's puffy eyes.

"Have a bad dream again, dear?" Virginia asked.

"Yeah, I guess it was all a bad dream," Cari said. "I haven't had one for a long time. I hope they aren't starting again."

"Here, this will help." Meg poured Cari a cup of coffee. "How about one of my cinnamon rolls to go with that?"

"Okay." Cari stirred her coffee.

"Want something in that?" Will offered her the cream pitcher.

"I guess."

"Classes today?" Virginia inquired.

"Not on Fridays. Am I ever glad. These summer classes are very different from the regular school term."

"Oh?" her grandparents asked in unison.

"Faster. We'll cover in four weeks what we would normally cover in nine weeks in a regular semester. We only take two subjects at a time, but then we do another two the next four weeks—a whole semester's worth of work in eight weeks."

"Do you get a summer vacation at all?" Meg wanted Cari's help with sorting the canned goods in the fruit cellar under the house.

"Two weeks at the end of August." Cari sipped her coffee.

"You'll need the break," Will said from behind the paper.

"I'll need a hospital room," Cari commented.

"Is this too much for you, Cari?" Virginia asked.

"No, Grandma, it's not. I just didn't sleep too well. I have some reading to do today. I think Jeff wants to go somewhere tonight, so I'd better try to get a nap sometime this afternoon."

Cari stood to go back up to her room. "You didn't even touch your cinnamon roll, honey," Meg scolded.

"I'll take it with me then," Cari said as she left the room.

"She doesn't look well," Virginia worried aloud.

"She's fine," Will said. "She's taken quite a load, but it was her own choice. Give her time to adjust."

Around noon Meg decided to take a sandwich up to Cari. After knocking lightly on her door, Meg quietly went in. Cari was curled up on her bed, her books open beside her. Meg turned on the small fan, noticing how warm it was upstairs this time of day.

She turned to take the sandwich back downstairs to the kitchen and noticed the cinnamon roll on the dresser untouched.

"Could we put off mowing until Monday?" Will asked Richard as he pulled into the driveway.

"Sure. I guess," Richard said. "Anything wrong, sir?"

"No, not really. Cari is sleeping, and we don't want to wake her."

"She all right, Mr. Rhoades?"

"Yeah, she's been through a rough time. Getting it all back together now, though. We just want to give her a peaceful afternoon. She didn't have a very good night, I'm afraid."

"I sure know how that is, sir. Didn't sleep too good last night myself."

That evening Cari listened intently to the music from the symphony orchestra. It was wonderful being there with Jeff. Meg had prepared a picnic basket for them, and they had come early to the grounds of the Redlands Bowl to eat before the concert began. Meg had included a bright tablecloth and matching napkins to go with the solid yellow paper plates and matching cups. Jeff had packed a large bottle of soda in ice and carried it in a galvanized bucket. It was perfect.

The weather had cooled a little, and Cari's nap had refreshed her. She had even gotten some required reading done after she woke up. Meg had told her that Grandpa had sent the "gardener fella" away and that he wouldn't be back to mow until Monday when she was in class.

Here with Jeff, Cari allowed herself to relax and enjoy the evening.

"Happy?" Jeff asked.

"Almost." Cari answered.

"Almost?"

"Yes, almost." Cari let her eyes wander across the landscape, taking in palm trees' silhouettes against the starry sky.

"What would make you completely happy, honey?" Cari had never heard Jeff use such a tender word before. She wrapped her arm across her stomach to try to still the fluttering she felt there.

"If my grandfather were well, if I had my own name back, and if I hadn't . . ."

"Shush." Jeff moved closer to her.

The concert was over, and most of the audience were gone. Just a few couples lingered on the lawn beneath the stars, taking full advantage of the atmosphere and making their evening together last as long as possible.

"There's no use in looking back, Cari. I pray that someday this experience will no longer stand in the way of your happiness. I pray for it, and want to be a part of the answer to that prayer."

Cari looked at this wonderful, thoughtful man. *He is so kind to me.* She reached toward his hand. He opened it to welcome hers.

Jeff wanted to hold her close and let all her pain pass from her body into his. If only he could. Instead he closed her small hand in his. It would take time, but he had waited a long time already. He was in no hurry.

Back home, he walked her to the back door of her grandparents' house.

"Your car is still out," he observed. "I'll put it away."

"It's okay, I've been leaving it out. I—well, it's a little scary driving into a dark garage at night. I like it better out here in the light."

"Well, I could use a little less light right now," Jeff teased as he laid his hand against her cheek.

"Come on to the porch, then," she suggested.

"Cari, do you smell cigarette smoke?" he asked as he followed her through the door.

"No, I don't think so." But she did, and she knew where it was coming from.

Later, Cari hooked the latch on the screen door and waited until Jeff backed the Jenkins' car out of the driveway.

"Richard," she whispered loudly.

"Over here."

"What are you doing here? Stay away from me."

"If I thought you really meant that, I would. But I know you."

"You're crazy!" Cari said.

"Yeah, crazy for you, Cari."

"Cari? You out there?" It was Meg's voice from the upstairs window. Richard stepped quickly into the dark shrubs next to the house.

"Yes, I'm out here. Just getting a book from the car."

Richard did not move until he heard Meg shut the upstairs window. He stepped forward and grabbed for the door handle.

"I'm telling you, Richard, leave me alone." Cari stepped back toward the kitchen door. "And stop following me around."

"Or what?" Richard taunted. "Will you tell that clean-cut boyfriend of yours all about our little summer romance?"

"Shut up." Cari fumbled backward, turned, and ran into the house.

CHAPTER TWENTY-SEVEN

*C*ari woke suddenly the next morning. She was sure she heard Grandma's voice calling her from below. She quickly crossed the room from her bed, grabbing her robe on the way. "What's wrong?" Cari saw the look on her Grandmother's face as she stood at the bottom of the stairs.

"What's the matter?" Meg came in through the dining room.

"It's Grandpa. He's had a terrible night. He's having trouble breathing." Virginia stood, shaking as she leaned on her walker.

"Why didn't you wake me?" Cari asked as she brushed by, leaving her grandmother to Meg.

"I tried." Ginny was nearly in tears. "I guess you didn't hear me."

Cari looked at her grandfather's ashen face. "Call the doctor, Meg." She was suddenly calm and completely in charge.

"Grandpa, try to sit up a little higher," Cari said, stuffing pillows behind him. "It might make it easier to breathe."

"Cari . . . we . . . need . . . to . . . talk." Each word was followed by a labored breath.

"Not now, Grandpa. We'll talk later."

"The doctor's on his way," Meg announced. "He is sending an ambulance, too."

"Cari . . . ," Will tried again.

"Hush, Grampy, hush." Cari sat beside him and held his head against her shoulder.

"He's trying to tell you something, dear," Meg said.

"He can tell me later. Right now he needs to save his strength."

"Gin . . ." Will waved in her direction.

"I'm here, Will. Right here." She stretched out her stronger hand and found his cold to the touch.

The doctor came in without knocking and found the little family circled around William's bed. "Now ladies, let me have a look at the patient." Cari heard the ambulance's siren and the squeal of its tires as it rounded the corner and made its way up the driveway.

Cari stayed as close as possible to William as they prepared to transport him to the hospital. "Go with him, Cari," Virginia said. "Meg will help me, we'll come along behind. I don't want him to go alone."

"I'm not dressed," Cari said.

"Hurry, then, my dear," the doctor said. "We want to check out his vital signs before we take him. You have five minutes."

For forty-five minutes Cari waited outside the emergency room while they examined William. What if he dies? She hadn't told him about the baby. He had a right to know; it was his only great-grandchild. How selfish she had been not to tell her grandparents. This baby was not only her offspring but theirs as well. How could she have been so indifferent to their feelings, their love—not only for her but for their son's grandson.

Cari leaned her head against a nearby wall. "Grandpa, please don't die. Dear God, please don't let him die." A simple prayer—the only kind Cari could muster.

Meg brought Grandma to the hospital after Will had been sent to the intensive care unit. "You can go in now," the nurse announced, "one at a time and only for a few minutes."

Virginia stood and slowly walked toward the curtained area where her beloved William lay. She leaned toward his face, which was mostly hidden behind an oxygen mask. "Will?" she said softly. "Can you hear me, my darling?"

"Gin . . . ," he could barely whisper.

A nurse brought Virginia a chair. "Try to keep him quiet. Talking takes too much out of him. We need to keep him as quiet as we can for the next few hours."

"Cari . . ." Will's face was covered with beads of sweat mixed with tears.

"Shhh." Ginny tried to calm him.

"Cari . . ."

"Who is Cari?" asked the nurse. "He's been asking for her ever since he came in."

"Our granddaughter," Virginia said. "She's just outside the door."

"Better get her then. Seems he won't rest quietly until he sees her."

"I'm right here," Cari said from the doorway. She came closer to the foot of the bed.

"He wants to say something to you, Cari." Virginia tried to get up and make room for Cari in the crowded room. The nurse sensed the struggle of the older woman and helped her into a nearby wheelchair. Meg took her out into the hallway.

"Cari . . ." Will was searching for her face.

"I'm here, Grampy. Try to stay still, okay? The doctor says it's important you try to rest."

"Go . . . to . . . workshop . . ." Will was exhausted and the three words were difficult to say behind the mask.

"The workshop?" Cari didn't understand. "You want something from the workshop?"

"Look . . ." Grandpa was breathing heavily.

"He needs to rest now," the nurse said.

"Under . . . canvas," Will said.

"What did he say?" Cari searched the face of the nurse.

"Something about under a canvas," the nurse said. "He needs his rest now. You can come back in a little while."

Cari went to where her grandmother was sitting. Meg had brought a little blanket and tucked it around her lap and was trying to keep her calm and encouraged.

"Cari?" Meg wondered who would need the most care now, Ginny or her granddaughter.

"I'm okay, Meg."

"What did he say, dear?" Cari didn't notice how slurred her grandmother's speech was becoming, but Meg did.

"He said he wanted me to look under the canvas in the workshop."

"Go, Cari," Virginia said simply. Meg noticed the slumping shoulders of her beloved patient. "Go now."

"But what about you," Cari said. "You will be stuck here."

"I've already called the Jenkins'. They're on their way. We'll be fine," offered Meg.

Going out the door, she didn't even see Sarah and James come in. Jeff had driven them and was parking their car when Cari drove out of the parking lot and headed for home.

As soon as the doctor saw the first signs of hope, he told Virginia to go home.

"He seems to be resting now. We've given him some medication, and he will be sleeping for a while. It's been a close one, but I think he'll pull through it. Virginia, you have had a long night. You need to go home now and rest too. You can come back any time you feel up to it. I'll let them know at the desk that visiting hours don't apply to you."

"We'll stay with him," James said to Virginia. "We'll be right here outside the door saying our prayers for William." He turned to Jeff. "Take them home, will you, son? We'll call if there is any news or change."

"Where's Cari?" Jeff couldn't believe she would leave her grandmother here with only Meg.

"Her grandfather sent her on an errand," said Meg.

Jeff noticed the silence that fell across Virginia. "Grandma Ginny?" He took her hand as he squatted by the side of the wheelchair.

"Home." Ginny's eyes filled with tears. "We need to go home to her, Jeff. This is not at all how Will wanted her to know."

"Know?"

"Please, Jeffrey. Take us home. Go to her. Try to understand. You love her, don't you, Jeff? She needs you now. Please, Jeff, she needs you."

"I'm here, Grandma. I'm here for her, and I'm here for you."

CHAPTER TWENTY-EIGHT

*C*ari arrived home and rushed in to find the key to the workshop missing from its peg on the back porch. She looked around on the floor, thinking it might have dropped as her grandfather hung it. Then she ran into the dining room and looked on the secretary where she and Grandpa had set up a bill paying system and stored all their important papers. There on a small shelf were Grandpa's keys tucked neatly into his black leather key pouch. She grabbed the little bundle of keys and headed out to the workshop.

Standing in front of the workshop door she looked at the keys, and recognizing the right one, she unlatched the padlock. She stepped into the room, and suddenly anticipation caused her heart to pound wildly within her chest. Battling tears, she fought her way forward, willing each step toward the canvas covering.

She placed her hand on the object without lifting the canvas and it moved from side to side under the weight of her hand. She stood back a little and watched the mysterious shape continue to rock slightly even though she no longer was touching it.

Afraid to look and terrified not to, Cari carefully lifted one corner of the canvas and pulled it slowly toward her. She couldn't believe what she saw. Rocking gently from side to side was a beautiful hand-carved cradle. She pulled the canvas completely out of her way and tugged on the large wooden cradle until it was out in the middle of the floor. She ran her hands over it and gave it a little shove to see it rock—back and forth, back and forth. It was then, just before her eyes filled over with tears, that she spotted a white envelope lying in the center—where a baby would sleep as her mother rocked the cradle and sang lullabies.

She took a deep breath that caught in her throat and shuddered as a sob escaped silently. She reached for the envelope.

Caroline. It was addressed in Grandpa's own hand. She turned the envelope over and carefully slid her finger under the sealed flap, trying not to tear it. Inside she found a letter.

My dearest Caroline,

It has been several months since you left so suddenly to be with your Aunt Hannah in St. Paul. Your grandmother and I were beside ourselves with worry until we found a way to make your mother tell us why you went and why it was so sudden.

It is no secret how much we love you, and you know how much pain we have gone through because of your stepfather's interference in our lives and with you, our only grandchild. Our lawyer advised us that we could file charges against your mother and stepfather. By sending you away without our knowledge and permission, they violated the court order giving us visitation rights. It was when we told her this that she decided to tell us the truth— to tell us about your baby.

The baby! Grandpa knew about the baby! Why didn't he say so? Why didn't he and Grandma call and let me come home then? Cari continued reading:

*Your mother denies knowing who the father is and assures us
that the decision to go to Aunt Hannah's was your own. She
also told us that you wanted to spare us the pain of finding out
about the baby and that someday you would tell us—when you
were ready.*

*Your mother says that you have decided to put your baby up for
adoption. I trust this is your decision and not hers—nor your
stepfather's.*

*I have made a small cradle for your baby should you decide to
keep it. You are precious to us, darling Caroline Grace. Nothing
you could ever do will ever change that. Your grandmother and I
pray every day for you and that the baby will be healthy and
strong. We pray that your decision is yours alone, and we pray
that whatever happens, you will come back to us here, home
where you belong.*

> *Eternal love,*
> *Grandpa William Rhoades*

Cari dropped beside the cradle and began to weep. She
felt as if her ribs would break from heartbreak.

"No. No! Grandpa," she sobbed, "my baby."

As Jeff approached the workshop, he could hear her
sobbing. He quickly crossed the lawn and opened the
workshop door. There he found her slumped on the floor
with her arms around the cradle as far as she could reach.

"Cari, my Cari." Jeff knelt beside her. As she lifted her
head and looked into his eyes, he felt his own heart break
open. He gathered her into his arms and pulled her onto
his lap as he sat on the floor. He wished he could make her
pain go away. He loved her so much.

"He knew, all this time he knew," Cari sobbed. She held
up the letter for Jeff to read. "Why didn't he tell me he
knew?"

"I don't know, Cari." Jeff stroked her head and smoothed her hair away from her tear-streaked face.

"I wanted to tell him myself. I wanted to, but I couldn't. I was afraid . . . I didn't want him to . . ."

"Afraid? Of what? Afraid that he wouldn't love you anymore? Afraid he would never want to see you again?"

"Yes, but I was also afraid he would make me tell him who the father was, and I wanted to forget. Jeff, I want to forget."

"I know you do, Caroline. I know." Jeff held her while she cried and soothed her as best he could. She felt his warmth and love, and she let it reach deep into the part of her heart that she had protected for so long. She let his strength surround her and his compassion wash over her. She sat on the floor with Jeff, her beloved Jeff, and let him hold her through the pain.

Finally, she lifted her head from his shoulder and wiped her tears with the back of her hand.

"Grandpa? Have you heard about Grandpa?"

"Yes, Sweetheart. I brought Grandma and Meg home."

"Home? Is Grandpa gone?" she asked fearfully.

"No, baby. He's resting quietly. He needed you to know about the cradle, I guess. When he sent you home, he finally calmed down and went to sleep." Jeff looked at the chestnut-haired treasure within the circle of his arms. "The doctor says it was close, but he will make it through this. Looks like you'll have a little more time with him after all."

"Why did he send me here?" Cari wondered aloud.

"He thought he was dying, I guess. I don't think he wanted that to happen with secrets between you." Jeff's forehead wrinkled in a frown.

"What's the matter?" Cari asked.

"I was just thinking that Grandpa didn't want to die with any secrets between you, and I don't want to live with any between us." Jeff looked deep into her deep, velvet blue eyes.

"Jeff," Cari said as she wrapped her arms around his neck.

"Caroline," Jeff whispered huskily into her neck, "I love you." Then he pulled her tighter into his arms and held on a few precious moments longer.

"Let's go see if there is any news." Jeff stood to his feet and pulled her up with him. Richard stepped back out of sight—away from the window where he had watched and heard every word between them. As soon as Cari and Jeff were inside the house, he found they had forgotten to lock the workshop door and he slipped inside. It was getting too dark to see much, but he found the letter and slipped it into his back pocket. *It might come in handy,* he thought—*yes, mighty handy.*

CHAPTER TWENTY-NINE

I just put her to bed, but I think she wants to see you, Cari," Meg said as Jeff and Cari came in the back door. "Go ahead," Jeff said. "You have a lot to talk about with her."

"Are you going to . . ."

"I'm not going anywhere," Jeff added. "I promised I would stay here until I heard from Sarah and James. Go on now, Grandma is waiting."

Cari went to her grandmother's bedroom and slipped in the door. Virginia was propped up slightly, and she held her hand out to Cari when she came in.

"Come here, my child," Virginia said softly. "Come and lay beside me."

"Grammy," Cari said as she carefully lay beside her aging grandmother, "you knew all along."

"Not all along. Only since early last January. We couldn't understand why you wouldn't come home for Christmas. We were willing to pay your airline fare here and back to St. Paul. Grandpa even offered to pay for someone to stay with Aunt Hannah so you could be away for a week or two. Your mother, though, she wouldn't hear of it. She became so angry with us. She even told your Grandpa to butt out and mind his own blankety-blank business."

"She swore at Grandpa?" Cari could hardly believe her mother would do such a thing. Even though curse words were common in their house, her mother respected her grandparents' Christian standards.

"She did. But later we realized she must have been hiding something. That no-good husband of hers took the phone and wouldn't let her talk to us anymore. That's when we called Mr. Lambert."

"The lawyer?"

"Uh-huh. But enough talk of your mother. Cari, dear, I want to talk about you. You've been through a terrible ordeal, and you felt you couldn't share it with us. Why? Caroline, why didn't you trust us to help you?"

Cari was trying to find the words to answer when Meg came in. "Sarah and James are back," she announced. "They took a cab from the hospital."

"Come in, Sarah." Virginia saw her friend peeking around Meg at the doorway. "Did you see Will before you left?"

"Only for a minute. They only want family to see him. However, the doctor came in and told the nurse we could see him for ourselves so that we could give you a better report."

"Well? How's he doing?" Ginny was anxious for any word about her beloved husband.

"He's doing pretty well, actually, considering what he's been through."

"Congestive heart failure," James's voice came from behind his wife. "With medication and rest, and he'll be better real soon. He's asking for Cari, though."

Cari stood up and looked at Ginny. "Go dear," Virginia said, "have Jeff drive you. Give Grandpa my love, will you? Tell him I'll see him tomorrow, I'm a little tired tonight."

Jeff drove Cari's Ford and dropped her off by the hospital entrance. She waited for him to park and come in before she went to the intensive care unit.

"Grandpa?" Cari peeked behind the curtain separating him from the other patients.

"Cari?" Grandpa said from behind his oxygen mask.

Cari bent toward him and found a way to nuzzle his cheek despite the elastic strap holding the oxygen mask in place.

"Let me take that off for a few minutes," the nurse said. "Is that okay?"

"Oh, yes. It's quite okay. He's doing very nicely, and tomorrow we'll move him to a regular room."

"Cari, you went to the workshop?" Grandpa's voice was hoarse and he sounded tired.

"Yes, Grampy, I did. I went and I saw the cradle." Tears of relief rolled down her cheeks and fell on his face.

"Now, my little Cari-bug, what are those tears about?"

"Grampy, I'm so sorry."

"Sorry? Now wait a minute."

"Shh. I'm telling you something important." Cari held her fingers across his lips. He covered her hand with his and kissed her fingers.

"Okay. I won't interrupt."

"Good. Grandpa, I didn't tell you because I was afraid to. Mama said it would kill you. You had such hopes for me, and I disappointed you."

"Now, no, Cari—"

"I thought you weren't going to interrupt."

"I could never be disappointed in you, honey. Never, never. Don't ever think such a thing. Promise?"

"Grandpa, how did I ever deserve such a wonderful grandfather as you?"

"Deserve? Cari, when are you going to learn . . ."

"Family members only, they told me," Jeff said from the foot of the bed.

"Jeff? That you?" Will asked.

"It's me."

"Take care of my little girl here." Will's eyes were full of love for Cari. "Take her home now. I've a big day tomorrow, and I need a good night's sleep."

"Big day?" Jeff looked at Cari for an explanation.

"Moving to a regular room." Cari was smiling for the first time today.

"Let's get out of here, and let the man have his rest then," Jeff teased.

Cari kissed her grandfather's cheek once more. "You need a shave, too."

The Jenkins had already left the Rhoades' house, and since Cari didn't want to be without her car—just in case there was an urgent call from the hospital—Jeff reluctantly agreed to let her drop him off and go home alone. He steered the car into the driveway, and before getting out, he turned off the motor and looked out the windshield ahead, deep in thought.

"It's been quite a day, Cari. It must be good to finally have the secret out in the open," Jeff mused.

"It's good. I'm just sorry that it had to take a crisis to get it out. I don't know what I would've done if Grandpa had died and I had to spend the rest of my life knowing that I never told him."

"Cari, there's something I must say to you." Jeff turned, took her hand in his, and began to play with her fingers. "It's not dying with secrets that is so destructive but living with them. Caroline, I told you today that I love you. I do, Cari, very much. I tried to restrain my feelings for you."

"You did? Why?"

"Because of the differences between us. Our backgrounds are so different, I don't even know my grandparents, yours adore you. I hate my mother . . ."

"Jeff!" Cari interrupted.

"Okay, I'm trying to understand her. But that's not for her sake, it's not even for mine. I want to understand her because it is important to you. But that's not the biggest difference—Cari, you know I'm ten years older than you."

"I know that."

"It's something to consider."

"Because you're older or because I'm younger than you? Jeff, is there a chance that this could be a problem for you? Because it's not a problem for me."

"It's not? Are you sure?"

"I'm sure. Now let's go back to that other thing you said."

"What other thing?"

Cari held her hand up to his face and turned his head gently toward her. "Face to face, eye to eye, I want you to say it again."

"Cari, my precious Cari, I love you."

Reaching home, Cari pulled the car into the driveway and turned off the engine and the lights. Sitting there in the dark, she leaned back in the seat and tried to recapture the full significance of the day's events. Grandfather's illness, the secret between them finally out in the open, and Jeff's declaration of love—it was overwhelming.

Grandfather's letter! She wanted to read it again and keep it in a safe place. She got out of the car, lowered the garage door, and went to the workshop. Inside, she turned on the light and went over to the cradle. She knelt beside it and ran her hands over the fine oil-finished wood. It was, without a doubt, her grandfather's finest piece.

She let her fingers feel every carved rosebud and the little hearts woven together in a delicate pattern at the head. She noticed little hearts carved on every spindle and a smaller heart pattern at the foot. She examined every seam and joint and noticed there were grooves and pegs but not one nail in the entire piece. She felt the smooth surface and let her mind picture a baby being rocked to sleep there. Maybe it won't be my first baby, but hopefully . . . well, someday maybe she would rock Jeff's child in it.

She found the envelope lying on the floor and opened it. It was empty! She looked around on the floor and under the workbench. She moved the cradle and crawled on the workshop floor, searching every inch of it.

"It's gone," she whispered. "Maybe Jeff picked it up."

"Looking for something?" She heard the words just as she caught the smell of cigarettes.

Scrambling to her feet, she realized Richard was blocking the doorway.

"Leave me alone."

"Oh, yeah, alone. You little slut. You led me to believe you were so pure. You told me I was the only one—now I find out you haven't been totally honest with me."

Richard stood to one side of the doorway and blocked it with his foot.

"Richard, go away."

"I don't think so, Cari. Not just yet."

"When?"

"When you admit you still have feelings for me—that's when."

"Okay. I still have feelings for you. I hate you!" Cari was trembling.

"I don't think you mean that, Cari."

"Yes, I do."

"Well, maybe we can change all that." Richard eyed her but did not move toward her. He just stood there, blocking her only way out of the workshop.

"You know, Cari," Richard said, and she noticed his tone changing, "I think I might just know a way to get me to stop hounding you."

Cari listened without saying a word.

"Yes, I think there is a way," he continued. "Want to know what it is?"

Cari didn't answer.

"Well, let me tell you, since you are so interested in getting rid of me. You either let me have a little—you know, *attention* from time to time or see to it that there is a nice little raise in my monthly gardening check. Not for me, mind you, for Sharon and the babies—you understand."

"How dare you?"

"How dare I?" Richard laughed and lunged across the workshop and grabbed Cari's arm. "How dare I?" He slammed her up against the wall then pressed his body close to hers.

"How would your lily-white boyfriend like it if he found out that in addition to that little brat you gave away, you also had—shall we say—feelings for me?" Richard's face was within an inch of Cari's, and she turned her face away from him. "It's one thing to forgive a girl for one mistake, but two?" Richard grabbed Cari's face in his rough hand and forced her head around and slammed his lips on hers.

Cari felt her knees buckle and the room began to spin. "See?" Richard said, lifting his face from hers, "I can still sweep you off your feet." He sauntered across the shop toward the door, and reaching for his back pocket, he pulled out the letter written by Cari's grandfather. Waving it above his head as he went out into the night, he said,

"Remember, a raise or a—well, you know what. Maybe I could even find it in my heart to give you back this letter from your old man."

Cari slumped down the wall to the floor. "Grandpa! Jeff!" she cried. "Dear God, what am I going to do?"

*I*t's strange how routine survives in the midst of crisis. Or is it that routine helps those in crisis survive? Meg wondered if the latter weren't true when the household quickly settled into a routine that helped them cope with the next few difficult weeks.

Cari went to class every morning, and Meg took Virginia to the hospital to see Will. Then Cari came home and spent a little time with her grandmother shortly before lunch. After lunch, Virginia took her nap while Cari studied or looked after the household accounts and paid bills. After dinner, Cari went to see Will and came home to give Virginia a report. It was a routine that worked well, except for one thing. Meg was aware that Cari was not sleeping well.

"You didn't turn the covers down on your bed last night, did you, Cari?"

"I fell asleep reading, Meg. Next thing I knew it was morning." But Meg knew different.

Since Will's illness, Meg had taken to sleeping on the daybed they had put in the kitchen for Virginia's daytime use. She felt that she should be in the main house should either Virginia or Cari need her. Since Cari's room was directly overhead, she could hear the floor boards squeak under even Cari's light step. Late at night, she heard the young girl move around her room. She could tell when Cari left the bed to go into the bathroom or to sit in the window seat.

One night Meg knew Cari had been awake most of the night because of the sounds she made upstairs. The next morning when Meg mentioned it, Cari shrugged it off.

"I lost a pair of earrings and decided to search all my dresser drawers," she explained.

When Cari was preparing for final exams, "studied late" was her answer to Meg's question about her late-night habits.

"She's losing weight," Virginia noticed aloud to Meg. "I'm worried about her. Has she said anything to you?"

"No, Ginny. If she were to talk to someone, it would be you, wouldn't it?"

"I don't know about that. Jeff, or Jen maybe. I think I'll call Jeff if it continues past finals."

"Hello?" A young woman's voice came from outside the front screen door. "Anyone home?"

Meg went to the door to find a young woman carrying a toddler slung across her hip and another yet to be born crowding her front. She wore rubber thongs and a sleeveless cotton dress. Her lifeless hair lay trapped in a rubber band behind her head. On her only available shoulder hung the strap of a worn plastic diaper bag with both zippers broken and the two gaping pockets stuffed with spare yellowed diapers. The baby was clad only in a diaper covered with a pair of plastic pants, and he had smudges of dirt on the backs of his hands and one cheek. Both of his bare feet were dirty.

"Hi, I'm Rich's wife. Is he here? I thought I would try to get a little money for milk for the baby."

"No, dear, I'm sorry, he's not. He comes on Mondays."

"Well," she hesitated, "I'm also a friend of Cari's. Is she home?"

Cari came down at Meg's announcement.

"Hi, Cari," Sharon said as Cari descended the stairway. "It's me, Sharon. I know I look different from when we last saw each other."

Cari's eyes widened at her overburdened acquaintance. "Hi, Sharon. It's been so long since . . ."

"Summer of '59, I guess. Two years." Sharon brushed away a stray lock of hair and tucked it behind her ear. "I heard you were back. I wondered . . . well, how you are and everything."

"I'm fine," Cari lied, "and you? How are you?"

"Well—" Sharon looked at her baby, then at her bulging stomach—"okay, I guess. Pregnant."

"Yes, I can see that." Cari stared at the disheveled young mother. "I'm sorry, Sharon, I've been studying, and seeing you is quite a surprise. Please come in. Let's go into the kitchen. My grandmother is resting in the other side of the house, and I don't think it would be a good idea to disturb her."

"I'm sorry. Maybe I shouldn't have come here. I just wanted to . . ." Sharon stopped as Meg came in with a basket of towels fresh from the clothesline out back.

"It's fine, Sharon. You don't have to apologize. May I get you something cold to drink? And the baby, would he . . . he is a boy isn't he?" Sharon nodded. "Would he like something in that bottle?"

Cari poured Sharon a large glass of fresh lemonade Meg had made with the lemons from the backyard. Then she rinsed the baby's bottle and filled it with milk.

Meg, busy with the folding on one end of the table, made Sharon a little uncomfortable.

"I really should be going. I don't mean to keep you from your studies. Did I hear you're going to be a nurse?"

"Yes, hopefully." Cari was still puzzled by Sharon's surprise visit.

"You think you could walk with me to the end of the street?" Sharon's eyes begged Cari to say she would.

Once outside, Sharon put the baby in a broken-down stroller. They walked slowly in the afternoon heat. A little distance from the house, Sharon rummaged to the bottom of the diaper bag and produced Cari's scarf.

"This is yours, isn't it?" she asked flatly.

"Yes, where did you get it?" Cari asked, even though she knew Richard had taken it from her that night in the garage.

"I found it in Rich's truck." Sharon stopped pushing the baby stroller and turned to face Cari. "You want him? If you do, you can have him."

"I don't want him . . ." Cari's eyes flashed anger, and Sharon knew.

"He's bothering you isn't he?" Sharon said in a tragically flat tone. She squinted in the bright sun. "It isn't the first time he has . . . well, you know . . ."

"Pardon me?"

"He has this problem—or rather I do. My husband chases." Sharon's voice showed little emotion. "He chased after me, got me pregnant, and he still chases."

"Why did you marry him?" Cari asked.

"Right there." Sharon pointed at the baby. "That's why I married him. Or really—that's why he married me." Then pointing to her bulging front she added, "And this is why he has to stay." Sharon reached forward to smooth the hair on her toddler's head. As she did, Cari noticed a series of small bruises on the inside of her arm.

"Sharon, did he do that to you?" Cari was stunned.

"That's nothing," she said with a hollow little laugh, "look at this." She pulled up her skirt a little to show Cari a bruise on the inside of her thigh. "He's got a temper. Somehow I just always seem to light his fuse. I try not to, I really do."

"Did you give him the scarf, Cari?" Sharon turned to face her again.

"No, I didn't—he took it."

"Do you want me to tell my uncle Mac?" Sharon asked.

"Mac?" Cari's mind began to race. Sharon didn't know that the problem was much more serious than a chasing husband. She had no idea that Cari's whole life depended on Richard keeping quiet about . . . well, Sharon didn't know about that either. "No! Really Sharon, I can handle this. Please let me assure you, I have no interest in your husband."

"Yeah, me neither."

"Sharon, what will happen when he discovers my scarf is missing from his truck?"

"He'll throw a fit." A frown crossed Sharon's weary face.

"Put it back." Cari handed the scarf back to Sharon.

"But it's not his, it's yours. He shouldn't go 'round takin' things that don't belong to him."

"It's not that important. I can get another one. Put it back, and don't even mention you know about it."

"You don't want him to beat me, do you Cari?"

"No Sharon, I don't. And believe me, neither do your babies."

Walking back to the house, Cari tried to think of a way to find an extra twenty-five dollars to slip into Richard's pay envelope—not for him, of course, but for Sharon.

CHAPTER THIRTY-ONE

*J*eff called on Saturday while Cari was napping. She was always napping, he told Meg when she refused to wake her. But Meg promised to have Cari call him back.

"Cari, are you all right?" he asked when she returned his call.

"Of course. Why do you ask?"

"You're always sleeping when I call in the afternoon. I've been worried about you."

"Look, Jeff," Cari snapped, "Grandma and Meg are always nagging me, I don't need it from you too."

She's really touchy lately, he thought. Grandma had told him she was when she called him on Thursday.

"Sorry, honey. I just . . . Hey, how about a night out. You've been so busy with Grandpa and Grandma . . ."

"And you've been quite busy yourself," Cari interrupted defensively. Jeff tried to ignore her remark.

"Would you like to go to a concert at the bowl?"

"I'm not in the mood for a concert. I'm not really in the mood to go out. If you want to, we could go up to the hospital and see Grandpa, then out for a drive. But I warn you—I don't think I'll be very good company."

Jeff was sure her last comment was accurate. "I'll see you right after dinner then," he said.

What could be eating at her? Was she under too much stress with her grandparents and school? Was paying the bills causing her irritability? There certainly was a sufficient amount of money in the checking account. Jeff saw to it that he had funds transferred each month to cover the budget Will had worked out. There was enough for Cari to have a generous allowance if she needed it, but she rarely took anything beyond what she needed to meet her simple needs. Something was wrong. Instead of things getting better with her secret open between her and her grandparents—they seemed to be getting worse.

That night Will was quite cheerful, and he reported that the doctor said he could come home on Monday afternoon. "He won't let me go on Sunday because he says the whole church would be over to check on me before the day was through. It's easier to keep a handle on visitors here, I guess."

"Monday, then. Grandma will be so happy to hear this."

"But she already knows, Cari. I'm surprised she didn't tell you."

"Me too." Cari's lip thrust forward in a mock pout. "My feelings are hurt."

Together they decided that James and Cari would come for Grandpa around three o'clock. Grandma wouldn't get her nap if he came home any sooner, and they conspired to use his homecoming as leverage to see to it that she rested. With their plans complete, Cari kissed her grandfather goodnight.

In the car Jeff turned on the radio and headed toward Palm Springs, about an hour away.

"It's a nice night," he said as he adjusted the triangle-shaped windowpane to direct as much air into the car as possible. "It's been pretty hot."

"Yeah, I know," Cari said, then fell silent.

They drove the entire distance with the radio playing, the wind coming through the car window, and Jeff wondering what could possibly be wrong with Cari. How could he persuade her to tell him?

Finding a drive-in restaurant, he ordered a burger and fries. Although Cari said she wasn't hungry, he ordered a burger for her too, hoping she'd change her mind.

"I'll eat it if you don't," he said, silencing her protest. And he did eat it.

After a silent ride back to Redlands, instead of pulling into the driveway when they reached Cari's house, Jeff pulled over to the curb and stopped the car a few houses away. He turned off the key, killing both the engine and the radio. Cari turned to him, and her wide open eyes asked Jeff what he was doing.

"I want some answers, Caroline. I want them now."

Cari stiffened and crossed her arms.

"No you don't." Jeff picked up her signals immediately.

"I didn't say anything," she said flatly.

"You didn't have to." Jeff slid from behind the wheel across the wide seat closer to her. "Cari, you are shutting me out worse than ever. I don't understand you at all. First, I'm afraid to love you, then I'm glad I do. Now I think you don't want anything to do with me at all."

Cari swallowed and looked out the window. "I don't know what to say," she said.

"I don't know what to think," he responded. "Cari, I know I've been busy with my practice, but you have been busy with school and with your responsibilities at home. Isn't our relationship strong enough for us to have a little respect for each other's pressures?"

"Of course."

"Have I hit the problem, or am I fishing without any bait on my hook?" Jeff asked.

He put his arm on the back of the seat and reached to touch her hair. As soon as she felt his hand near her, she shivered. "Cari, come here." Jeff tried to pull her close and could feel her resistance. "What's wrong? Have I done something to hurt you again? Have I said something? What have I done?"

"Nothing. It's not you . . . it's . . . I guess it's just me."

"You?" Jeff's eyebrows shot up.

"Well you know, there's school. You know how that is. I have exams on Tuesday and Wednesday. Sociology and math. I'm not sure I understand math very well at all. Sociology is okay—you know, the study of group behavior—cultures and the like. But math is harder."

"You're smart. You'll do fine. Remember, not every grade has to be an A. Bs are good too."

"I know. I just want to do well. Grandpa is paying the whole bill, supporting me while I go to school—books, clothes, tuition, everything. I want to do well for him."

"Has he complained?"

"No."

"Has he asked you to bring home a perfect four-point GPA?"

"Of course not."

"Has he ever threatened you to make you study harder?"

"Jeff, you know he hasn't." Cari was getting impatient with his questions.

"Then the pressure is all coming from you, isn't it?" Jeff concluded.

"Yeah, I guess."

"Is school the only thing bothering you?"

He's bothering you, isn't he? Cari could still hear Sharon's question. "What else?" Cari asked.

"I thought you'd tell me," Jeff said.

"There's nothing to tell."

"You didn't say there was nothing else bothering you," he persisted.

"Jeff . . . I said there's nothing else to tell."

"Okay, have it your way. I need to tell you something, though."

"Oh?"

"I have to be in L.A. next week. I thought about commuting, but it really makes more sense for me to stay and get my work done and not spend so much of my time on the road."

"I never thought being a lawyer . . . I mean, I didn't think it meant you having to be out of town." Cari was not happy with the thought of Jeff leaving. She didn't see him every day, but that was because of school, her grandparents, and his work. They managed to have a phone conversation, even if it was brief, once or twice a day. In the five-and-a-half months since Jeff came home from taking his bar exam, she had simply assumed he would always be nearby and available.

"Being a lawyer means there could be quite a bit of traveling, my dear." Jeff blew on his fingernails and then rubbed them against his lapel.

"I see." Cari grew silent again. Even during her long sleepless nights, Jeff had been only a phone call away. If the situation with Richard became impossible, who would she call?

"Promise me one thing," Jeff said as he pulled her into his arms.

"What's that?" she said, finally yielded to his encircling arms.

"Try to miss me, just a little."

"Okay, I'll try," she teased.

"Know what else I'll be doing in L.A.—besides my regular business?"

"What? Dating old college girlfriends?"

"There are no old college girlfriends."

"I'll bet."

"No, no social activities for me. I'll be searching court records for a client—a very special client—who wants to divorce her stepfather."

"Oh, Jeff, thank you." She turned up her face and even in the darkness Jeff could see her mood brightening. A kiss might even make her smile. It did.

CHAPTER THIRTY-TWO

*T*he next week was a difficult one for Cari. Jeff was gone, and even though he called her every night, she missed him just knowing he wasn't near. And Grandpa came home. The short trip from the hospital tired him, and his frailty frightened Cari. Her math final came on Tuesday, and she didn't sleep well the night before.

Alone in her room, she hugged her knees to her chest as she sat in the window seat. She could see the lights of the small city from her second story perch. The friendly twinkling did not soothe her as it normally did. She watched the lights of the airplanes blinking as they made their approach to their destinations in the various airports of the Los Angeles area without the familiar excitement of wondering where all the travelers were going to or coming from.

Near dawn, she thought she heard stirring downstairs. Stepping as quietly as she could so Meg wouldn't hear, she opened her door and listened. Nothing. Everything was quiet, and the soft light from the base of Grandma's floral glass lamp sent warmth and familiarity up the stairway to Cari.

Settling herself back in the window seat, she watched as the dawn began to break across the mountains in the distance. From where she was she could see down the long streets lined several decades before with tall, slender palm trees that stood in silhouette against the pink and yellow sky.

Meg would soon be up, and within minutes fresh perking coffee would send its aroma throughout the whole house. The familiar clanking of pots and pans meant that Meg was preparing oatmeal, hard boiled eggs, or both, even though this promised to be one of the hottest days of the summer. Chilled grapefruit would be halved and waiting by each place, each section cut and loosened and a candied cherry in the center. Cinnamon toast made with Meg's homemade bread would be offered with ice cold milk.

The thought of it nauseated Cari. Each morning she had prepared her excuses, but they were beginning to sound hollow. Soon she would have to tell them the truth, so just the thought of eating made her sick.

How could she eat with Richard's threats ringing in her ears?

Across town, Richard poured the last of a jug of milk on a bowl of cornflakes. Sharon sat heavily on the chair opposite him. "Now what'll I give the baby?" she asked.

"Give him a beer," he said, then broke into a sarcastic laugh.

"Can I have some money?"

"Money? For what?"

"I'll go to the store and get some milk before he wakes up." Sharon held her head in her hands.

"I'll give you a buck. Make it last the day." He threw the dollar bill into the air.

"I'll try."

"And comb your hair. You look like a witch."

Sharon put on one of her two cotton dresses and ran a brush through her hair. She looked around the apartment and found her rubber thongs and slipped her swollen feet under the straps. Waddling toward the door, she bent to reach for the dollar bill Richard had thrown on the floor. He remarked, "I guess I don't have to worry none about whether you'll come home. No one else would have you. You look like a cow."

Sharon closed her eyes for a moment, to shut in the tears and to protect herself from the hate she felt growing inside her heart, very near the child growing inside her as well. Before she could shut the door, she heard the baby cry from the bedroom. "Hey, take the brat with you. I'm a father, not a babysitter."

In L.A., Jeff waited for his bus. He had a nine o'clock appointment with Raymond Stetler, a young lawyer who had finished school a year or two ahead of him. He had some questions about some very strange information he had found the day before while searching the court records for Cari's adoption.

The ride between Jeff's hotel and the downtown law firm would take about thirty minutes—just enough time to review the file he had begun on Caroline Grace Rhoades Nelson.

"Hi there, Jeff," Ray Stetler greeted him warmly. "City lights beckon you from way out there in San Bernardino? Ready to go to work for us after all?"

Jeff shook Ray's hand and relaxed. If anyone could dig through this maze of legal potpourri, Ray could. "That's not exactly why I am here." Jeff's wide smile always appealed to Ray's warm sense of humor.

"What could possibly bring you into the smog capital, and what do I have to do with it?"

Jeff began to explain the case in the file. A young girl adopted by her stepfather at the age of five wanted to be an emancipated minor. Jeff continued to fill him in on the details of Cari's life and her desire to be able to use the surname of her grandparents, her father's parents.

"What's the problem then? These kind of adoption records should not be hard to break open. Only anonymous adoption records are sealed. This is obviously an open adoption." Ray reached for the file, and Jeff surrendered it to him.

Looking over the file's contents, Ray paused. He picked up a certified document and let out a low whistle. "Well, look at this. You don't see one of these too often."

"That's just it. This is a total shock to me. I'm sure the grandparents don't even know about this. The grandfather is really my client, the girl is . . . well, more like . . . This is a favor to her."

At nine-thirty in the math classroom at Valley College, Cari said one simple prayer: "Dear God, let me get a *B*."

Finishing her test just as the professor called, "Time," Cari wiped her hand across her forehead and rubbed her eyes.

"How'd you do?" Sam asked.

"I'm glad you're here," Cari said to her new friend. "I don't think I would have even come if you weren't."

"You take life too seriously, Caroline. If you fail, you fail."

"Yeah, right. And if you fail?"

"My daddy disinherits me, that's all." Samantha laughed and led the way to the car. "Time for a Coke. We deserve it."

"It's not even lunch yet." Cari checked her watch. *Wonder what Jeff is doing?* she thought.

"So what. We're big girls. Not old enough to drink but certainly old enough to have a soda before lunch if we want to."

Cari's stomach was feeling a little better, and she decided not to upset it again with a cola. She ordered a 7-Up instead.

"Hey, tomorrow's the last day for us, at least until Monday. Let's celebrate. Let's go to the beach."

"Sorry. I'd really like to," Cari said, "but I promised to help Meg with some deep cleaning projects this week."

"You need some fun, Cari. Don't you ever have fun?"

"Sure I do," Cari answered, but she couldn't remember the last time.

Cari arrived home to an empty house. *Where is everyone?* "Grandma? Meg? Grandpa?" She moved quickly through the house and found a note on the kitchen table.

Cari, dear, the doctor wanted to see Grandpa this morning for another cardiogram. Your grandmother wouldn't hear of having the doctor test him without her along, so I went too. Doctor assures us it is routine, but the results may indicate a change in medication. We should be home before too long.

—Meg

Alone. She hadn't been completely alone in over two years. Someone had always been in the house with her. The thought of being alone was too frightening, and she headed for the phone to call Jen. No, Jen was at work. Jeff was in L.A. She was alone.

"Hi." No other voice could send shivers down Cari's spine like that of Richard Potter. She spun around to face him just as he closed the distance between them. "Alone at last," he growled.

He grabbed her arm and pulled her toward Grandma's room. Pushing her to the bed he threw his body across her as he pinned her arms above her head with one strong hand.

"I found the extra twenty-five dollars in my pay envelope, Cari. But it's not enough to satisfy a man, if you know what I mean."

"Don't, please don't."

"You always sing the same song don't you, Cari?" Richard said through clenched teeth.

A car door slammed in the driveway. Richard clamped a hand across her mouth and listened. Standing, he pulled Cari along with him toward the sliding glass door. "I'll be back," he muttered, and he instantly disappeared through the fruit trees, around the back of the workshop, and over the fence.

"Cari, dear. What is the matter?" Virginia thumped her walker in front of her as she approached her room. "You look terrified."

"Did we scare you, honey?" Will was coming in slowly, escorted by the doctor.

"I told you we could wait until she got home," Will scolded his friend of many years. "But you insisted that we do this dang test this morning. Now look, we've scared our precious Caroline half out of her wits."

"Didn't you get my note?" Meg asked.

"Note?" Cari squeaked.

"I left you a note, right on the kitchen table." Meg went to retrieve it and soon returned. "Here it is. I'm so sorry, dear, it must have blown off to the floor."

Virginia put her arms around Cari. "Why, honey, you're trembling. It's all right now. Please don't be scared. Your

Grandpa is doing just fine. Tell her, Mark, isn't he doing better?"

Mark Lohengren had been the family doctor for as many years as Cari could remember. He and Grandpa had played golf together on as many Wednesday mornings as they could spare from their busy practices. Cari trusted him and turned to him now. "He's doing fine, Cari. My child, you must try not to get so upset. You'll be the heart patient next." He patted her shoulder and returned to his favorite patient.

"I'll be going along. I have other patients, you know. But I must admit, none as dear to me as this old bird here." He pulled at Will's toes through the blanket. "See me to the door, young lady?"

"Cari, what's wrong with you?" Dr. Lohengren said as soon as they were away from the bedroom door. "What gave you such a fright?"

"Dr. Mark, I wish I could tell you. I really do." *I need to tell someone,* she thought. "Maybe it's just the stress of finals, and on top of that coming home and finding the house empty." She tried to compose herself a bit more and took a deep breath, hoping it would help. "I'll be all right. Don't worry about me. It's him we all need to worry about."

"Cari, I meant it when I said he is better. But you must never mistake what I have said. He is better, but he will never be well, I'm afraid. I'm glad you're here. You are the light of his life—you and Ginny."

Cari saw the doctor out and locked the door behind him. Then she went to the kitchen, and even though it was mid-afternoon, she locked the back door. When the opportunity presented itself, she locked the screen to Grandma's sliding glass door as well.

Jeff! When can you come home?

CHAPTER THIRTY-THREE

*A*fter he hung up, Jeff tried to identify what he heard in Cari's voice. Each night she seemed to be getting a little more distant. Last night she blamed it on the upcoming math final. Tonight she used the sociology final as her excuse. It didn't make sense. Jeff knew how smart she was. She was mature for her years, sensitive to her grandparents, and though she resented her mother, he was convinced that there was a way to build a bridge between mother and daughter. No, it wasn't school. Something else was wrong. He decided to take what he had learned and return to Redlands. He could come back next week if necessary. Besides, the day after tomorrow was Cari's birthday, and he needed a little time to arrange a small celebration with Jen's help.

Phoning Jen he said, "Do you think you could find an excuse to go spend the night with Cari? I just talked to her, and she didn't sound good to me."

"She probably just misses you, Jeff," Jen said.

"I hope so—and I hope that's all it is, but I'm worried about her. Could you do this for me, or rather, do it for Cari?"

Meg also worried about her young charge. She had two elderly patients to look after, and Cari's emotional state presented almost more than she could handle. She placed a call to Mac.

"Meg, my darlin', what a wonderful surprise so late at night," Mac said when he heard Meg's voice on the phone.

"I'm calling to ask a very special favor, Mac."

"Anythin', you know that, Meg, luv."

"Could you . . . well, would you . . . I don't know quite how to ask this."

"Spill it out, Meggie."

"Could you come spend the night?"

"Margaret, my pet, what a wonderful invitation. But you are knowin', of course, what an impropriety that would be in the Rhoades household?"

"Mac, go on with you. It's not what you make it out to be. I'm worried. I'm sleeping in the main house now, with everything bein' so upset and all. It's Caroline. She's been pretty upset about something. I thought she might rest better if there were a strong man nearby."

"You don't have to flatter me to get me to sleep near you," Mac said tenderly. "You know how I feel about you, Meggie. I'd do anythin' for you. Anythin' at all."

Meg answered the door a little later and was surprised to find both Mac and Jen standing there together.

"What was to be company turns out to be an invasion," laughed Meg. "Go on, Cari's upstairs."

"No, Cari's right here," Cari said from the door to the dining room. "What's going on, a party?"

"A raiding party," Meg said.

"I brought my stuff," Jen said, holding out a small bag and a dress on a hanger. "I'm staying the night."

"But Jen, I have a final tomorrow. I can't . . . I mean, I won't be much company."

"Math or sociology?"

"The good ol' social science. Math was this morning."

"How'd you do?" Jen asked.

"Prayed for a *B*, but I'll be happy if I pass."

Cari noticed Mac standing there with a silly grin on his face looking at Meg.

"Mac? You want us to leave you alone with Meg, here?" Jen teased.

"No, no hurry." Mac took a chair at the table, and Meg poured him a cup of coffee. "Got all night."

"All night?" the girls chorused.

Meg didn't say a word but turned toward the sink and began to scrub at an imaginary spot with the dish rag.

"Yep. With all these women in the house, Meg decided what you needed was a bodyguard."

"Some bodyguard," Jen said. Then turning to Cari, "You know who will get all the attention from our bodyguard."

Meg snapped the dish rag at Jennifer, catching her on the thigh. "Mind your tongue, young lady, or you'll have me to deal with."

"Don't threaten me, Meg," Jen retorted, "or I'll summon my bodyguard. Take care of her, Mr. Guard." Jen pointed from Mac to Meg.

Mac stood and crossed to Meg and wrapped his large arms around her, pinning her arms to her sides. Then, right there in front of the girls, he planted a loud smacking kiss on her lips. Meg's face turned bright red, and she stood back with her mouth gaping open.

"Look, Jen. Meg's speechless!"

"Yeah, she's blushing too!"

"Mac! How dare you do such a thing in front of the children!" Meg scolded.

"Oh, sorry." Mac laughed and caught her again. "Go away children."

Meg wriggled loose and shooed him out to the guest house. "Mind you, this door will be locked—all night!" Meg warned. The three heard Mac's laugh as he walked away to take his station for the night.

"Meg, I didn't realize . . . !" Jen feigned shock.

"Get away from me, you little imp." Meg rolled up the dish rag for another swat at Jen.

Jen ran around the table and toward the dining room door. "My, my, my," she said, "the lady has a boyfriend and a temper to boot!"

"Off to bed now." Meg directed her gaze to Cari. "Try to get some sleep."

"With Jen here?" Cari said. "I doubt it." *But with Mac here, maybe I will,* she thought.

The next morning Mac was already sitting in the kitchen drinking coffee, and Grandma had joined him. Meg was bustling around the kitchen as usual when Cari and Jen came down. Cari reached for a cup, and Meg took it from her. "No coffee without something to eat."

"Okay," Cari said, "you win. How about a piece of toast and jelly. Would that make you happy?"

"No, an egg would make me happy," Meg countered.

"Don't push your luck, Meg," Cari said, "or I'll go out of here with nothing and get a Coke on my way to school."

"You win," Meg said, but she was more than satisfied that Cari was eating anything at all.

"How about you, Jen?" Meg asked.

"Well now, Meggie, my darlin'," she said, imitating Mac. "Anythin' your little heart desires, anythin' at all."

"Don't get fresh with me, Jennifer Whipple. I'd just as soon send you outa here starvin'." But Meg was already reaching for a small frying pan to make her favorite pest a small omelet.

In L.A., Jeff boarded the bus for Redlands. He was sure his news would be a wonderful birthday present for Cari. He also was sure he should hold off telling her anything until he could return to Los Angeles next week. In San Bernardino, he impulsively got off the bus and took a cab to Valley College. Cari was taking her last final that day, and he was sure he could find her without much trouble. Asking directions, he found the room where her test was being given and settled down on a bench nearby. As soon as the students started leaving he moved closer to the door to wait.

"Hi," Jeff said when he saw Cari.

Cari was startled. "Jeff!" She threw herself in his arms. "I'm surprised to see you here. I thought you wouldn't be back until day after tomorrow."

"I couldn't stay away any longer. Besides, you didn't think I'd miss your birthday, did you?" Jeff was glad he decided to come home. "I have to go back next week, but only for a couple of days," he told Cari.

"Cari?" Samantha stood back a little.

"Oh, I forgot. I have a date with Sam."

Jeff's face registered surprise. "Sam? I've come all this way, go to all this trouble to surprise you, and then you say you're seeing some other guy?"

Cari threw her head back and laughed. "Jeff, don't be silly. You've never really asked me not to see anyone else."

"Caroline, I didn't think I had to." Jeff was clearly getting upset.

"Cari—" The girl's voice was getting more insistent. Then deciding to rescue Jeff, she stuck out her hand. "Hi, I'm Samantha—Sam for short."

Cari watched with delight the expression on Jeff's face and then laughed as he picked her up and swung her around. "Hey," Sam said. "We can cancel our date. We can do it later."

"Nothing doing," Jeff said, "let's make it a double." Then taking both girls, one on each arm, he asked, "Where is the old Ford parked, ma'am?"

CHAPTER THIRTY-FOUR

*J*eff took Cari home and then borrowed her car for an errand. He arranged to meet Jen downtown to plan Cari's birthday celebration, and together they went to the "Goodie Shop" next to J. C. Penney's to order a cake. Jen followed Jeff into Wilson's jewelry store and watched from a distance as he again picked out a small gold disc and walked back to order the inscription.

"One of these days, Mr. Bennett, you'll plan ahead," Mrs. Wilson teased. "I think you're serious enough about this girl to look into some *real* jewelry."

Jeff tried to look embarrassed, but he wasn't. He wanted the whole town to know how he felt about Cari. Promised that the present would be waiting for him the next day at noon, Jeff left the store with Jen and headed toward Cari's car.

"Want to get some pizza?" Jen invited.

"Thanks, but I want to get back to Cari." Jeff had hated the two and a half days he had been away. "I also need to stop by the office."

"Work, work, work," Jen said. "Are you typical of others in your field?"

"Fairly typical, I'd say. But look who's talking, Miss Career Woman."

"Don't you forget it, Mr." Jen stuck out her chin. "Not nothing, not no one will be able to stop me."

"You'll need to work on your grammar, kid," Jeff teased.

"So I've been told."

Jeff went back to the office and checked his mail. He was glad that the real estate deal he had been working on was on hold as both parties had asked for time to consider offers and counter-offers. The Jennings contracts seemed straightforward enough and the Smith divorce . . . *I hate divorce,* Jeff thought, *but if someone doesn't look out for Peggy Smith's interests, she'll get taken to the cleaners. She'll be left with three children to raise, and she needs an honest lawyer to see to it that she gets a fair shake.*

Before leaving, he checked his appointment book and left a note for the office secretary to change the one appointment he had from Monday afternoon to Friday afternoon. Then he penciled large X's through the remaining days to free himself up to go back to L.A. on Monday morning. He put a memo on Mr. Lambert's desk, left the office, and made his way to the Jenkins' before he headed back to Cari's.

"I'm glad to see you, Jeff." Sarah looked worried. "I think we need to talk."

"What's the matter? What's wrong?" Jeff asked. Sarah poured a cup of coffee for herself and one for Jeff and asked him to sit down at the table with her. James arrived from work and joined them.

"It's something I can't quite put my finger on," Sarah began. "James senses it too." Jeff knew them to be level-headed people, not given to imagination or worry. Her tone made him feel uneasy.

"Did you know Meg asked Mac to stay over at Cari's last night?"

"No, I didn't. I saw Cari this morning and she looked a little better than I've seen her in a while. Maybe having Mac there had something to do with that." Jeff became thoughtful. "Why does having Mac there make you uneasy?"

"It's not having him there that worries me. It's *why* he had to be there that worries me."

"Did you ask Meg about it?"

"No. I thought I'd talk to you about it first."

"Thanks, I appreciate that," Jeff said.

He arrived at the Rhoades' house just as Meg was setting the table for dinner. "Will you be here for supper?" she asked.

"Am I invited?"

"Do you need to be?" Meg winked at him.

"No, I don't."

"Good," Meg said as she reached into the cupboard for another plate.

"Wait, I thought you had my place already set," he said, counting the places around the table.

"Nope," Mac said as he came in the back door, "that's for me. I've been invited."

Seeing his chance to talk to not only Meg but Mac as well, Jeff decided to be direct. "Why did you stay here last night, Mac?"

"Because this little woman here called and ask me to."

"Meg?"

"It's kind of hard to explain," Meg hedged.

"Well, try."

"Yesterday when we came home from taking Will to the doctor, Cari was home alone for . . . well, it couldn't have been more than a few minutes." She looked from Jeff to Mac.

"Go on," Jeff said.

"It's something I sensed. It's hard to explain. Cari was beside herself. Scared to death, I'd say. I left her a note on the table telling her where we were and when we'd return. Then I guessed she hadn't seen it when I found it on the floor. I assumed it had blown off the table and she missed it." Meg stopped for a minute and wiped her hands on her apron.

"That's why you called Mac?"

"No, not exactly. When I helped put Will to bed, I noticed the sliding door open a few inches and the screen part of it was open all the way. I was sure I had fastened that door when we left. I can't be sure, mind you, but I am careful that way."

Jeff got a drink of water at the sink and then turned to lean back on the cabinet. "Anything else?"

"When the doctor left, I saw Cari lock the door behind him. I didn't think anything about it at the time, but later I discovered that she had also locked the screen door on the back porch."

"What's so unusual about that?" Jeff asked.

"Wait, there's more," Mac said. "Go on, Meggie, you're doin' fine."

"When I returned with Will's medicine and a glass of water, Cari was locking the sliding door screen too." She leaned toward Jeff. "It was only three o'clock in the afternoon, Jeff."

"Did you ask her about it?"

"No. It wouldn't do any good. She's a master at excuses and even better at clamming up," Meg said.

"Yeah, I know," Jeff agreed.

"Well, anyway," Meg continued, "the note."

"The note?"

"I found it on the floor, but it was crumpled up. You know, like someone started to throw it away. Just blowin' off the table wouldn't have crumpled it like that."

"There's one more thing," Meg said as Jeff drained his water glass. "Cigarettes."

"Cigarettes?"

"I thought I could smell cigarettes by Ginny's bed."

"What do you make of all this, Mac?" Jeff turned to the older man.

"Could've been a prowler. That's my guess anyway. I thought it wouldn't hurt to have a man on the grounds for a night or two—even longer." He winked at Meg.

"Cigarettes," Jeff mused. "We don't know anyone who smokes, do we?"

"No one that comes around here, anyway," said Meg, "except for the gardener, but he's only here on Mondays."

Jeff and Mac exchanged looks but didn't comment.

"Where's Cari now?"

"Upstairs getting herself all prettied up for supper." Meg poked at the roast in the oven. "She'd better hurry. This roast is as tender as a down pillow, but another half hour, and it will be shoe leather."

Jeff walked in through the dining room and paused at the bottom of the stairway. Looking up to where he knew Cari was, he had to discipline his mind to make his feet carry him past the stairs and in to see Virginia and Will.

"Jeffrey. Come sit here beside me." Virginia moved a little to make room for Jeff to sit at the foot of her bed.

"How're you two doing?" Jeff asked.

"Better, now that I have an excuse to keep Will where I can see him," Ginny laughed.

"Good to see you, son," Will said. "We've been wanting to talk to you."

Jeff could see the concern on their faces. "What's wrong?"

"We don't want to worry you," Will began.

"Nor Cari," Virginia interrupted.

"But we think there might have been someone snooping around the house yesterday."

"Oh?" Jeff looked surprised for their benefit.

"Yesterday Virginia watched Meg close and lock the sliding glass door. When we came home, it was open a bit and Cari was scared to death," Will said.

"Meg sensed it too, but she wouldn't do anything but assure us we were wrong. She called Mac, and he stayed the night out in the guest house." Virginia relaxed a bit more on her pillows. "We're mighty grateful he did, I tell you."

"I think we all slept better just knowing he was here," Will added.

"Think we could get him to stay for a while longer?" Ginny asked.

"I don't think staying will be the problem. Getting him to leave, however, might be a bit more difficult," Jeff said with a smile.

"Isn't it wonderful?" Virginia's eyes sparkled. "We might see something develop between those two."

"Might? Would be pointless to try to stop it if you ask me," Will added.

"You two, look at you. Lying here all day watching those daily soap operas has made you into incurable romantics."

"It's not the TV, Jeff." Will winked at Virginia. "It's having this beautiful lady with me 'round the clock. It makes me think everyone should be as happy as we are."

Jeff admired the couple's love for each other, obvious even after more than forty years of marriage. But he had other things to think about at the moment.

213

Back in the kitchen, he interrupted Mac teasing Meg while she was making a salad.

"Behave yourself, Mac, or I'll send you packing."

"Packing? For a honeymoon I'll be a-packin'?"

"Hey, you two," Jeff said, "behave yourselves."

"It's him that needs to behave," said Meg.

"Mac, do you think you could move into the guest house for a while?" Jeff asked.

"A while?"

"I think we'd all feel better with a man on the place. Maybe for a couple of weeks or so?"

"If I had my way, I'd be movin' in permanent," Mac said as he put his large arm around Meg's generous shoulders.

"Sure would solve a lot of our problems," Jeff said.

"Don't the two of you go gangin' up on me," Meg said. "I'm thinkin' it over and I won't be rushed."

"I'm pushin' sixty-five, Meggie. You young girls may not see the need for a rush, but I do." Then turning to Jeff he became more serious. "I'd be glad to move in for a while."

"Then I'm moving out!" Meg said. "I'll not be worried about walkin' in on an ambush every time I want to brush my teeth."

"How about the room upstairs?" Jeff said.

"Will and Virginia's?" Meg said. "It's empty, that I know for sure."

"We'll move the day bed up, or . . ." Jeff started thinking out loud.

"No need, Jeff. I have some of my own furniture in storage. Why don't we see about moving some of the guest house furniture upstairs and moving some of my things into the guest house?"

"Oh, Meggie, my darlin'." Mac pretended to be distressed. "Is it not enough that I will be tortured just being near to you? Now I have to live surrounded by your belongings? Please, darlin', let us set the date before I go out of my mind. Have you no mercy?"

"Yes, I think I do. A little anyway. We'll discuss this later." Then quickly she began to put the finishing touches on supper. "Call Cari and help me take these trays to the darlins in the other room, will you, Mac? Let me see you make yourself useful, and I might be persuaded to give your proposal some serious consideration."

Mac's grin spread almost from ear to ear as he picked up a tray in both hands. As he crossed the dining room and front hallway he bellowed up the stairs, "Cari, get down here and eat!"

CHAPTER THIRTY-FIVE

*C*ari woke the next morning and realized that she
had slept soundly for at least a few hours. She felt refreshed
and was glad to know that Mac was going to stay in the guest
house for a while. Plans had been made, and this morning
was to be spent moving some of the guest house furniture
into the other upstairs bedroom, separated from hers by
the bathroom and a few storage closets along the small
hallway at the top of the stairs.

Coffee already sent its inviting aroma throughout the
house, and Cari could hear voices below. Mac was visiting
with Grandpa, and Virginia was in the kitchen with Meg.
With Mac around, Cari began to feel somewhat secure. Of
course, Jeff's return from L.A. helped too.

"Cari"—it was Meg calling softly from below—"Jeff's on
the phone for you, dear."

Cari grabbed her robe and ran down the stairs. "Hi," she
said.

"Hi yourself, birthday girl. I wanted to be the first one to
say happy birthday to you. Am I?"

"Are you what?"

"The first one to say happy birthday to you?"

"Yes, come to think of it, you are."

"Good, then my day is getting off to a perfect start." Cari
loved his voice and the way he made her feel special just by
calling. "What's up for today?" he asked.

"I'm helping Meg move upstairs this morning," she said.

"Could you use another strong back and willing pair of hands?" Jeff offered.

"You bet, that would be great," she said.

"Do you think we'd be finished by . . . well, let's say two-thirty or three?"

"Could be, why?"

"I want to take you somewhere, that's why."

"Where?"

"You'll find out later."

"Jeff?"

"Trust me," he said and hung up the phone.

Cari did trust Jeff. Though she had been determined never to trust any man again—except her grandfather, of course—Jeff had won her trust very easily. Not only did she trust him, she was almost sure she had fallen in love with him.

The morning was spent as planned with Mac helping Meg and Cari move Meg's things upstairs along with a few necessary items of furniture. They carried up a bed, of course, as well as a lamp and a table. A picture hung over the bed made the room look homey and warm—an observation made by Mac which caused Meg to smack him across the head with a magazine. Her clothes barely filled one half of the roomy closet, and Mac noticed out loud that there was plenty of room for his things, should she give the invitation. The morning, filled with the hard work of moving, was made lighter with the bantering between the older couple, obviously crazy about each other.

Meg's chest of drawers was moved a drawer at a time. Mac poked around in what he called "Meg's dainties" and made her blush more than once. "Get away from my things," she would scold.

When the project was finished, all but the "woman's touch," Jeff excused himself, promising to be back at two-thirty sharp.

He stopped at Wilson's to pick up Cari's third gold charm. Checking the inscription, he looked at Mrs. Wilson. "Perfect," he said and reached for his wallet to pay her.

"Young man," Mrs. Wilson said over her half glasses, "it's not my place to interfere, and maybe you don't want any advice . . ."

"And if I do?" Jeff said.

"If you were to ask me," she said leaning over the counter closer to Jeff, "I'd suggest a little ring—maybe an engagement ring?"

"Well, I might just consider that someday soon, Mrs. Wilson, but for now . . ."

"Then, may I ask what in the world the young lady is stringing these gold charms on?"

"The key ring I gave her at Thanksgiving. You have something better?"

"My dear, Jeffrey, follow me." She beckoned him with her index finger. "I have the perfect thing."

Jeffrey again reached for his wallet to pay for the delicate charm bracelet she showed him and waited for Mr. Wilson to solder the latest charm on it. "In the interest of true love," Mr. Wilson said, "and at the direction of my dear wife, if you will return tomorrow or the next day, I would be more than happy to transfer the other two charms to the bracelet—no charge. But remember, one day soon we are hoping to sell you a diamond."

Jeff smiled, tucked the velvet box back into its paper bag, and left the store. On the way out, he stopped for a moment and looked over the wedding sets in the store display window. He smiled at the couple watching him from inside the store and waved to them as they nodded to each other.

"We'll make it a point to go to that wedding, my love," Mrs. Wilson said to her husband.

Lunch at the Rhoades' was served a little late. Meg prepared a simple meal of canned soup and bologna sandwiches. Grandpa's appetite was returning, and he complained that there was hardly enough there to keep a bird alive, let alone a recovering heart patient.

Meg quickly satisfied him with some of her home-canned peaches and a piece of cinnamon toast. "That's more like it!" he said.

"William, don't be so demanding," Virginia scolded. "There's more important things to do around this house than to wait on you hand and foot." But everyone knew nothing was more important to Virginia than William. The adoration between them was what kept Caroline believing in marriage in spite of what she had seen between her mother and George Nelson.

At two-thirty, Jeff came just as Cari had finished showering and putting on a fresh outfit of white bermuda shorts and a light blue cotton sleeveless shirt that tied in a knot at her waist. Her brown hair, longer now, was combed back into a pony tail and tied with a scarf. She had combed her bangs straight down across her forehead and wore white T-strap flats over bare feet.

"No matter what you wear, you are adorable," Jeff commented when she came down the stairs. Her wide smile made his heart beat stronger, and he took her by the hand and led her out the door.

"See you later!" she called over her shoulder.

Taking Sunset Drive around the rim of the mountains surrounding the little city, Jeff carefully maneuvered Cari's Ford around the last hairpin curve to Lookout Point. It wasn't a good idea to come here at night, but in the afternoon the place was deserted. They got out of the car and kicked their way through the beer bottles strewn all around. Jeff took Cari's hand as they sat on the stone wall built during the Depression by a WPA crew. They sat in silence, looking at the cities stretched out as far as they could see. It was one of those rare July days when a Santa Ana wind blows the smog away, leaving the sky looking blue and fresh. There was not a cloud anywhere.

"Cari," Jeff began, "I want to ask you something important. Please don't say no until you have heard me out completely. I know there are a million reasons you can find to tell me I am crazy for wanting to do this, but just promise me you'll at least think about it, okay?"

I'm not ready for this, Cari thought as her heart leaped into her throat. Jeff felt her stiffen beside him.

"You don't even know what I'm going to say, and already you're resisting me. Please, Cari, trust me. Hear me out."

She looked at the mountains in the distance. "I'm listening."

"You remember how you said that I didn't look at my family situation from my mother's perspective?"

Cari looked around at Jeff. "I remember."

"Well, I've been thinking. You were right. I've given it a lot of thought and have even called her a time or two, just to, you know . . . to open communication. It's going slow, but it's a beginning at least."

"I don't understand why you're bringing this up now."

"You know I told you I would be searching the records in L.A. about your adoption."

"There's no connection between your mother and mine, Jeff."

"No?" Jeff asked. "Not even through us?" Cari didn't respond to the comment but looked at Jeff with her eyebrows in a concerned frown.

"Let me finish. I've wondered if you have ever looked at your situation in the same way you have told me I should look at mine."

"What?" Cari jumped from the stone wall and stood a few feet away facing Jeff. She planted her hands firmly on both sides of her waist and began kicking a dirty beer bottle with her toe.

"Cari, you're not hearing me out. Before you jump to conclusions about what I'm trying to say, let me say it, okay?"

Cari closed her eyes a minute then looked away, and Jeff saw the set of her jaw as she clenched her teeth. "This better be good," she grumbled.

"Cari, I have been doing some digging." Cari looked at him again. "I have reason to believe it will be easier than we first thought to let you use the name Rhoades. But I need to talk to your mother."

"You must be kidding," Cari said.

"I'm serious. Very serious."

"What about him?"

"Him?"

"George." Cari's face puckered with the sourness of his name.

"Well, what about George?"

"He won't let you near her. He can be mean, Jeff. I don't want you hurt."

"What about her?" he countered.

"She's made her choices."

"Cari, I'll tell you what, I'll take Ray Stetler with me. He's a lawyer friend of mine and he's a big, tough brute of a guy. Would that make you feel better?"

"Well, I would feel better if you went with someone. He's strong, this Ray?"

"Very," Jeff answered.

"Okay, I guess if you think it will help. I want this over quickly. I want to use my own name again." Cari grew thoughtful. "It might be rough on her after you leave though."

"We'll try to go when he isn't home. Do you know when and where he works?"

"Early mornings. He delivers produce for Liberty Produce Company, or at least he did. He goes on the truck about four-thirty and gets home by noon. She leaves for work at twelve-thirty."

"Cari, one more thing about your mother." Jeff looked her straight in the eye and found it difficult to concentrate on the rest of his sentence.

"Yes?"

"I need her address."

"I'll write it down for you, her phone number too if you think you might need it."

Jeff knew he'd pressed her as far as he could—or for that matter, as far as he needed to for now. He changed the subject. "I have something for you."

"You do? What color is it?" She was glad to stop talking about her mother.

"Guess." But Jeff couldn't wait to give her the bracelet with the small circlet hanging from it. He produced the box from his pants pocket and opened it himself. Taking the bracelet from its hiding place, he fumbled with the latch as she stood speechless with tears swelling in her eyes.

"It's the most beautiful thing I have ever . . . I love it!" she said. She stood looking at it and wiping her tears to see it better. Then turning over the gold circle, she saw the scrolled monogram—*C* on one side and *G* on the other with a larger *R* in the middle. Turning it carefully over, Cari caught her breath as she saw in small block letters, Caroline Grace Rhoades.

"It's to give you faith, Cari," Jeff said as he pulled her into his arms under the bright blue afternoon sky. "I think very soon you will be using your own name again."

Cari lifted her face to his and waited for the kiss she knew was coming. Jeff jumped from the wall and stood holding her in his arms as he kissed her, then he scooped her up and carried her back to the car. "There's a party to go to tonight. We'd better go back."

"Do we have to?" she asked, still aloft in his arms.

"Yes, baby, we have to."

CHAPTER THIRTY-SIX

*O*n Saturday, Jeff and Cari took the bracelet back to Wilson's, and Cari barely let them take it off her wrist to solder the other charms on. Later that night they took Jen and Samantha to a movie and out for burgers and sodas. Sunday morning was spent in church, and Jeff held Cari's hand during the sermon as Sarah looked on and smiled.

On Sunday afternoon Jeff took Cari to Prospect Park, and they returned to their Christmas bench only to find it occupied by another couple. Cari pretended to pout until they found another place to sit. The bench was tucked between large eucalyptus trees and graceful palms swaying in the summer breeze. Ivy covered the ground all around the area, except just in front of the bench, where it was worn away clear to the sand by people's feet. Jeff proclaimed this their summer bench.

"Starting school tomorrow?" Jeff asked, and Cari squirmed beside him.

"I'm thinking of taking the rest of the summer off," she announced.

"Oh, really?"

"Maybe you haven't been aware of it, Jeff, but I didn't do so well this last quarter."

"In school or otherwise?"

"School," Cari lied.

"I see," Jeff said.

"You sound like a lawyer," she complained.

"Don't change the subject. What were your grades?"

"It's not the grades, it's the pressure," Cari explained.

"The pressure?" Jeff looked at Cari, trying to read her face.

"The pressure," she said simply.

"The pressure to get good grades?" he asked.

Cari sighed. "The pressure to do well, yes."

"If you take the next few weeks off, then what?"

"Then I'll go back to school in September," Cari promised. "I want to spend more time with Grandma and Grandpa. The two of them are a handful for Meg."

"They won't be a handful in September?"

"I'll go back to classes in September, Jeff, I promise."

"Will this delay your graduation?"

"Maybe not. I'll have to wait and see."

"Cari," Jeff began, changing the subject, "I'm going back to L.A. tomorrow morning."

"I thought so."

"Grandpa wants me to use his car."

"I know, he told me."

"Do you think that's okay?" Jeff felt strange borrowing anything, let alone such an expensive car.

"Grandpa says he is sick, but he has three hundred and eighty six horses sitting in the garage that beg to be run," Cari said. "I'm sure not going to drive it. I have my own car, thank you."

"And a nice car it is, I might say," Jeff added.

"When will you be back?" Cari asked.

"It shouldn't take more than a day or two. Tuesday night at the latest."

"Will you come right back and tell me what happens?"

"I will. I promise if you promise."

"Promise what?"

"Promise to be there when I get back."

"I don't know," Cari teased, "I might have a date with Sam."

Cari jumped up from the bench and ran away from him as fast as she could. Jeff followed and caught her easily. Boosting her on his back, he gave her a piggyback ride to the car. Cari didn't ever dream she could be so happy. Jeff never dreamed he could love someone as much as he loved Cari.

The next morning Meg met Cari at the breakfast table with a disturbed look.

"Meg?" Cari took the coffee offered. "Something wrong?"

"It's Sharon."

"Sharon?" Cari sat down and reached for a piece of toast.

"She went into labor last night," Meg said. "That husband of hers was out, and she has no phone. She had to walk to three houses before she found anyone home to call her mother. By the time anyone could get there, she was really far along."

"Did she make it to the hospital?" Cari suddenly lost her appetite.

"Yeah, she made it, but it's been touch and go for her and the baby all night." Meg wiped the table nervously with the rag. "She finally delivered a little while ago. She had a girl. She's not very big, just under five pounds. Mac is there now with Sharon and her mother. Her husband never did come home as far as we know."

"Meg, that's awful." Cari shuddered to think of Sharon delivering Richard's baby.

"What about the little boy?" Cari asked.

"Well, that's what I want to ask you. The neighbor kept him during the night, but Mac called and asked if we could watch him today, just while Sharon's mother stays at the hospital."

"Here? A baby here?" Cari felt the panic welling up in her throat.

"Virginia says it's okay with her. They'd like to see a baby here again, even just for a few hours." Cari's heart felt a stab of guilt.

"I don't want it to be hard on either of them," Cari said.

"And they don't want it to be hard on you," Meg answered.

"He's not really a baby, he's more of a toddler, isn't he?" Cari asked.

"Yes, he's walking and saying a few words."

"Sharon says it's okay for him to be here?" Cari asked.

"Sharon isn't caring, right at the moment, where he is, but she doesn't want him with his father. No chance of that happening anyway. So it's okay then? I told Mac I'd call him back when I knew for sure."

"Sure. Let's give the baby a day at the Rhoades' house."

"Thanks, Cari. This means a lot to Mac and me."

"And you both mean quite a bit to me—to all of us."

When Meg returned with the baby, she announced that Sharon was asking to see Cari.

"She needs a friend, dear," Virginia said. "She's alone except for her mother. Couldn't you go for a few minutes?" Cari couldn't resist her grandmother's request.

"I haven't been near any babies since . . ." Cari's eyes filled quickly with tears.

"I know dear." Virginia gathered her granddaughter in both her arms. "But maybe it's time. Maybe this visit to Sharon will help you as much as it will her."

"How's she doing?" Cari asked Meg.

"Better tonight. The baby's still not out of the woods, but the doctor has hope. We're all praying for the best."

Cari didn't go near Sharon's little boy at first. But when the baby began to play and smile at her, she found her heart softening toward him. As the day wore on, she began to be fascinated by how much he looked like his mother and how much of his own personality had developed already.

Later in the day Cari found her way to the hospital's maternity floor and tried not to look at the babies in the nursery on her way to Sharon's room.

"Sharon?" Cari whispered as she entered the room. Sharon was sleeping, and her mother sat in a chair by her bed.

"She wanted me to wake her if you came. You're Cari, aren't you?"

"Yes, I am."

"Cari?" Sharon's voice was weak and thick with weariness.

"How you doin'? You look, well . . ." Cari stammered.

"Like I've just had a baby. I know, awful. How's my little boy?"

"He's just fine. He's been playing peek-a-boo with Grandpa Will for most of the afternoon."

"Did he get a nap?"

"Yes, he did. Grandma and Meg saw to that. Meg set up a playpen in the living room where everyone could keep an eye on him. Instead of one babysitter he has three."

"I sure appreciate it."

"It's fine, Sharon. Glad to help."

"Where's Mac, Mom?" Sharon asked her mother.

"I'm not sure, sweetheart. He'll be back later, though. He loves you like you were his own daughter."

"He's out looking for Richard, isn't he?"

"I have no idea. He didn't tell me where he was going."

"That's where he is though, I know it."

"It's . . . I mean she's a girl, huh, Sharon?" Cari didn't feel comfortable in the hospital, and she was even less comfortable with the discussion of Richard's whereabouts.

"She's very small, Cari." Sharon stretched and winced in pain. "I haven't held her yet. Maybe tomorrow."

"Is she okay?" Cari asked.

"Yeah, just small."

"Here, Cari, sit here for a while. If you can stay a few minutes, I'd like to get a cup of coffee." Sharon's mother motioned toward the chair she had been in when Cari came in.

"Sure. Take your time. It's been a long day, I bet. I'll stay here a little while." Cari didn't want to walk back past the babies just yet.

"I'm glad you came, Cari." Sharon reached toward Cari, and the two young women held hands for a moment. "I have something for you," Sharon said.

"For me? Sharon, you're the patient here. I should be bringing you the presents and stuff."

"This is important. Get my purse out of the closet." Cari found Sharon's purse and noticed it was worn and dirty. "In the bottom, you . . . well, the lining is torn. Under it. That's it. There's something that belongs to you."

Cari reached into the ragged purse and the lining loosened under her tug. Folded neatly there was a smudged piece of paper. Cari carefully pulled it out, afraid to ask what it was, afraid to know.

"It's your letter," Sharon said, "the one Richard took."

"Sharon, how did you get this?" Cari couldn't believe her eyes.

"I found it when I was putting your scarf back in his truck." Sharon's eyes clouded with pain and tears. "I didn't know, Cari. When we walked together and you told me to put it back, I had no idea what he had done to you."

"I don't know what you mean." Cari was crying too.

"Yes you do. I figured it out. We got pregnant the same summer, didn't we, Cari?"

Cari tried to control her sobs but couldn't. Sharon raised up on one elbow and held out her arm to Cari. She moved into the open circle of the understanding arm, and the two young women found comfort in each other.

"Does he know?" Cari asked, straightening up and wiping her tears.

"I don't think so. If he gave it a little thought he might come up with the answers, but he doesn't think of anyone but himself."

"Does he know you have the letter?"

"Yes." Sharon's face clouded with the memory of his rage. "We had a terrible fight. That's when it began."

"What began?"

"My labor. Richard threw a beer bottle and hit me in the back. Then he ... well, he shoved me and I fell. That's when my contractions started."

"This is my fault," Cari said.

"How in the world do you figure that?"

"You were fighting over me."

"No, Cari, we were fighting because that's what we do. Or at least that's what he does. I'm not fighting anymore. I've made a decision. I'm not going back. Mom said I could come home. I don't know how we'll do it, but she wants me and the babies to live with her."

"I think you are brave, Sharon."

"No, you are the brave one, Cari. You did the right thing by leaving and seeing to it he could never hurt your baby."

"You have no idea . . ." Cari's eyes spilled over with her tears.

"I'm going to see to it he never hurts one of mine, ever again." Sharon's voice was firm and determined.

"Sharon, you are the only one who knows—besides me and my mother—who the fa . . ." she paused, unable to say the word.

"Believe me, I understand why you don't want anyone to find out—I'm not going to tell anyone, Cari, I promise."

"Do you think we could be friends?" Cari asked.

"I'd like that. I really need a friend." Sharon smiled, and Cari saw a deep inner beauty in Sharon's face, a beauty that comes only through shedding tears and conquering pain. "You want to know what I named her?" she asked. "Frances. After my mother. If it's okay, I'd like to name her Frances Caroline . . . after you."

"Me?" Cari couldn't believe she had heard right.

"Yes, I want her to grow up to be loving and forgiving, just like my mother, and brave, like you."

"Sharon, I don't know what to say."

"About what?" Mac's rich voice boomed as he came in the doorway with his cousin Frances.

"Frances Caroline," Sharon said. "That's my baby girl's name."

"Want to see her?" Frances asked Cari. "Want to see our namesake?"

"Yes," Cari said, "I believe I do," and she carefully tucked the treasured letter in her purse, gave Sharon a warm hug, and walked with Frances to the window of the nursery.

CHAPTER THIRTY-SEVEN

*J*eff turned William Rhoades' car onto Highway 10 and headed for Los Angeles. His appointment with Ray Stetler was at ten. He had enough time to get there if the traffic moved along smoothly, but was glad he gave himself an extra thirty minutes. His phone conversation with Cari that morning had set his spirits singing. She had surprised him by saying that she would be praying for him and praying that her mother would be receptive.

He had wanted so much for Cari to share his faith and deep belief in God. He even had her to thank for showing him the bitterness he held against his own mother. He had mentioned to Cari that he had contacted her, but he had not told her how he had prayed prayers of repentance for the resentment he had harbored for so many years. He wasn't sure what this change of heart would do for the strained relationship with his mother, but he was sure it was making a difference in his own heart and in his relationship with God. *Forgiveness isn't so much for the forgiven as it is for the forgiver,* he thought. *I'm proof of that. And if I'm right, Cari may soon find forgiveness for her mother, too.*

Entering Ray's office, he was greeted warmly by the secretaries in the outer office and then by Ray. Coffee was offered, as usual, and together the men planned their strategy. They considered every option of approaching

Cari's mother and decided that waiting until tomorrow morning was the best plan since it almost guaranteed that George would be away from the house.

Ray offered Jeff an unoccupied office to go over his notes and review the details of this most interesting case. Later, Jeff looked into the firm's small library of legal books and case studies and found more information to make his presentation to Eleanor even stronger.

That evening Jeff had dinner downtown with Ray and his wife and left them in time to call Cari from his hotel room before he went to bed.

"Are you ready for this?" he asked Cari.

"Am I ready?"

"Your whole life could change very soon."

"How soon?"

"Well, it will begin tomorrow, one way or another."

"I'm ready."

"Cari?"

She loved to hear him say her name when he was about to ask her something important. "Yes?"

"Have you given any thought to what I said about your mother's perspective being quite different from your own?"

"Some." Cari had tried not to, but the thoughts often came crowding into her mind uninvited.

"And?"

"I'm not sure what to say. I'm trying to see the whole thing from her side, but it's hard. It doesn't make any sense. She wouldn't let me stay with Grandma but made me stay locked in my room in the apartment while she worked. We never saw each other anyway. Why couldn't she have let me go?"

"I'm hoping to have an answer to that question very soon."

Jeff heard a small jingling sound on the other end of the phone as Cari changed the receiver from one ear to the other. "Are you wearing your bracelet?"

"I never take it off."

"Never?"

"Only to take a bath."

Jeff decided to change the subject before his mind wandered. "Anything new? How are the folks?"

"Doing real well. In fact, there is something new. Sharon had her baby."

"Sharon?"

"Sharon Potter, you know, the gardener's wife."

Jeff didn't like the gardener for some reason. "How'd you know about that?"

"Her mother is related to Mac, remember?"

"Oh yeah."

"Sharon and I knew each other from youth group a few years ago. She came to see me a little while back." Cari paused. "I went to the hospital, Jeff. I went to see her baby."

Jeff wished she'd waited for him to get back to do that. "Was that hard on you?" he asked.

"A little. The baby is so small. Less than five pounds. I think she was early. Sharon looked so tired and beaten. She said she wasn't going home. She is going to go live with her mother."

"She's leaving Richard?"

"I think so."

Jeff sensed Cari's silence. "Anything else?"

"She named the baby after me."

"She what?"

"She knows about me, Jeff. She figured it out. She said I was brave." Cari started to cry. "I wasn't brave, Jeff. I was scared. I had nowhere to turn."

"She had a husband, right? You didn't."

"She married Richard after Mac found him and made him marry her."

"Oh," Jeff said, "I see."

"There you go with the lawyer sound again."

"How do you know what a lawyer sounds like?"

"I happen to know one very well, and he sounds just like you," she said. Changing the subject, she added, "I'm sleeping better. Isn't that good news? I even ate a breakfast that Meg was pleased with today."

"Now that is good news."

"Oh, one more thing. Sharon's son stayed here today for a while so her mother could stay longer at the hospital."

"How old is he?"

"Fourteen months. He was born in the middle of May last year."

Jeff's chest tightened with pain for her. "Cari, are you doing all right with all this?"

"It took a while, but I think it was good for me—even though it hurt to see Grandpa play with him and Grandma fuss over him. I not sure what it all means to me, but seeing Sharon so whipped and sick, I'm thankful my baby and I didn't go through anything like what she's going through."

Jeff wanted to pack his bag and go home to her right then. "I miss you, Caroline."

"I miss you, too," Cari said softly.

"I'll be home tomorrow night, and hopefully I'll have news."

"I'll be waiting." Cari didn't want to hang up. "Jeff?"

"What?"

"I love you," Cari whispered.

"What did you say?" he asked, sitting upright on the hotel room bed.

"I said I love you."

Jeff's eyes watered a little, and he could tell from the little sniffles on the other end of the line Cari was crying too.

CHAPTER THIRTY-EIGHT

*T*his is KFI, your radio station for more news and weather in the greater Los Angeles Basin. Hot and dry today in L.A. with a high of eighty-nine degrees." Jeff already felt the heat and turned on the air conditioner in Will's car. "In the valleys it will reach ninety-five, and in the inland empire the low one hundreds." *I wish Cari's car had air conditioning,* Jeff thought. He turned off the radio and watched for the exit to Culver City. Ray was meeting him at Eleanor Nelson's so that the two men could go their separate ways as soon as the meeting was finished.

Jeff looked at the map again. He checked his location and his watch. "Right on time," he said aloud. "So far so good."

Pulling up in front of the apartment complex, he saw Ray right behind him. The two men had planned their rendezvous carefully, and though Jeff felt nervous, Ray was perfectly calm. Jeff was glad he had asked him along.

"Mrs. Nelson?" they asked the lady through the peephole in the door of her apartment.

"Yes."

"My name is Jeffrey Bennett. I'm an attorney representing the interests of your daughter, Caroline. This is Ray Stetler, my associate. May we speak with you?"

"What about?"

"As I said, we are here about Caroline."

"What about Caroline?"

Jeff felt anger begin to knot up in his stomach. Ray saw him clench his fist and quickly intervened before Jeff could scare the poor woman off, making their trip useless. Gently pushing Jeff aside, Ray held up a business card for Eleanor to see.

"Mrs. Nelson, Mr. Bennett and I would really like you to open the door and let us talk to you about your daughter's affairs. We have recently been assigned to manage her trust fund, and we have some questions we think only you can answer since her grandparents have taken so ill."

"Will and Ginny? They're both sick?"

"Will's having trouble with his heart," Jeff said. "Ginny, well, you probably know, suffered a major stroke."

"I thought she was getting better."

"She was, but this latest problem with Will has taken its toll on her as well." Ray stepped away from Eleanor and gave Jeff a thumbs up sign.

"I see. Well, okay." They heard Eleanor unlatch the safety chain from inside the door, slide back the dead bolt lock, and turn the locking button on the door knob. Opening the door, she stepped back tentatively and waved them in.

"I'm sorry the place is such a mess. I wasn't expecting anybody."

Ray scanned the room for a place to sit while Jeff stood staring at Eleanor. Scooping old newspapers and magazines from a small swivel rocker, Eleanor offered Ray the chair and moved toward the sofa to pick up an arm load of clean laundry waiting to be folded. "Mr. Bennett, won't you sit down?" Her gentle manners stood in sharp contrast to her harsh appearance.

Eleanor was wearing a stained white seersucker house-coat with large yellow and orange flowers appliquéd on the front. Her feet were covered by green terry cloth slippers, and her matted hair was dyed red and tinged with grey roots. She obviously had plucked out all her eyebrows, favoring painted ones instead. Yet, in spite of the way she looked now, Jeff knew that this woman had once been beautiful. He could see Cari in her.

"Mr. Bennett, you wanted to talk to me about Cari?"

"She looks like you," Jeff said.

"You've seen her lately then?" Eleanor's faded elegance belied her surroundings. Eleanor sat on the other end of the sofa and Jeff noticed how gracefully she moved. *She doesn't belong here,* he thought.

"Yes, we've seen her, or rather, Jeff has." Ray felt a responsibility to keep Jeff on target.

Recovering from the initial shock, Jeff found a place atop the magazines on the coffee table to put his briefcase. Opening it, he pulled out Cari's file. "As I said, I have been recently assigned the management of Caroline's financial trusts. She has asked me to represent her in another matter as well."

"Another matter?"

"Yes, Caroline wants to petition the court to become an emancipated minor."

"A what?"

"Emancipated minor," Ray repeated. "That means that she wants the court to grant her the same powers and privileges as an adult."

"She'll be twenty-one in a year. Her twentieth birthday was last Friday," Eleanor said quietly.

"I know," Jeff said. *You remembered.*

"Can't she wait? She could cause a lot of trouble for both of us if she pursues . . ."

"Trouble? How so?" Ray asked.

"Well, family trouble. My husband, he is her legal guardian you know."

"That's what doesn't make sense," Jeff said.

"Oh?" The ghosts of Eleanor's eyebrows shot upward.

"You see," Jeff continued, "as I was searching the county records, I found the transcripts of three proceedings. First, there was the adoption application when Cari turned five. Second, there was the injunction, the protest registered by her grandparents two months later."

"Yeah, they fought George tooth and nail on the adoption."

"With what result?" Ray asked.

"It was an all-out custody battle."

"How did it turn out?"

"They ended up with visitation rights. Cari was to visit them summers and during school vacations. They also got her on Thanksgiving weekend."

"And what did you get?"

"Child support."

"Pardon me?" Ray asked.

"You know, monthly support."

"You mean, you gave them time with Cari in exchange for . . ."

"It wasn't really like that, Mr. . . ." Eleanor looked at the business card she still held in her hand. "Stetler," she finished.

"And how was it?"

"As Cari's legal parent, George—that's my husband—didn't want Cari to have anything to do with her grandparents since they were my first husband's parents and all. Without the support checks, he wouldn't have agreed to let her see them at all."

"Legal parent?" Jeff asked.

"Sure. The adoption."

"What adoption?"

"What are you talking about? It's right there in your papers, isn't it? If you found the records of the application and the record of the custody hearing, you must have also found the final adoption decree."

"I found the first two, the application and the custody hearing records, but the last one is not an adoption decree."

"What?" Eleanor looked pale.

"I found this," Jeff handed Eleanor a certified copy of the court's decision.

"What's this?" Eleanor held her throat with her hand and then reached for her glasses. She started to read the document Jeff handed her.

"You can skip to the bottom of the last page, Mrs. Nelson." Jeff pitied the woman for what she was about to find out.

"Petition for adoption denied," she read aloud. She removed her glasses and rubbed her eyes as she looked at first Jeff, then Ray. They let her have a moment to absorb what she had just read before they said anything further.

"Mrs. Nelson—Eleanor," Ray leaned forward, "what can you tell us about this?"

"I can't tell you anything. I don't believe it. All these years."

"You mean you didn't know about this?"

"No, of course not. Do you think I would have . . . I had to work on the day we went back to court. George was out of work—laid off—and he insisted he could handle this alone. He didn't even have to reappear in court—he just went to the lawyer's office."

"Alone?" asked Ray.

"Sure."

"Did he ever show you the adoption decree? The document?"

"No. He said he put it in a safety deposit box."

"Do you know where that box is?" asked Ray.

"Bank of America, I think. But I doubt it is still there."

"Oh?" asked Jeff.

"I assume he cleared it all out when he left."

"He left?"

"Alaska. He went to Alaska. He got a job with a fishing company," she explained.

"When did this happen?"

"Just after Cari left." Eleanor still held the document in her hand. "I can't believe this. All these years I thought he could take Cari away from me . . ." Jeff noticed the tears spilling down her face. "He didn't have a leg to stand on to back up any of his threats . . ."

Eleanor put her elbow on the arm of the couch and leaned sideways to put her head in her empty hand. Softly she began to cry; then the sobs began to be deeper and louder. Jeff moved closer to her. He had heard those same sobs from Cari, and his heart broke for Eleanor the same as it had for her daughter.

Putting his hand on her shoulder, Jeff said, "Eleanor, tell me what George threatened."

Regaining some composure, Eleanor wiped her nose with her empty hand. Jeff offered her his clean handkerchief. "Thank you," she said and she wiped her nose with it. "George told me that if I let Cari go live with her grandparents, he would sue me for divorce and that because he was *legally* her father now, he would get at least joint custody, hanging her grandparents out to dry—or so he said. He also said that because he was *legally* her father, he would be entitled to half of Cari's inheritance should anything happen to her or me."

Jeff's eyes flared, and he moved forward to sit on the edge of the couch. Anger toward a man he had never met began to boil deep within his stomach.

"Eleanor"—Ray's tone was calm and he shot a warning glance to Jeff that said, *get a hold of yourself*—"we want to help you, and we want to help Cari. If this is all true, and according to the court records it is, there is no reason to pursue the emancipation petition. You see, as I understand it, it's not you Cari wants to be rid of, it's George."

"That's right," Jeff said. "Cari thinks she is legally George's adopted daughter. She has been living under the same scam that you have."

"You mean," Eleanor said, "she doesn't know about this?"

"Not yet," Jeff said, "but she will when I get back to Redlands."

"When will that be?" Eleanor wiped her face again with Jeff's handkerchief.

"Tonight," Jeff told her. "But first we need to talk about George."

"Okay," she said. Jeff could sense a small flicker of hope in her wide trusting eyes. "I just hope I have the information you need."

"You said he left for Alaska right after Cari left for Minnesota?" Jeff asked.

"Yeah. He said that since there was no more money—"

"No more money?" Jeff interrupted.

"When Cari left, her grandparents stopped sending her support checks. George was very angry. He slapped me around a bit, blamed me for her problem . . . Do you know why she went to Minnesota?"

"I do."

"I thought he was responsible for her condition. I never liked the way he treated her, and as she got older . . . it was awful."

"Why didn't you send her to her grandparents?"

"Because George threatened to sue me for divorce and take Cari away from me," Eleanor said. "He's such a liar. He couldn't have done that if the adoption didn't go through, right?"

"I doubt he could've even if the adoption had been granted," Ray said.

"All these years," Eleanor said, "I have been trying to protect her from him. I stayed with a man who beat me, chased other women, couldn't keep a job . . . and I didn't have to." Eleanor looked defeated. "Now I've lost her after all. She hates me because of George. She's finally where she wanted to be all along. I could've let her go there years ago. I would've too, just to get her away from him."

Eleanor stood and crossed the room to the small kitchen area along an opposite wall. She reached in the small cupboard and took out a bottle of aspirin. "I have a headache," she said, swallowing two of the pills and washing them down with a small glass of water.

Turning back to Jeff, she looked thoughtful. "Mr. Bennett," she started.

"Jeff," he said.

"Jeff, maybe she should be given her independence. Not just from George but from me."

Ray stood to leave. "I must go. Jeff can stay a while longer, but I have an appointment in Long Beach early this afternoon. To make it I will need to leave now."

Eleanor walked Raymond Stetler to the door. "Thank you for coming, Mr. Stetler. Did you say your office is in L.A.?"

"Yes."

"Do you know a good lawyer here in Culver City?"

"I will have my office call you with a referral, how's that?"

"Thank you."

"Jeff, old man, I'll be talking to you. Have a great life out there in the suburbs." The two men shook hands.

"Thanks for all your help, Eleanor," Ray said, and with a wave he was gone.

Jeff said, "Do you have to be somewhere? Work maybe?"

"No, not until seven. I clean the offices across the street," Eleanor answered.

"Can I buy you lunch?"

"Lunch? My goodness. Might I have a few minutes to tidy myself up first?"

"Take as long as you like. I'll check the phone book and call for reservations."

"Reservations?"

"You deserve a celebration, and I'd like to give it to you."

"Then I might need just a little more than a few minutes." She was actually smiling. "It's been a while since I've been to a really nice place. I want to look my best."

Later, sitting across the table from Eleanor Nelson, Jeff couldn't believe his eyes. Cari was the picture of her mother—minus the hard lines etched on her face by years of abuse.

Jeff heard all about the way she met George. He was all smiles and charm at first, but the beatings began on their honeymoon. She told him about teaching Cari to lock herself in her room while she was at work and how she had to work at night because George wouldn't allow money for a babysitter.

She talked constantly, and Jeff listened patiently for over an hour and a half. *She's been a prisoner for years,* Jeff thought. When George left her, she didn't know anything else, so she locked herself in her apartment as if it were a prison cell with no key. Jeff looked at his watch.

"I'm sorry. I'm keeping you. You need to get back to Cari. Will you see her tonight?"

"Yes, I most certainly will." Jeff was excited about all he had to tell Cari, but mostly he was excited about just seeing her.

Jeff paused before asking Eleanor, "Are you interested in seeing her?"

"I miss her so much. Of course I want to see her. I want to ask her forgiveness for putting her through all this with George." Eleanor traced the fold marks in the table cloth with her finger. "I don't know. Maybe she won't want to see me."

We'll see, thought Jeff.

"You're sure George wasn't responsible for . . . well, for her trip to Minnesota?" Jeff asked.

"Positive. Cari told me his name."

"His name?"

"You know, the boy that . . . It sounded like he was a lot like George. I couldn't let her face the same kind of life I had. I made her go to Aunt Hannah's. George had told me that she was a Christian fanatic and that Cari would be kept on a tight leash in her house."

"A fanatic? Cari never mentioned that Hannah was a fanatic," Jeff said.

"I know. George thinks Will and Ginny are fanatics too. I knew Cari would be safe if Hannah was like them."

"Why did you pressure her to give up her baby?"

"I knew that she would someday end up living in Redlands. If she had the baby with her, she would always have a connection to—what's his name—you know, the baby's father." Eleanor gracefully refolded her napkin and laid it across her empty plate.

"The father," Jeff tried to sound calm, "he lives in Redlands?"

"Yes. Cari met him on one of her summer vacations there. Bad news too. All charm and manipulation. He convinced Cari that being with him . . . well, you know . . . that it was all her fault. It wasn't—he forced her." Eleanor's eyes teared. "She got a ride home with him from a youth activity one night, and he forced her. Then he told her she wanted it, that it was all her fault. Can you imagine? Her fault. Said she was leading him on and all."

Jeff swallowed hard. "Go on."

"She knew him, Jeff. It wasn't as though she accepted a ride from a stranger. He was a part of their group. He said she had been flirting with him. He said he could read the hidden meanings behind her friendly manners. Cari didn't lead him on, she didn't know how! She trusted him, Jeff. That's all she did, she trusted him."

Jeff's stomach didn't seem to be digesting his food too well; he felt nauseous. "Did she tell you she told him no?"

"Of course. But some guys are . . . well, they don't know how to take no for an answer. In fact there are some who think when a woman says no she is really begging for it. I should know, I married one."

"Did Cari also tell you his name?" Jeff didn't know if he could stand knowing who it was, but he had to ask.

"Yeah, she did. I forced it out of her because I was convinced it was George." Eleanor frowned and sipped her now cold coffee.

"Want some more coffee?" Jeff asked, wishing she would tell him the name of Cari's attacker.

"No, thanks. Do you think he's still around?"

"Who?"

"Richard—Richard Peters, no *Potter*. That's it, Richard Potter."

Jeff felt his food drop to the bottom of his stomach then rise rapidly, threatening to come up again. He fought it back down. "Richard Potter? Are you sure?"

"Do you know him?" Eleanor asked.

"Yes, I'm afraid I do," Jeff said. "He's the gardener."

"He's what?"

"Will hired him to keep up the yard."

"You mean he's near Cari?"

"On a regular basis, I'm afraid." Jeff summoned the waitress. "I have to get back. You understand."

"Please be careful, Jeff," Eleanor said once they were outside her apartment complex. She got out of the car, and before shutting the door she said, "Take care of her, will you?"

"I'm going to try, Eleanor. I'm sure going to try."

CHAPTER THIRTY-NINE

*H*ey, I know you're ner-
vous," Jen said, "but can't
you sit still for a few minutes? I have something to tell you."

Jen had come over to see Cari the minute she knew for
sure. She found her friend pacing in her room upstairs.
First checking on Will and Virginia, Jen went up and sat
cross-legged on Cari's bed, ready to make her big announcement.

"I'm sorry, Jen. I expected Jeff back by now."

"He's on the freeway, remember? It could take him a
while. If there's not an accident to stop the traffic, it will be
some stupid construction project."

"Thanks. That makes me feel a *lot* better."

"I didn't mean that Jeff . . . Cari, stop it. I'm getting
nervous just watching you. I've spent all day trying not to
be nervous, please, don't ruin it for me."

"What are you talking about?"

"I have a new job!"

"What? I didn't know you were looking for a new job."

"I wasn't, well, not really." Jen pulled Cari down to sit
beside her on the bed. "You remember frumpy old Mrs.
Martin?"

"From Woolworth's?"

"Yeah, you know, the lady born without a smile. Well, she
went to apply for a position at Penney's, and while she was

there, she discovered they were also looking for someone interested in display who could also float."

"Float?"

"You know, work in any and every department without notice. Someone who is bright, flexible, and talented." Jen stuck up her nose and brushed back her long red hair.

"A snob? They were looking to hire a snob?" Cari teased.

"Stop it. I got the job! Isn't that wonderful?"

"What does that mean? School starts in a little over a month. Isn't it kind of strange to change summer jobs in the middle of summer?"

"It's not a summer job." Jen held her breath for Cari's reaction. "It's permanent." Jen grabbed her ears in case Cari started bawling her out the way her mother did.

"Permanent?" Cari asked calmly.

"Permanent." Jen answered.

"As in not returning to school?"

"You got it."

"Ever?"

"Well, I don't know about ever, but certainly not this semester. What do you think, Cari? Tell me honestly. Isn't it just great, too good to be true, beyond your wildest dreams, and all the other superlative statements you can think of?" Jen held her face in her hands and fell backward onto the pillows.

"Basic college writing did you a lot of good!" Cari joked. School without Jen. After all these years of wanting to be together, their goals were beginning to lead them down separate paths. Cari didn't like the uncomfortable feeling that thought gave her, but she loved Jen so much she wouldn't have dreamed of discouraging her.

"This might be a good opportunity for you, Jen. Who knows where it could lead? J. C. Penney is one of the largest chains in the whole world—besides Wards and Sears. You could be running the whole corporation within what . . . five years?"

"Two," Jen said, and the two friends laughed.

"Two." Cari shook her head. "You might just do it too."

Looking out her window to the driveway below, Cari said, "What could be keeping him?"

"Where'd he go?"

"L.A."

"What for?"

"For me." Cari turned to face Jen. "You might as well know. Jeff says it is possible to file a paper or petition of some sort and become a legally recognized adult."

"What?"

"It's called being emancipated."

"That's for slaves."

"Yeah, right. Listen Jen, it's more like getting a divorce from your parents. After I told him about my life with George Nelson and how I wanted to get my grandfather's name—my own name—back, he told me he thought he could do this for me."

"Boy, having your own personal attorney must be handy." Cari threw a pillow at Jen. "Hey, just how personal is he?"

"I'm afraid of how much I love him, Jen," Cari confessed.

"Oh, no! I knew it. You two have gone and fallen in love. It's an epidemic in this house! First Meg and Mac, now you and Jeff. I'm getting out of here."

Jen grabbed her purse and headed for the door. "Not so fast," Cari said. "I need you to wait for Jeff with me. It's too hard waiting alone."

Jeff clenched his jaw and rubbed his forehead. He checked his rear-view mirror, adjusted the side mirror, and turned the radio dial in search of a new station while he waited for the construction worker to wave his lane ahead. He reached over and thumped his briefcase with his fingers and thought of the contents and what the information was going to mean to Cari and her grandparents. *Finally,* he thought as traffic started to move, *now maybe we'll get somewhere.* He waved at the flagman directing traffic as he went by.

He headed toward Redlands and pushed the speed limit, all the while keeping an eye out for the highway patrol. *Getting a ticket will cost me more time than speeding will save.* And as he tried to get home as soon as possible, Jeff thought about what Eleanor Nelson had told him.

Richard Potter. Cari has had to face him almost every week this summer. I wonder how she has managed. How come he hasn't caused trouble—or has he?

Changing lanes to avoid a slower driver, Jeff picked up speed again. *Obviously Mac knows nothing about this,* Jeff reasoned. *I wonder what Meg has told him about Cari. I wonder what Meg knows.*

Ahead someone had been pulled over, and Jeff checked the speedometer and slowed slightly. *I'll have to speak to Mac before I fire Richard . . . Cari will have to tell me how much she wants him to know.*

Noting slow traffic ahead in his lane, Jeff moved into another. He was so anxious to see Cari, to bring her the news that the emancipation was unnecessary. *Caroline Grace Rhoades,* he thought. *She had been Rhoades all along.*

Turning off the freeway at the first Redlands exit, Jeff drove by the office first. He checked his mail and decided everything there could wait until tomorrow. Picking up the phone, he called the Rhoades' house.

"She's right upstairs, Jeffrey," Virginia said. "I'll get her."

"No, Grandma, wait. I'm on my way over."

"See you soon, then, dear."

"Grandma?"

"Yes?"

"I have some good news, good news for all of you."

Meg greeted Jeff at the door when he arrived. "Cari's upstairs with Jen. Shall I call her?" Meg asked.

"No, not yet," Jeff said. "I want to talk to Will and Ginny first."

Jeff knocked on the Rhoades' bedroom door. At their invitation, he stuck his head in. "I have to go upstairs to talk to Cari. Do you mind, Will?"

"Of course he doesn't mind," Virginia said.

Will looked at Jeff and shrugged his shoulders. "You heard the boss. Go on up."

"It could be a while; I've got a lot to tell her," Jeff warned. He took the stairs two at a time and headed in the direction of Jen's voice. Reaching the door he knocked lightly.

"Come in." Jeff's stomach flipped at the sound of Cari's voice.

"Cari? It's Jeff."

"Jeff?" Jen ran to the door and flung it open. "This is an honorable house, Jeffrey Bennett. Did you get permission from the Lord of the Manor before you came up here?"

"I did, my lady," Jeff said as he bowed low before her. "May I speak to the mistress of this room, please?"

"Is this a private conversation, my lord?"

"Yes, fair one, it is."

"Rats!" Jen said. "I know when I'm being dismissed. But mind you, I'll be right downstairs."

Jeff crossed Cari's room in two long strides. His heart was almost exploding with his news and his love for her. She jumped up and stood on the bed. As he came closer, she nearly leaped into his arms.

"Jeff, Jeff," she cried. "I missed you so much. I've been so worried, I could hardly wait until you came home."

"I've missed you too, sweetheart. And do I ever have news."

"You saw my mother then?"

"I did, but let me begin at the beginning." Jeff set his briefcase on the small vanity bench, took a few papers out of it, and settled himself in the window seat.

"I'm trying to be patient, but it's hard." Cari's voice quivered.

"I'm sorry, honey. I don't mean to drag this out. First, let me say I found some very interesting things when I searched the court records."

"Like what?"

"I found the application for adoption. Then I was able to find the court transcripts of the hearing when your grandparents filed for custody. They record the actual words each of them said in the courtroom that day. I examined all the questions and found the settlement your grandparents agreed to pay in exchange for your right to visit them each school vacation."

"My grandparents paid money?"

"Yes, didn't you know that?"

"No."

"They sent monthly support for you," Jeff explained.

"That's really strange. I never knew that. Grandma always bought all my clothes and once a week they sent me five dollars in a letter. They sent monthly support besides?"

"Yes."

"Wow. I didn't know."

"Wait, there's more. Much more." Jeff leaned toward her, and she responded as he kissed her briefly on the lips. "Much more."

"Go on."

"No decision was reached that day. The adoption decision came later—in February. It's normal for an adoption to take six months in the court from the time of application to the granting of the decree."

"The what?"

"The adoption decree. The final documents are prepared, the adoptive parents appear before a judge, and he grants the petition. That's the usual case, anyway."

"Is my case unusual?"

"Very."

"How, Jeff? Tell me."

"Your stepfather's petition for adoption was denied." Jeff watched anxiously for Cari's reaction.

"Denied?" Cari's eyes widened, and Jeff saw her mother's face in that expression.

"Denied," he repeated. "Do you know what that means?"

"No, what?"

"It means that you never were adopted by George Nelson. The court turned him down."

"But, my mother . . . she made me change my name . . . she registered me as Cari Nelson in school . . . he said . . ."

"Cari, your mother didn't know."

"She went on and on about how George was my father now and that he—what did you say?"

"I said, she didn't know."

"How could she not know?" Cari was standing now, and tears began to fill her eyes.

"He fooled her, he fooled your grandparents, he fooled everyone."

"How?" a sob caught in Cari's throat. "I don't see how he could do that."

"It really was very simple," Jeff said calmly.

"Simple? I was never *legally* his daughter, yet he held me there like I was? And you stand there and call that simple?" Cari's tears were more than Jeff could bear. He reached in his pocket for his handkerchief and realized that her mother had not returned it to him after she had cried out these same questions earlier in the day.

Looking around the room—Cari's room—he spotted a box of tissues on the nightstand and handed her two of them. She blew her nose loudly and wiped her tears away.

"Cari, calm down and listen to me."

"Calm down?" Cari's eyes blazed with anger as she began to pace back and forth in front of where Jeff sat in the window seat.

"I can't continue with this explanation until you are quieter," Jeff told her.

She sat down on the bed to face him "Okay." She blew her nose again. "I'm quieter."

"After your grandparents filed a protest—that's what they did—the courts denied the adoption. They said no to George's petition."

"I don't understand. How did he . . ."

"He went to the lawyer's office by himself. Your mother had to go to work. Then he told her that the petition was granted. He told her that the courts had made him your adoptive father. But it was a lie, Cari, a lie."

Cari stood up and faced Jeff, who was still sitting in the window seat. "A lie," she repeated. "My whole life has been a lie."

"No, Caroline, it has not."

"But I went to school, I traveled, I'm registered in school now as Caroline Nelson—that's a lie." Cari grabbed her purse and rummaged for her wallet. She got out her driver's license and social security card, both of which read *Caroline Grace Nelson,* and threw them on the bed. "Look, Jeff, I'm not Caroline Nelson. I've never been Caroline Nelson. It's all a lie."

Jeff watched the truth soak into Cari's understanding as he had watched Eleanor earlier. Cari sat down on the edge of the bed, her back to Jeff. She began picking shreds of tissue from the damp wad she held in her hand and dropping them on the floor.

"Okay, she didn't know," Cari said. "But she could have left him. He was cruel to her. I heard them fighting, mostly over me, many times a week. He would scream that he was my parent, my *legal* parent and that what he said went. Didn't it ever occur to her that she was also my *legal* parent?"

"He threatened her, Cari."

"He did what? How?" She was surprised.

"He said he would divorce her and sue for custody of you. He convinced her that he would take you away from your grandparents and that he would only share custody with her fifty-fifty. She did it for you, sweetheart, do you understand that? She thought she had to stay with him to protect you."

Caroline wrapped her arms around her middle and began to quietly moan. Soon deep sobs were ripping from her heart. "Dear God! Where were You?" Then turning to Jeff, her eyes swollen and her lips dry and puffed from crying, she said, "Where was God in all of this? You try to get me to have faith in Him—but He stood by and let this happen to me—to her. Tell me Jeff, where was God?"

Jeff answered softly, "He was there, with you, and with your mom."

"And He stood by and did nothing while we lived a life of pure hell with that man?"

"Caroline." Jeff moved to take her in his arms. She was tense and rigid at his touch. "Caroline, baby, listen to me. God does not stop bad things from happening to good people. But He will give them the strength to come through it and a vision to help make sure it doesn't happen to other people. I've watched Him do that in your mother, and I'm watching Him do that in you, right now."

"I don't know what you mean," Cari said.

Jeff suddenly noticed how late it was getting and how quiet the rest of the house was. "Cari, can I have a few minutes to think about how to answer your question? It's been a long day and I'm hungry."

Cari ignored his request. "Jeff, I can't believe I've been a Rhoades all this time. Do Grandpa and Grandma know this?"

"Not that I know of. I thought you'd want to be the one to tell them. Are they still awake?"

"Grandpa has been napping every afternoon, so he doesn't go to sleep very early. He's getting stronger every day. Grandma wouldn't want this kind of news to wait until morning. Please, can we go down and at least tell them?"

"Think Meg would be willing to fix me a sandwich?"

"Meg is always ready to feed someone."

Jeff stood and suddenly became aware of how much he liked being in her room. Cari reached for the door and then spun around to face him. "Jeff," she said as she flung herself in his arms, "I love you so much."

"I love you too, honey. And we're getting out of this room and going downstairs right now."

I can't believe it. This is a real answer to our prayers," Will said when Jeff had finished telling them the news about Cari's adoption. "We thought the court system had failed us, that it had failed Caroline."

"Poor Eleanor," said Virginia.

"Yeah, wow," said Jen.

Cari still wasn't capable of such benevolence toward her mother—not just yet. She was waiting for an answer to the questions she had asked Jeff upstairs.

Meg was happily making Jeff a sandwich and a smaller version of the same thing for Cari just in case she could persuade her to eat something. It was nearly nine o'clock, and Cari hadn't eaten since noon—and very little then.

Jen stood and hugged Cari. "Well, my pet. Seems your knight in shining armor came through for you. It's almost enough to make me want to shop for a husband—almost, but not quite."

Cari laughed at her friend and hugged her back. "You will meet someone and fall so hard it will cause the San Andreas fault to erupt."

"Faults slip, not erupt," Jen corrected. "No, not me. I'm headed for a big career in retail. J. C. Penney is only the beginning. And by the way, since I start there tomorrow

260

morning at nine sharp, I'd better get home and set my hair."

Cari walked Jen to her car parked on the curb. The two girls were so happy about Cari's news that they didn't notice the dark figure step back into the oleander bushes along the driveway.

Back in the house, under Jeff's watchful eye, Cari attempted to eat Meg's sandwich. She at least drank a glass of milk, and Jeff didn't push her any further. He was thinking of how to explain to Cari not only that God was there but that He worked in all of this.

Meg excused herself and hugged Cari for the third time. She tucked in her patients and asked Will if he needed one of the sedatives the doctor left for him. He refused, assuring everyone he would sleep better than he had in a long, long time. His Cari was home, and in a way, he felt closer to his son—Cari's father—too.

Jeff and Cari sat across from each other at the kitchen table, and Jeff took her hands. "Cari," he began slowly, "I don't know if I'm the one who can explain this to you. But I love you, and I'm the only one here, so I'm going to try."

"I just don't understand how God can stand by and not do something about what George did."

"I'm not so sure He was just standing by."

"I don't know," she said.

"What, or maybe I should say *who* do you think prompted your mother to buy the lock for your door? And who do you suppose led her to put the phone in your room? What, or who, convinced George to settle for such a small amount of monthly support when your grandfather was willing to pay much, much more? And why did George let you come for summers and holidays at all? Your grandparents would have continued sending the money. They never wanted you to go without or be in need."

"But I didn't get the money, George did."

"But, honey, don't you see, they would have never known that?"

Cari listened to Jeff, this wonderful man she loved so deeply. He continued, "Just suppose God had not been there. Suppose George had never been restrained, what then?"

"I can't even bear to think of it."

"You see? Maybe God didn't stop him where you think he should have been stopped, but he was stopped." Jeff took a long drink of orange juice right from the glass bottle in the ice box. He winked at Cari. "Don't tell, Meg I did that—promise?"

"I promise. But Jeff, why did my mother say all of those things to me when she sent me away? It was awful. She was crying and yelling and calling me names."

"It was for George's benefit, I think. She wouldn't let you go to your grandparents because George would have thought about the money and caused all kinds of trouble, you being a minor and this happening to you while you were staying with them. Remember, she thought he was your legal parent. I also think there is a deeper reason, something she may not have thought through at the time but knew instinctively."

"What's that?"

"She thought you would end up living in Redlands just as soon as you were old enough anyway. She didn't want you to give the father of your baby anything he could hold over you in the years to come. She knew how difficult that would be for the whole family—and surprisingly, for your baby, too."

"Oh, my gosh," Cari said, "I didn't ever consider that she did what she did for my sake. I thought she hated me."

"That's how she had to behave to get your stepfather to believe her. Think about it. Did she ever have a single minute alone with you once they found out about your condition?"

"No way. George wouldn't give us any privacy at all. He kept ranting and raving about the cost of feeding one brat and telling us he sure wasn't going to take on another—not without more money, anyway."

"There, you see? Your mother was protecting your grandparents too. And can you imagine what your life would have been like had you stayed there and kept the baby?"

"Oh, my God, Jeff."

"Exactly—God. He was there all the time. And somewhere in Minnesota was a childless couple praying for a baby of their own. Your decision to place your baby with them was an answer to their prayer. Do you see God in this at all, now?"

"I think I do. I never thought of it this way before." Cari squeezed his hand. "He also knew I needed you. You have helped me see so much."

"He knew I needed you too, Cari. Your experience has helped me see my own mother so much differently. I have some very interesting questions to ask her since talking to your mother."

"My mother." Cari's face tensed, and her eyes drifted away from Jeff's. "How is she?"

"Lonely, very lonely. Did you know she is alone now?"

"Alone? Where's George?"

"Alaska, or at least that's what he told her. He left her just after you went to Minnesota. When your grandparents sent your support to Hannah instead of George, he skipped out on your mother."

Cari leaned her head onto her hand, resting her elbow on the table. "How does she look?"

"Beaten. She looks much older than what I'd calculate based on the age listed on your birth certificate."

"My birth certificate? You've seen my birth certificate?"

"I'm a very thorough lawyer, Miss Rhoades. I even know how much you weighed and how long you were when you were born."

"Caroline Rhoades. I am so happy to have my name back."

"I am pleased to report that you never lost it," Jeff replied.

"How do I go about changing it on all my other stuff, my driver's license, social security card, and school registration?"

"I'll work on that for you, my dear. Just trust me," Jeff said, trying to imitate W. C. Fields, "just trust me."

"I do," Cari said softly, "I really do."

"How much?" he asked, suddenly serious.

"How much what?"

"Do you trust me?" Jeff's voice was husky and thick.

"With my life," she whispered.

"With your whole life?" he asked.

"My entire, whole life."

"Cari?"

"What?"

"Will you marry me then?"

"I love you, Jeff. I trust you. I really want to marry you."

"Is that a yes?"

"That, Mr. Lawyer, is a yes."

Jeff came around the table to where Cari was sitting, took her hand, and pulled her into his arms. He looked at her tenderly—his little love, his precious treasure. Slowly he lowered his lips to lightly rest on hers for a long, sweet moment. Then he picked her up and swung her around. Setting her down he quickly touched her lips with his own once again. Nuzzling her neck, he whispered, "Mrs. Wilson will be so happy about this."

CHAPTER FORTY-ONE

*D*id you sleep?" Jeff asked Cari the next morning on the phone.

"I think so. I had the wildest dream, though."

"Oh? Want to tell me about it?"

"A lawyer asked me to marry him."

"That's interesting. What did you say?"

"I said yes. At least I think I said yes."

"You did."

"How do you know?"

"I had the same dream."

Cari laughed, and Ginny thought there wasn't any sound this side of heaven sweeter than that, except for Will's snoring.

"What are you planning to do today?" Jeff asked.

"I am helping Meg with laundry. Mac's been keeping her pretty busy with Sharon's baby, and she went over to help him move Sharon's stuff today."

"Any sign of her husband?" Jeff wondered when he would be able to tell Cari that he knew what Richard had done to her.

"Not that I know of." *Thank God,* Cari thought. *Maybe He's watching over me after all.*

"Interesting, don't you think?" Jeff wondered aloud.

"What's interesting?"

"He walks out on his wife and on his landscaping jobs."

"He beat her, did you know that?"

"He what?" Jeff was obviously alarmed.

"He beat Sharon the night little Frances was born."

"I didn't know . . . are you sure?"

"She told me that day I went to see her after Frances was born."

"Is she out of the hospital?"

"Meg said she was coming home tomorrow, I think." Cari wasn't sure. Her mind was too full with thoughts of Jeff and her future as his wife for her to concentrate on much else.

"Cari? Would it be all right if I called your mother again?"

"What for?"

"I think she wants to see you. Could I tell her you might be ready to see her sometime soon?"

"I have been thinking about that all night."

"I thought you said you slept."

"Well, I did off and on."

"What do you say? Would it be okay if I called her?"

"Grandma told me that whenever I am ready, Mother is welcome to come here. They feel really bad about what has happened to her. She was their daughter-in-law—they loved her."

"Are you ready?"

"I'm not sure I will ever be ready."

"Cari—"

"Wait, Jeff," Cari interrupted. "I said I'm not sure I will ever be ready, but I think I need to—no, I want to."

"I'll call her."

"I trust you, Jeff."

"I love you, Cari."

Jeff hung up and anxiously called Eleanor. She sounded out of breath. "Eleanor, you okay?" Jeff asked.

"Yes, Jeff, I'm fine—really fine. That lawyer friend of yours called me last night and gave me the name of an attorney right down the street from here. I saw him this morning at 8:30. I took what little money I had, and he said he would file divorce papers for me on the grounds of desertion. I'm packing my stuff now. I don't want to be here when George gets the papers, if they can even find him."

"If they can't they'll run an ad in the paper in the city where he was last known to be. If he doesn't answer, you get your divorce by default."

"That's what my lawyer said. Anyway, I don't want to take any chances. I've been packing all night. The landlord said I could leave most of my things in the storage room here until I'm settled somewhere, and then I can send for them. He's so nice. He never liked George."

"Where're you going, Eleanor?"

"Haven't thought that far yet. I've just closed my last suitcase. Thought I might get a hotel for a few days and think about my future."

"Cari said she wants to see you."

"She did?"

"Want to come this way? I mean if you have no plans, you could stay in a hotel here just as well as there," Jeff encouraged.

"Yeah, I guess I could." Eleanor was quiet, and Jeff wondered what she was thinking.

"Eleanor, do you have enough money to get here?" he asked.

"Oh, I think I do. I have about a hundred and fifty dollars left. I cleaned out all my old purses, where I used to hide money from George. I even found some I forgot I had. I didn't go anywhere, and I don't eat much."

Jeff remembered how thin she looked.

"Take the bus to San Bernardino then. Catch the one that gets in at 6:30 tonight. I'll have someone there to meet you. His name is James Jenkins. He's a very nice man. He's been my father now for over seventeen years. How will he know you?"

"I'm wearing a blue suit, kind of a medium blue, and a yellow blouse. Wait a minute, Jeff—give me your phone number, just in case."

Jeff gave her the number and decided against telling Cari her mother would be arriving soon. He planned to make a motel reservation for Eleanor, but when he told Sarah what he was doing, she insisted on clearing out the spare room and making up the bed.

"She'll be much more comfortable here," Sarah said, but Jeff wasn't sure. All he knew was that if anyone could make her feel welcome, Sarah could. *She has a way with strays,* he thought. *I should know.*

With the arrangements all taken care of, Jeff went to the office to see if he could get some work done. At noon he received a call from Mac.

"Sorry to disturb you, son," Mac said.

"Not disturbing me a bit. In fact, I was hoping to talk to you today."

"It's about Sharon's husband. He came back last night."

"He did?" Jeff dropped the gold pen Cari gave him for Christmas.

"He broke into the apartment, or used his key—the place is such a mess we can't tell."

"What do you mean a mess?"

"He took a knife and slashed what little clothes Sharon had left there. Cut the mattress and sofa up to nothin'." Mac paused and Jeff could hear the weariness in Mac's voice. "I made a terrible mistake makin' him marry her. I know that now. I feel responsible for her and those babies. There wouldn't be a little Frances to worry about if I hadn't interfered."

"Mac, you didn't know."

"Well, too late to look back now, I suppose. It's just the violent way he tore up their apartment. He broke all the dishes in the middle of the floor. He must have really tied one on to do all that."

"What are you thinking, Mac?"

"I'm thinkin' there ought to be some way to restrain him from comin' around Sharon and Frances. Two women would be no match for this crazy man."

"Let me see what I can do," Jeff said. "I'll talk to the sheriff and see if there's enough to swear out a warrant or, at the very least, a restraining order."

"Thanks, Jeff, I'd really be grateful to you. Would it be okay if I came over and went with you to the sheriff station?"

"You bet. I've got some free time now if you can make it."

Jeff hung up the phone and called Cari. "She's out back, Jeff. Hanging up the laundry. Want me to go get her?"

"No, Grandma, that's okay."

"She's sure a happy girl. You put that smile on her face?"

"Maybe I did," Jeff said. "Is that okay?"

"More than okay. Isn't it time you made an appointment to speak with Grandpa, though?"

"You know, Ginny, I think it is."

Mac arrived within minutes, and Jeff and he drove together to the sheriff's station.

"Pretty mean accusation, Mac. Is Sharon willing to press charges?" the sheriff asked.

"You bet. Her mother—that's my cousin—and I are willing to put her in safe hiding for a while if necessary. It's important that the man is put away where he can't hurt anyone."

"She still in the hospital?" Sheriff Stanton asked.

"Yeah, till tomorrow."

"Do you think we ought to put someone up there?"

"I don't know. No use scarin' the poor girl. She's been through enough."

"How about posting an extra officer in the lobby and alerting the hospital's own security men?" Jeff offered.

"Good thinking, Jeff. We're mighty glad to have you come into our community, a nice levelheaded fella like you."

Jeff didn't feel levelheaded. He had an uneasy feeling that something was wrong. He couldn't shake it, even with reason. He thought of Cari and her invalid grandparents home alone. He thought of her hanging out the clothes in the backyard. The hair on the back of his neck stood on end. He grabbed Mac by the arm and said, "Let's get out of here."

"Where're we goin' in such a big hurry?" Mac asked.

"I just have a feeling, that's all. Go get Frances and Sharon's son and take them to the Whipples' as soon as you can. Don't even stay there to explain, let Frances do that. Then meet me at Will and Virginia's. I don't like leaving them there alone, not with Potter on the loose and in such a state of mind. Bring Meg home, too. We need her there."

Jeff turned his car toward Cari's and prayed for her safety.

CHAPTER FORTY-TWO

*W*here's Cari?" Jeff asked Ginny.

"Out back, hanging another load of laundry." Ginny looked a little concerned, but she hid her feelings as best she could from Will.

"She talked about the cradle this morning, Jeff. That have anything to do with you?"

"I think it has to do more with you, Will. She is finally realizing how much we all love her."

"Go on out, Jeff," Virginia said. "If she's not at the clothesline, she's in the workshop."

Jeff tried to still the rumbling in his stomach. He left Cari's grandparents watching "The Price is Right" and tried to walk casually around the house to the clothesline. The laundry basket was empty. *She finished hanging the clothes*, he thought. *She must be in the workshop.*

Jeff quickened his steps, rounded the guest house, and went to the back of the garage where the workshop was. He ducked under the overgrown branches of the lemon tree and saw the workshop door standing wide open. He briefly stopped to listen and didn't hear her inside.

His heart pounded, his temples throbbed. He touched the door, and it squeaked on its hinges. "Cari?" Jeff called her name softly. No answer.

Jeff stepped inside and looked around to get his bearings. He had only been in the workshop once before, but he knew Will well enough to know he would have never left it in such disarray. A small tool chest was overturned and the contents scattered across the floor. A trash container was also upset and wood scraps lay all over the floor.

He spotted the cradle—lying on its side, one of the rockers loosened and the other broken. "Cari!" He yelled.

Jeff spun around and ran out the door. Something caught his eye. Cari's scarf was snagged on the chain link fence. He went toward it and saw the fence had been cut from the bottom to near the top and the fencing was curled back on both sides, leaving just enough room for a man to walk through. From a distance, no one would have noticed; but up close, it was obvious—the hole had been cut as a passageway.

Jeff turned and ran back to the house just as Mac was getting out of his car. Before Mac and Meg could go in, Jeff pulled them into the guest house.

"She's gone," Jeff said, breathing heavily. "I have been in the house; I've looked in the yard and in the workshop."

"Is she in her room?" Meg asked.

"I don't think so. It looks like there was a scuffle in the workshop . . . the cradle . . . it's turned over and broken."

"The cradle?" Mac looked confused.

Jeff took a deep breath and ran his hand through his hair. "And Mac, there's a hole in the fence back there big enough to ride a horse through."

"Oh, dear Lord," Meg said. "I'd better attend to the folks."

"Call the sheriff, Meg. You better call the doctor too. No telling what this day might bring."

"You don't have to tell me what to do. You go after Cari, Jeff. Mac, you go with him. I'll take care of things here."

Jeff and Mac returned to the workshop. "I thought you said a scuffle, son. This looks like an all-out brawl happened in here."

Jeff's heart sank at Mac's assessment. "Where shall we start?"

"Let's go the way he did." Mac led the way and out through the hole in the fence.

The men spread out and started walking down the furrowed rows between the orange trees. Jeff thought he could hear voices in the distance. Mac heard the same thing and came silently alongside Jeff. They dropped to their stomachs and looked as best they could under the trees. The Valencia oranges were heavy with ripeness and pulled the branches almost to the ground.

"There!" Mac pointed, and Jeff turned around to look. "See the pickup wheels over there?"

They could hear a man's voice but couldn't make out what he was saying. The thick orange grove deadened the sound.

Mac motioned for them to spread out. On the far side of the grove, Jeff caught a glimpse of a police car. *Dear God,* he prayed, *don't let them rush him, not until we get Cari.*

He and Mac moved through the grove now, about a hundred feet apart. When they got closer, they could hear Richard's taunting voice. "You never did like me, did you Cari? You were just leading me on, teasing me all the time. Sharon, though, she liked me. Ask her sometime, since you have become such good friends." Richard pulled Cari around to the back of the truck. "Get in, Caroline," he ordered. Then in a mocking tone he said, "You'll not get your pretty little dress dirty in the truck."

"Don't, Richard, don't," Cari pleaded.

"You don't mean it, Cari." Richard laughed, and Jeff thought he would vomit in the dirt beneath him.

"Please, let me go. Don't hurt me, Richard, please!"

"Don't hurt you? You mean like this?" Jeff heard Richard's hand strike something with a thud, and Cari cried out. "Or like this?" Another slap, and Cari screamed. Jeff could stand no more and bolted toward them, running as fast as he could.

"Stop!" Never in his life did the hate run as cold in his blood as it did then. "Richard! Leave her alone!"

Jeff ran from between two trees and into Richard's hardened fist. Jeff fell backward, rolled over and scrambled to his feet just as Richard lifted his foot into Jeff's midsection.

Mac circled behind, and Jeff saw him out of the corner of his eye. *Turn him around so Mac can get him from behind,* Jeff thought instinctively.

Richard picked up a crowbar from the back of the truck and stepped toward Jeff. "No!" Cari screamed. "No!" With no thought for her own safety, she jumped from the pickup bed, grabbed the crowbar, and fell with Richard to the ground. Richard easily flung her off and hit her across the face with the back of his free hand. Jeff, on his feet again, lunged at Richard as Mac grabbed him from behind. With a mighty yell, Richard flung them both around. He managed to free himself from their hold and ran headlong through the orange grove toward the street.

Jeff lifted Cari from the dirt and saw the blood running from her split lip. Mac sprinted to catch Richard from behind and tackled him just as he broke the edge of the grove. Before Richard could catch his breath, two uniformed police officers had him in handcuffs.

Jeff carried Cari back to the house. She was barely conscious and was calling Jeff's name.

"I'm right here, baby, I'm right here." Jeff was sobbing by the time he climbed back through the hole in the fence, carrying her into the kitchen.

Meg met them at the door and helped Jeff lower her to the daybed. Virginia came in and walked over to her side. "I'll get the doctor," she told them, her voice shaking.

Meg put out her hand and restrained the old woman. "No, my friend. You sit here with your granddaughter. I'll get the doctor. He's in with Will," she said to Jeff.

Mac came in the house for a moment to check on Cari, then left again to speak with the police out in the driveway and file the report.

"My good doctor," Meg said cheerfully, "is the patient well enough for you to leave for a moment?" She nodded toward the kitchen.

"I'm sure he is, aren't you, Will?"

"Of course," William said slowly, "now that you've given me your magic potion. Come back next week and wake me, will you?"

"In the kitchen," Meg whispered to the doctor. "Take your bag with you." Meg sat down in the chair beside Will's bed and tried to make small talk to keep him occupied. "That's what I plan to do on my vacation this year."

"What's that?" Will asked.

"I plan to visit one of them TV game shows and win lots of money."

"What do you need money for, Meggie? Marry Mac, and you'll have all the money you could want."

"Sure'n I bet," Meg said, but her mind was in the kitchen where the doctor was attending Cari and on the crisis they would have on their hands with Will if he knew how badly she had been hurt.

"How is she?" Jeff asked the doctor.

"She's not as bad as she looks, thank the Lord." Virginia was beginning to wash Cari's face and hands with a cool cloth. "Cari?" Virginia's heart was breaking for her only granddaughter. "Cari, can you hear me?"

"She's had a bad fright, in addition to the bruises," Dr. Lohengren said. "We have no way of knowing for sure if she has any internal injuries. I could call an ambulance, but with Will's condition, I'd like to wait a little bit, and if it's necessary, we can take her by car."

"Jeff?" Cari looked wildly around the room. "Jeff?" She was shaking uncontrollably.

"I'm here, baby, right here."

"Is Richard . . . ?"

"He's gone, Cari. The police came and arrested him."

"Jeff," Cari started to cry. "Jeff, he's the fa—"

"Shhh, I know. Your mother told me."

Virginia looked at Jeff with her eyes wide and her eyebrows raised in a stiff arch high on her forehead. Jeff nodded to Virginia. "I'm afraid so," he said quietly.

"She didn't tell us."

"She couldn't," Jeff defended her. "Not till now."

"How did you find me?" Cari asked between her tears. "How did you know?"

"God told me, Cari. I know it was God."

"I prayed, Jeff. When Richard grabbed me, I prayed."

"He was there, Caroline. He was right there."

James arrived, and after being filled in on what had happened, he said, "Someone better tell Will the truth. If you don't, he will think his condition is worse than you've led him to believe."

"I think you're right," Virginia said. "Can you do it? You're so good with him."

James checked his watch. "Sorry, can't stay. I have to be in San Bernardino in forty-five minutes. Better get going."

"Coming right back here, then?" Jeff asked, and James nodded.

Meg and Virginia stayed with Cari while Jeff and the doctor told Will about Richard.

Cari wouldn't let Jeff out of her sight. She refused to be moved upstairs, needing to be near him and her grandparents. They moved her to the living room, where Jeff stroked her hair while she slept off the light sedative the doctor gave her after he decided her ribs were bruised and not broken.

She roused once in a while, and Jeff would whisper that he loved her and that she was safe—and she would fall asleep again for a few more minutes.

In a couple of hours, James came back with Eleanor. Her clothes and hair were neat, and she wore makeup. She looked completely different from the woman Jeff met yesterday. In her blue suit, she looked lovely, even motherly, Jeff thought. She sat in a chair near the couch where Cari was lying.

Cari roused and Jeff kissed her injured lip gently. "Cari? Can you wake up a little?" Cari stirred and changed positions. She caught the sight of Eleanor through her blurry eyes. "Mama? Mama?" Cari began to sob as she carefully turned her beaten body to face her mother.

Eleanor needed no further invitation. She fell to her knees in front of the couch and carefully wrapped her arms around her bruised daughter. "Mama," Cari said through her tears, "you came. I prayed you'd come."

Jeff encircled the small figures of both Cari and her mother within his arms. After all they had been through, they still loved each other—and he would love them both.

*J*eff stood at the altar of the beautiful little church facing those he had come to love so deeply. He tugged at the sleeve of his tuxedo unconsciously as he waited for Cari to appear.

The Wilsons had taken a seat halfway back, and Mrs. Wilson dabbed at her eyes with a hanky long before the soloist even began her lovely rendition of "Entreat Me Not To Leave Thee." Every once in a while she would look at her husband with tenderness, and together they smiled at the secret knowledge that they had reserved just the right ring setting for Cari long before the young couple had come in to make their selection.

Meg sat a few rows back near the center aisle, still radiant following her Labor Day elopement with Mac. Frances sat next to Meg. The two women were more like sisters than cousins-in-law.

Diedra had been ushered in and sat in the second row, leaving space for Sarah and James. Jeff had insisted that Sarah occupy the place reserved for the mother of the groom, but had graciously invited Diedra to sit next to her.

Ray Stetler stood beside his friend, glad that Jeff was getting married, but sorry that such a talented attorney was not going to join his firm in Los Angeles. Mac looked stiff and uncomfortable in his tux, but counted it a privilege to be a part of the wedding party—though he was old enough to be Jeff's father.

Cari had requested there be no flower girl or ring bearer, and Jeff didn't argue with her. She had grown more open and trusting these past three and a half months. Spending time with her mother, watching her grandparents and Ellie grow closer and reaching toward each other in genuine love and forgiveness had provided a wonderful environment for her own healing to progress at a miraculous rate.

Sharon made her appearance at the back of the church wearing the deep forest green velvet dress so carefully selected for a Thanksgiving wedding. She had burst into tears when Cari asked her to be a bridesmaid. Jen, as the maid of honor, followed—keeping the proper distance that had been carefully told to her during the rehearsal.

"This is as close to being a bride as I might ever be!" Jen said on more than one occasion. The deep green velvet and the fall colors contained in the bridesmaids' bouquets set off Jen's red hair beautifully and complemented Sharon's blond hair and fair skin.

Jeff's hands felt wet and dry at the same time, and his heart nearly stopped when the strains of the church organ changed to the wedding march.

Ellie quickly stood and turned to help Virginia stand as well. The two women held hands as they turned slightly to get a better look at Cari, standing beside her grandfather, ready for the walk down the aisle lined with baskets of fall-colored flowers and leaves.

Cari was stunning in the long, full wedding dress she and her mother had so carefully chosen. Seed pearls and imported Belgian lace covered the tightly fitted bodice. A string of her grandmother's pearls were perfectly displayed above the scalloped neckline—the same pearls her mother had worn when she married Cari's father. The large, full skirt, caught tightly at the waist, made soft swishing sounds as she walked beside her cherished grandfather. Her chestnut hair was crowned with a band of pearls and white sequins holding the layer of sheer white that delicately covered her face. Several more layers of the same sheer white material were also gathered at the crown before cascading down her back, filling the aisle far behind with more pearls and lace, which gracefully flowed behind her as she walked toward her beloved Jeff.

Reaching the pew where her grandmother and mother waited, Cari paused, Will beside her.

After a few opening remarks the minister asked, "Who gives this woman to be married to this man?"

Will stood a little straighter and said, "Her mother, her grandmother, and I."

Cari pulled a deep red rose from her bridal bouquet, handed it to her mother, and kissed her on the cheek. She then pulled a second one and gave it to her grandmother. In a sudden unplanned movement, Will surrounded the three women with his arms and they stood for an unforgettable moment. No one except their closest friends knew the years of pain and then the miracle that had happened to this little family. Jeff shuffled his feet and stared at the floor. Tears flooding his eyes, he caught the gaze of his own mother and winked at her.

"Ahem!" The minister cleared his throat. "I think there is a young man here who is wanting to get married tonight."

A quiet ripple of laughter swept over the wedding guests.

"That's okay," Jeff said. "I've waited this long, I can wait a moment longer."

Finally Jeff moved toward Caroline, took her hand in his, and together they walked toward the minister.

With all their secrets laid in the open and all their fears now quiet, they faced the future together. The promises they now spoke in front of those witnessing the ceremony were ones they had already made to each other many times before.

Jeff slipped the small gold circlet on Cari's hand, then turned to face his lovely bride. Just before he kissed her, he whispered, "See, Cari? God does answer prayer."

*N*eva Coyle is a full-time freelance writer who is very active in the ministry of her local church. She is also the co-author of the best-selling book, *Free To Be Thin*. *Cari's Secret* is the first in a series of Christian romance novels set in her hometown of Redlands, California.

Neva is happily married and the mother of three grown children. Two of her children are adopted, and much of the story line in *Cari's Secret* grew out of discussions in her own household as the family worked through various questions asked by her children when they were growing up. Neva is also a proud grandmother.